Dark

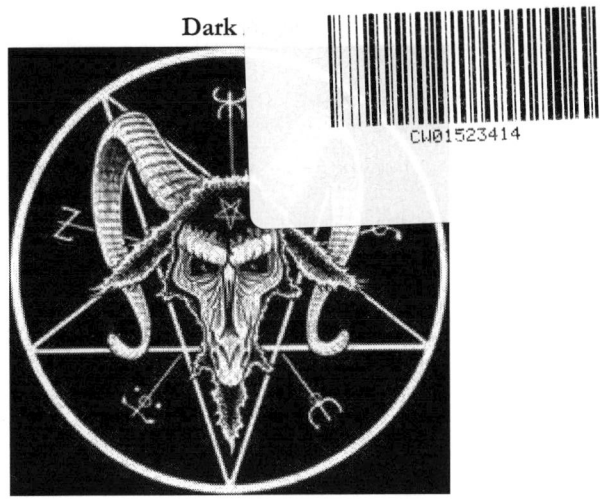

The Anglesey Murders
BOOK 5
By Conrad Jones

ISBN : 9781698017532

COPYRIGHT@CONRADJONES2019

PROLOGUE

I'd like to say that I slept like a baby, but I didn't. My dreams were tortured by the haunting sound of an infant crying. I searched everywhere that I could in the dream, but I couldn't find her. I knew she was a girl. I don't know how I knew it, instincts; I guess. One minute her crying was close to me, the next it was miles away, just a whisper of distress on an icy wind which whistled through the derelict structure. It had been a hotel once. It was built to mimic a castle, with towers and turrets, battlements and arrow slits. Though its shape was imposing against the seascape, it was painted white, like a vision from a fairy tale. Once a place full of laughter, wedding feasts and christening parties but now in my dreams, it was a burnt-out shell perched on a rocky outcrop overlooking a stormy sea. The white fascia had turned to mottled green, blistered and peeling. Smoke-burns snaked from the empty windows like eyelashes above blackened sockets. They seemed to offer a view into an infinite black abyss. Nettles and thorny weeds pushed their way up through the crumbling floors. When I looked towards the ceilings, I could see an angry sky through the gaping holes in the roof. The slates and rafters had collapsed, leaving the timbers hanging dangerously. Lightning forked earthwards, momentarily illuminating the heavy black clouds like a massive camera flash. The ear-splitting thunder threatened to shake the decaying building to the ground. Echoes of the past reverberated from the crumbling walls, ghostly laughter mixed with sounds from the past; tears of joy and tears of sadness.

As I walked through the remnants of the bar, I glimpsed the ghostly hotel owner sitting alone on a stool crying into his whisky. His head lolled onto his right shoulder; his broken neck no longer capable of supporting its weight. His eyes bulged almost ready to pop and his tongue hung from the corner of his mouth like a fat black slug. He didn't seem to notice that the wooden bar was nothing, but a charcoaled frame, the optics long gone, the staff moved on to different jobs years ago. Next to him was the rope with which he eventually hung himself to escape the pain of losing his philandering wife and the insurmountable debts that she'd left behind. Although it was a dream, I shouted at him, nonetheless. I needed help to find the girl. No matter how loud I shouted, my pleas for help went unheard. I felt the desperation of the years gone by, dragging me down like a weight around my waist slowing me down as I ran in search of the source of the tortured cries of the infant. I knew the child was a stranger to me and yet something told me that there was a connection somewhere. I had to find her. Every door was locked, and every window barred. When a corridor opened in front of me, I ran as fast as the weight would allow me, but I never made any progress. It was like running on a giant treadmill through mud. The desperate sobbing was ripping my heart out. I had to find her. My nightmare was interspersed with gravelly laughter from behind me. It was evil laughter whispering in my ear, a ghostly echo like an itch that you can't scratch. I knew it was Fabienne Wilder who plagued my dreams but every time I turned around; she was gone; the laughter replaced by the soul-destroying sobbing of a baby in distress and a lingering stench of decomposition. It was the same dream every time I closed my eyes. I couldn't stop the landlord slipping the noose around his neck and I couldn't find the child. My frantic search left me exhausted when I awoke. It seemed that there truly was no rest for the wicked and wicked was what I'd become.

***

It had been a year since I escaped the clutches of the Order of Nine Angels and I was no closer to finding Fabienne Wilder, their human goddess, Baphomet. If you still don't know who they are or are unsure if my tale is true, I've put their history at the back of the book. Or google them if you dare. Despite everything that the police and the Internet giants have tried to do, they still have websites and Facebook pages and as one closes down, another springs up to replace it. They're more prevalent now than ever. The more I searched for them, the more I got to know how they function and the more I understood her too. She is the evil which drives them. She is their tangible link to the insidious evil that they worship. Because she is real, a tangible God, they believe that their efforts are not in vain. They can touch her, hear her sermons and see her depravity with their own eyes and that gives them faith in the sinister way.

Unlike the traditional faiths, they have a tangible focus on this planet. She walks among them, encouraging them to live their lives with no boundaries. The laws we respect, our civilised values and moral framework are considered 'mundane' to them. Most of her followers are involved primarily for the unbridled sex which their religion allows, but once they're drawn in by the promise of pleasure with no limitations, they soon realise that Satanism is not a game. She takes over their hearts and minds and there is no way out. She holds the threat of them being exposed hanging over them permanently and demands more and more until they either submit completely or break. The weak ones are deemed as a threat to the Order and tend to disappear. She is far more powerful than traditional religious icons because she is alive. Because she is alive, it's easier for them to believe. Jesus is long dead and yet Christians the world over worship him. Could you imagine the power he would hold if he walked the earth? Well, she does walk among us and her followers revel in her existence. They believe that she is the devil incarnate. Baphomet, the Dark Goddess.

My dilemma was that the police were searching hard for me, and the evil cult the Order of Nine Angels searching harder still. They were holding a girl alleged to be my daughter hostage; a daughter who I'd never met. She was supposedly the product of a relationship that I'd almost forgotten about. Although it was serious at the time, it ended in tears and I'd shut it out of my mind. I'd met Pamela on a course at work and she blew my mind when she walked into the room. I thought she was the one, but I couldn't convince her that she felt the same. In the end, I gave up trying and we parted on reasonably good terms. Finding out that she was pregnant months after we had split up, her mother took the decision that it would be better to pretend that her new boyfriend was the father. She was obviously so heartbroken that she'd fallen into bed with him a week after the split, so at first wasn't sure if Constance was mine or not. Or that's what she told the newspapers when she went fishing for a lucrative exclusive. My notoriety had shaken a lot of old 'friends' from the woodwork. Each one brought a nugget of information from my dull past, most of it bullshit but the Press pay well for lies and exaggeration. With the new boyfriend out of the picture and the recession biting single mothers hard, Constance's mother, Pamela jumped on the bandwagon with a story that in terms of impact, blew the rest out of the water.

'Murder Spree Crime Author is the Father of My Daughter'.

The silly cow had no idea that the Niners were looking for anyone related to me so that they could force me out of hiding. I'd painstakingly wiped out my Internet footprints so that they couldn't target anyone that I cared about. It had been a difficult process cutting all ties with my family and friends, but their safety was paramount, and I knew that the police would be tapping their calls to try to track me down. Pamela had no idea how widespread this insidious religion had spread or how powerful they were. Her daughter Constance was snatched within a week of the headlines being published. I didn't know if she was telling the truth about her being mine or not, but either way I couldn't leave a young girl in the clutches of paedophile Satanists. I had to find her.

I had a head start on them this time around. Months before, I'd tracked some of the Niners to a remote farmhouse aptly named, Brunt Boggart, old English for 'burnt witch'. The farm was built on the site of the ancient execution of a local woman who was accused of being a witch and her legacy was documented throughout history. Every building ever built there mysteriously burned down and the families were plagued with sickness, death and misfortune. It seemed that the Niners searched out such places to hold their ceremonies. To cut a long story short, I interrupted one of their gatherings and three of them were sent to meet their dark lord, despatched with my twelve-gauge shotgun. The mobile phones which I'd taken from the dead Niners proved to be very useful tools in my search for the kidnappers. I knew that it could be weeks before they realised that their sicko friends were killed in the fire at Brunt Boggart. The bodies of the Niners that I'd shot were in the cellar and the building had collapsed on top of them. The emergency services would have no idea that the farm had a cellar as it wasn't marked on the structural plan. The damage was severe, so nobody looked for it. It would be months later when developers cleared the site that the cellar and the charred remains of three men were found.

During that time, I had free rein of their phones. I'd sent a series of texts from the dead men and eventually tracked down one of the Niners who were holding the girl.

'Fabienne W wants me to bring 'presents' for the daughter.'

It was vague enough to confuse anyone who had no knowledge of the hostage but clear enough to provoke an answer from her captors. Sure enough, a reply came back from a number stored under the name Andrew. I asked where he wanted them dropped off and he replied that I should bring them 'to the mill'. The farm at Brunt Boggart had been chosen for its remoteness. I guessed that somewhere close by in that green-belt area, I would find a mill. Google Earth helped me to pinpoint an abandoned sawmill a mile away from the farm. After studying it on Google and watching from a distance for a few hours, I knew that they were there.

The mill was a single storey structure with a vaulted loft space constructed of timber and breeze-block walls with a corrugated iron roof. A window above its double doors was protected by a mesh grill. There were two cars parked on a gravel path which didn't move all the time that I watched. Another vehicle arrived and a bald man in his fifties stepped out of the mill and shook hands with the driver who handed over a carrier bag with a logo resembling a fish printed on it. They chatted for a moment then the bald man went back inside, and the vehicle left. I assumed it was a delivery of fish and chips to keep the captors and the hostage from starving to death. I knew that it would only take five minutes for me to cross the field between us. Rapeseed was growing waist high and its intense yellow flowers were almost dazzling to the eye; its scent sweet. I ducked low and headed towards the side of the mill where there were no windows.

There was a path around the mill, made from tons of compacted waste sawdust. Waist-high grasses leaned over from either side, threatening to swamp it forever. I headed for the rear of the building hoping that the images on Google were recent. They were and I thought I'd seen a way in but until I saw it up close, I wouldn't be sure. A conveyor belt protruded from the rear elevation, its cogs and wheels red with rust. The hatch above it was padlocked but below it was a flywheel, half in the building and half out. The axle was fitted to the rear wall, its belt twisted and warped by time and the elements. The mill had once supplied wooden beams to the coal industry, which were used to support the miles of tunnels deep beneath my feet. When the pits were closed, the mill went bust with them and it had never been sold on. There was a gap between the flywheel and the wall which I'd guessed was big enough for me to squeeze through. It was a tight fit, but I was inside the mill in seconds.

The smell of freshly cut wood had long since been replaced by must and mould, damp and decay. Armoured grey wood lice in their thousands scurried beneath my feet making the floor look alive. Every footstep seemed to crush a hundred of them, their crunching bodies threatening to give away my arrival. The loft above me was supported by a suspended wooden platform, thick curtains of grey cobwebs dangled from every crack in the floorboards. An antiquated giant bandsaw dominated the ground floor and I had to skirt around it to reach the front of the building.

I heard muffled voices upstairs. All male. Three at least. A rotten wooden staircase was the only access, its handrail splintered into several sections some of which dangled uselessly in the air. The aroma of fish and chips drifted to me. They were having their dinner, which was a bonus. I had hoped that my rescue mission would be simple and straightforward, after all, they weren't expecting me. I planned to bamboozle them so much that they wouldn't know what had hit them until it was too late.

I crouched at the bottom of the stairs and pulled on a black ski mask. I took a deep breath and sprinted up the stairs, taking the steps three at a time. I heard the conversation stop and a few surprised expletives were exchanged as my footsteps alerted them to my presence. As I reached the landing at the top, I shouted as loud as I could.

'Armed police,' I bellowed. I held the Mossberg tightly against my shoulder and knelt down to make myself a smaller target. 'Get your hands up in the air now.'

The ski mask frightened them and combined with the dark military clothing which I was wearing, I hoped that they would think that I was part of an armed police unit long enough for me to disarm them. There were three men sat in a semicircle below the only window; the bald man who I'd seen outside, a grey bearded man in his sixties and an old biker-looking guy with sideburns and a ponytail. I couldn't see any weapons, another bonus. The chairs were arranged around a small screen television, that was perched on an old crate. Ponytail stood up, his chips in one hand, raising his other above his head. His mouth was open revealing the half-chewed contents. I couldn't take my eyes off them to look for Constance.

'Don't shoot,' Greybeard joined Ponytail and stood up. 'I can explain everything.'

'Get your hands up, now.' I screamed. They jumped visibly and complied; three bags of chips spilled in the dust. 'Where is the girl?'

None of them spoke but their eyes involuntarily flickered to a point behind me. 'Get on the floor, face down and do it now.'

Two of them responded quickly but Baldy hesitated and eyed me suspiciously. I fired a shot above him. The lead shot blew a hole in the roof bringing down a landslide of grit and filthy debris. It was more than enough to discourage him from arguing. He hit the floor like a sack of spuds giving me the opportunity to glance behind me. A young girl was sat on the floor tied to a roof support. She was gagged and blindfolded. Her long blond hair hung lankly to her shoulders. She was struggling against her restraints causing a small avalanche of dust to fall from the pitched ceiling, showering her with a powdery grime. 'Stay calm, Constance,' I shouted. 'I'll have you out in a minute.'

'He's not the police,' Baldy hissed to the others.

'What do you mean?' whispered Ponytail.

'He's on his own.'

'Shut up.' I shouted. I walked over to them and put my haversack on the floor. 'I'm the man that barbecues Niners,' I looked at their reactions, 'one wrong word from any of you and I'll blow your balls off, get it?' They nodded that they understood, the colour draining from their faces. 'Get up, Baldy,' I aimed the gun as I spoke. He was the mouthy one and therefore the one most likely to cause me problems. 'Sit on the chair.'

He sat down as instructed. 'She'll find you eventually,' he sneered. 'You have no idea what she is.' The look on his face was one of disdain, disgust and an almost perverse superiority. 'You're a dead man but you haven't realised it yet. Do you know what she is? I don't think you have a clue what she can do to those who cross us.' His expression of disgust really bothered me.

'She doesn't scare me.' I lied.

'She'll eat you alive, you fool.'

'She hasn't done so far.'

'Do you have any idea how many of us there are?' he scoffed like a schoolboy bragging about how big his dad is. 'Taking your daughter is just a message.

It's nothing to what we can do to you. You do not understand what we are capable of.'

'Maybe not but the mistake that you're making is not understanding what I'm capable of.' I saw fear in his eyes as I raised the gun. I pulled the trigger twice and blew the annoying expression off his face, along with his head. Ponytail whimpered like a wounded dog and Greybeard retched. Blood and globules of grey matter splattered their faces. Constance let out a scream, the sound muffled by the gag. 'Constance,' I called, 'I need you to stay still and do not panic, no matter what you hear. I'll come and untie you in a couple of minutes. Do you understand me?'

She nodded silently although I could see her legs were trembling and a puddle of urine began to spread beneath her. I turned my attention back to the horrified Niners. 'I was going to tie you up and leave you here until the police arrived but I'm beginning to get the impression that you lot think that I'm some kind of cockroach running and hiding under a rock somewhere.'

'I don't think that,' Ponytail stuttered.

'I'm not hiding from you perverts,' I explained calmly. 'I'm hunting you.' I smiled, but they didn't return the gesture. 'I guess I'm going to have to spell it out to that bitch and the rest of you, that if you try to hurt the people that I know or my family then you'll pay tenfold with your lives. Get up, Ponytail.'

He put his hands together as if in prayer. 'Please don't kill me.' His eyes were closed so that he couldn't see the ruined body of his friend. 'I'll do anything you ask if you let me live.'

'Okay, let's see shall we,' I tossed a bundle of cable ties onto the floor in front of him. 'Tie him up with those, two around the ankles and two around the wrists.'

Ponytail scurried off on his hands and knees. His hands were shaking so much that he fumbled clumsily with the zip ties. He avoided looking at the headless corpse which was still sitting upright on its chair. The cloying smell of excrement mingled with the coppery smell of blood. Baldy's bowels had relaxed upon death, releasing his waste into his trousers. 'Your friend is starting to stink already,' I commented on Baldy's deterioration. 'Do you think he's gone to help Fabienne's boss on the dark side?'

Ponytail just stared at me his lip shaking like an epileptic pink slug beneath his moustache. He obviously didn't have an opinion to share with me. 'I don't think he's gone to hell to be a dark angel,' I offered mine regardless. 'I think he's just a dead paedophile with shit in his pants.'

Tears ran from Ponytail's eyes.

'Was he married?' I asked.

Ponytail nodded.

'Kids?'

Another affirmative nod.

'I feel sorry for them, don't you?'

He nodded.

'Not because their father is dead,' I said making sure that he understood my point, 'because they'll find out what their father really was. That's the sad part. You see, I don't get it,' I kept the gun on him and crouched down to his eye level. 'How can you have kids of your own but abuse someone else's child?'

Silence.

'Take his phone off him,' I ordered once the bonds were fixed to Greybeard. Ponytail rummaged through his pockets and brought out a Samsung. 'Put it on camera mode.' His hands shook as he scrolled through the apps until he found it. 'Select video mode.' His eyes widened in shock as the realisation of his dilemma dawned on him. 'What's wrong?' I asked. 'Don't you want anyone to realise what you've done? Family, wife, kids, boss, workmates?'

'I'd rather die.' His eyes glazed over and he stood up. He dropped the Samsung onto the floor and stamped on it with his right foot. The screen split and the casing clattered across the dusty boards in several pieces.

'Okay.' I sighed. His eyes focused on me as the enormity of what he'd said hit home. I squeezed the trigger twice more blasting him off his feet, two bloody rents in his chest pumped his life fluid onto the floor. His lacerated lungs hissed like a punctured balloon in a bath of water. 'Some people just don't like disappointing their loved ones, eh?' I said to Greybeard. 'How do you feel about it?'

'I don't want to die,' he croaked, his voice breaking. 'I tried to get out of this, years ago.'

'You didn't try hard enough,' my sympathy was non-existent. I searched Baldy's pockets and took his Blackberry. The stench was now palpable. 'I'm going to call the police now and when I've explained where we are, you're going to tell the operator who you are and what you've done. Understand?' He closed his eyes and nodded. I dialled 999 and asked for the police. 'I need the police at the saw-mill near Benllech,' I paused, 'Constance Bonner, the kidnapped girl from the Midlands is being held here. There have been gunshots and there are two dead.'

The operator began asking a stream of questions, but I placed the phone on the floor next to Greybeard's head. 'Tell them who you are and why she was kidnapped,' I aimed the gun at his head. 'If you lie once, your brains will be all over that wall.'

'My name is David Moor and I'm involved in the kidnapping of the girl.'

'Tell them her name,' I ordered.

'Her name is Constance Bonner.'

'Tell them why.'

'She was kidnapped because she's the daughter of Conrad Jones.'

'Tell them who you belong to.'

'I'm a member of the Order of Nine Angels.'

I left him sobbing in the dirt and ran to Constance. I cut through her bonds and lifted her to her feet. I removed the gag and pulled off her blindfold. Her eyes showed terror in them. I realised that I still had the ski mask on. Pulling it off, I reached for a bottle of water and put it to her lips. She gulped thirstily from it. I could see her mother in her features, but I didn't recognise any of mine. Not that it mattered now, but I knew there and then that she wasn't my blood. I kept my body between her and the carnage behind me. 'I want you to close your eyes while I carry you down the stairs, okay?'

'Okay,' she said her voice a whisper.

I lifted her like a doll and carried her quickly down the creaking steps. The double doors were unlocked, and I put my back against them and pushed them open. The fresh air was invigorating, a stark contrast from the reek of death. I put her down on the weed strewn tarmac that led to the road. The sound of the first responding police car whined in the distance. 'Now I need you to trust me okay?'

'Okay,' she whispered again. 'I want my mummy.'

'The police are coming,' I cocked my head and smiled. 'Can you hear them?'

Constance nodded and bit her lip. 'I thought you were the police.'

'No, but I had to tell the bad men that,' I shook my head. 'Now listen to me. I need you to run down this road until the police car reaches you, okay?'

'I'm scared,' she tightened the grip on my hand. 'I want to stay with you until they get here.'

'I know you're frightened but I'm going to stay here and make sure that none of the bad men follow you, okay?'

'Okay.'

'Now run.'

Constance took one last teary look at me and then bolted down the road. She moved quickly for one so young. I waited until a curve in the road hid her from view and then I sprinted into the rapeseed and headed back the way I'd come. I knew that she'd be safe now. My hunt for Fabienne Wilder would continue but I knew then that I had to intensify my search for her before she got to my family and friends again. Once she was dead, I could try to restart my life somewhere. That was my plan, but as usual my plans would turn to dust in front of my eyes.

CHAPTER 1

With Constance safe, I had to reassess how to find my target. Their belief that Fabienne was indeed a goddess was undoubtedly the root of their loyalty. They feared her and revered her too. She's their living Jesus. I didn't believe that she is and my goal was to remove her from the face of the earth. When I found her, I planned to kill her very publicly so that her followers couldn't fail to know that she was dead and gone. I wanted to make sure that pictures of her dead body were broadcast across the world so that they would realise that she was nothing more than an evil bitch with a sick twisted mind.

***

That was the plan then and things went quiet for a while. In my search for her, I've moved from one place to another running from the law and hunting her followers along the way. The Order of Nine Angles is the most depraved religious tract on this planet and because I'd exposed some of their members in a book, they'd tried to kill me. I am both hunter and hunted. Up until a few months ago, there was no sign of Fabienne and her Niners, as they like to call themselves. I'd almost given up finding her until I met Max Blackman.

Although I was becoming expert at tracking them down using the mobile phones I took from the dead ones, I hadn't had a sniff at the whereabouts of Fabienne Wilder for months. She'd sent me a message, months before telling me that she was carrying my child, but I'd heard nothing since then. Looking back, some may say that it's because she told me that she was pregnant that I'm plagued by my recurring nightmare, but I know the dreams began months before she called me. Maybe I knew that she was pregnant. I don't believe that she's immortal but there was definitely a mental connection between us. I'm forever sceptical about such things but then I'm always sceptical about things which have no plausible scientific explanation. Whatever it was, my search for her had gone cold.

It was quite by accident that I stumbled across Blackman, although the circumstances in which he became infamous had sent ripples of fear across the world. The newspapers and television were plastered with the news of the arrest of a Welsh man called Dewi Critchley. He was originally arrested for the kidnap and rape of a young man who lived locally but when the police searched his farmhouse, the dismembered remains of numerous unidentified males were found. Human organs were found in the fridge and freezer and Critchley was in the process of cooking a human liver in the oven. They'd discovered the lair of a serial killer that they did not know existed. Echoes of Dennis Nilsen and Jeffrey Dahmer sounded across the Western World, another cannibal killer discovered by accident.

Critchley was big news, but the story only began to interest me when it became clear that he was an occultist. The more the evidence was uncovered, the more convinced I was that his murders were committed to satisfy his ritual fantasies. Initially, there was only a drip feed of information from the police, but I was immediately suspicious that he was a Niner. An altar had been discovered in his cellar along with human remains and ceremonial paraphernalia. Ornately carved goblets contained congealed human blood and a selection of razor-sharp ceremonial knives were collected and sent away for DNA examination. I saw television pictures of the cellar under forensic examination. They'd sprayed luminol, a chemical that exhibits chemiluminescence, creating a striking blue glow when it comes into contact with blood trace. It reacts with iron found in haemoglobin. The glow lasts for about thirty seconds, but the effect can be documented by a long-exposure photograph. The cellar floor was awash with blood splatter. Investigators said it was equivalent to testing the killing floor of a slaughterhouse.

Dewi Critchley had converted the cellar beneath his farmhouse into a full-blown satanic temple. His farmhouse was situated on the green slopes of the Dee Valley, close to Snowdonia on the outskirts of a village called Carrog. The village consists of a few dozen houses, a post office, a church, a primary school and a pub, all clustered around a 17th century stone bridge spanning the river. Wooded slopes rise steeply on either side, turning into dramatic rocky crags near the summits. The surroundings are picture postcard and the beautiful setting is the last place that you would expect such evil to be cultivated. The truth is that buildings and places are not evil it's the people who dwell there that manifest its power.

When I searched the Internet for historical news of occultism in the area, a string of reports in the local papers reported the desecration of churches and graveyards going back to late 1980s. The more I searched, the more I found. As I've said many times, google it if you don't believe me. Search for 'witches in North Wales' and a dozen articles appear on the first page. The spate of vandalism was put down to a handful of bored teenagers, but the more I looked into them, the more it was obvious that the vandalism and daubing of occult symbols on churches was only the tip of a black iceberg. Satanism had a foothold in the mountains and valleys of North Wales.

Over the following weeks, the police released numerous updates about the gory findings at the farmhouse and photographs of Critchley were published as his neighbours scrabbled to earn a few pounds from the ravenous press, by rooting out their old pictures. They ranged from class photographs at school, to images of him in the background at family functions. One of them pictured Critchley dressed in a goatskin robe during some kind of fancy-dress party. The numeral 9 was painted below his left ear in what looked like blood. The Press assumed it was an upside down 6, as in 666, the mark of the Devil, but I recognised it as the mark of a Niner. That was all the proof I needed to convince me that he was a member of the Order of Nine Angels. My ears pricked up when I realised that he was definitely involved with the cult and I followed the news closely as I packed up my meagre belongings.

I needed to be close to the investigation. Carrog is a tiny village and it has only a few beds for tourists. I knew that the Press would have block-booked whatever accommodation was available and I also knew that my presence there would not go unnoticed, so I drove to the larger neighbouring town of Llangollen. I found accommodation in a small guest house close to the edge of the River Dee, which ran through both Carrog and Llangollen. Niners are never individual practitioners of the dark arts; they worship in groups. Whenever I'd found one of them, there was a cluster of other members nearby. I knew that Critchley wouldn't be acting alone, so I waited for an opportunity to arise to find his affiliates. Somewhere in the investigation there would be a name, or an address loosely connected to the case that I could follow without drawing attention to myself.

The police hunt for me was no longer front-page news, but I was still high up on the wanted list. I had to be very careful, but this was too good an opportunity to miss. All I needed was one loose end to catch onto and I could uncover an entire sinister nest. There was no way that Critchley would have practised alone, and I wanted to talk to his fellow sinister members. If I found any of them, then I knew that it would be a conversation that they wouldn't enjoy or survive. My experience had taught me that when you find one of the evil bastards, they're only too willing to give up a few more names to save themselves, especially when they're looking down the barrel of a shotgun. I killed them regardless of the information they gave me. That might sound callous and cold-blooded, but in my mind, they'd lost the right to mercy when they became Niners. They've been trying to kill me for years now and the trail of dead Niners that I've left behind means that if I'm ever caught, I'll serve life in prison. Once digested into the prison system, I would be an easy target for them. The prisons are full of the right-wing extremists who affiliated with the Niners. They live for violence and they would get me in the end. I'd already lost everything so finding and eradicating them was the only thing that I had left. Critchley had lifted the lid on a nexion so there I was in Llangollen, hunting Angels.

Llangollen is a small market town with a population of 6,000 inhabitants, which is tripled in the summer months as tourists flock there to enjoy the romantic beauty of the Welsh mountains. When I arrived, there was a buzz about the town. News of the horror in the nearby village had acted like a magnet for journalists from all over the world. The pubs and guest houses were crammed with huddles of reporters and television crews gossiping, swapping and searching for titbits of information about the case. It's easy to hide in a crowd, so I blended in and enjoyed the anonymity of it all. I listened to dozens of conversations every day, sifting through the names and places attached to the case, waiting for an obvious place to start.

The locals were suspicious of each other. They'd worked out that Critchley was not worshipping Satan alone. Family feuds going back decades were resurfacing as accusations were met with counteraccusations. I witnessed several scuffles between the natives, usually fuelled by the consumption of ale and a festering dislike for each other that went back generations. Of course, the Press soaked it all up. There was an atmosphere of morbid excitement over the town. The one thing that struck me though, was the lack of possible victims being named that came from the local area. Over twenty bodies had been discovered yet none of them seemed to be linked to the local area. There were only a few names mentioned in regard to relatives reported missing over the last ten years. That told me that Critchley was a clever man. Had he preyed on the local community; his depravity would have been discovered much sooner. Ten days after his arrest, Critchley was found in his cell with his throat slashed. According to the news reports, a fellow prisoner had sharpened his toothbrush by filing it to a point against his cell wall and then had slashed Critchley repeatedly, taking out one eye and severing the jugular. He was rushed into the prison surgery but died from blood loss before they could help him. His death left a lot of unanswered questions and also reinforced my fear of entering the prison system. I'm convinced that Fabienne had him silenced before he could identify himself as a Niner.

As with any story, for a few short weeks the tabloid newspapers were all over it. The television stations replayed new additions to the story daily on all the major news programmes. With a story moving this fast, there was no time to look back in detail. New revelations were made every day. The body count at the farmhouse was growing as the police excavated the site and pieced together Critchley's ten-year rampage. With the bones and flesh that remained there, forensic scientists discovered that he had been killing for over a decade. Identifying the victims was the priority and missing persons' lists were being cross-referenced and analysed. As the names of the victims began to be confirmed, the focus shifted to their families. Some say that closure is a blessing which some victims' families are denied, but in this case, I'm not convinced. Given the choice of having a missing sibling or child or being informed categorically that they'd been sexually abused, slaughtered and eaten by a raving psycho and his buddies over an extended period of time, missing sounds preferable. Victims' families were interviewed relentlessly, their shock and grief televised for a news hungry world. Speculation as to how their relatives had arrived at such a brutal end was rife.

Critchley's arrest was shrouded in mystery. At first the police were cautious about revealing how they'd stumbled across the carnage at the farm. Eventually it came to light that they'd been alerted when an allegation of rape and kidnap was reported by a young local man named, Geraint Hughes. It appeared that he had managed to escape Critchley, but only after he had been subjected to a brutal assault and sodomised repeatedly by a number of men who he couldn't identify. His testimony cemented the ritual side of the story. Over the following weeks, the police revealed that they were interviewing a number of other possible victims, who had come forward once the story hit the headlines. One victim on the periphery of the investigation was Max Blackman and I identified him as the person that I would talk to first.

Initially terrified, Max Blackman told the Press that he was a victim of abuse at the hands of Critchley and that he was nearly a murder victim, but some of his statements didn't add up in my mind. In his version of events, he escaped a hideous death at the hands of the cannibal killer Critchley, who before his death, had confessed to the mutilation-murders of at least twenty-two men and boys. Max alleged that he was held prisoner in Critchley's farmhouse of horrors which he described as a dwelling with a cellar littered with human skulls and body parts. Finally, after eight hours at the knife-edge of death, he fled half-stripped, bleeding and handcuffed, into the nearby woods. After running for his life, he reached the road which led into town, where he flagged down a passing car. The driver had taken him to the hospital where his wounds were stitched and treated but he wouldn't reveal how he had received them. He told the police that he had been too scared of Critchley to report the attack at the time.

The first day after Critchley's death rocked the world, the nationals ran a small, page one article on Max Blackman and his escape alongside the main headlines from the farmhouse. The account of Max's getaway was short and shallow. There were few details in his account. It was dwarfed by the huge headlines and photos of Critchley's arrest and the search for his victims' identities. While some lesser known reporters from small publications hounded Blackman for a few days, other more established reporters ignored him and pursued the grim body count, the grieving relatives while religiously attending daily news conferences held by the lead officer on the case. It was as if those in the know disregarded anything that Blackman had to say.

There was a subtle but clear change of tack in the manner in which Blackman was perceived. The police were giving out no more information about Max's experience inside the farmhouse with the murderer. There was no *inside* story. It didn't sit right with me, but he had said enough for me to want to talk to him alone. I wanted to know more. If he had been subjected to such a terrible ordeal, then why wasn't he receiving the same amount of sympathy and exposure as Geraint Hughes was? Following Critchley's death, Hughes had been interviewed on every breakfast news programme and afternoon talk show that I could mention and some that I can't remember. There was no doubt that Hughes had suffered terribly and if he made some money out of his plight, then good for him. But I couldn't understand why Blackman had been shunned by the Press. They knew something that I didn't.

Something about Blackman made my skin crawl. He was lying about all or parts of his testimony, but I couldn't put my finger on what or why. After the initial wave of public sympathy for him had waned, the Press seemed to back off his plight and the police decided to drop his allegations from the prosecution's files. It seemed that I wasn't the only one who doubted him. It would be another week before the media would turn its collective attention away from Blackman completely. By then Max was talking to any small newspaper that would give him a few pounds to hear him whining, but his story was lost in the middle pages.

The local Welsh journal mentioned that Max Blackman lived in the same valley that the bodies were discovered in, about two miles away from the farm. There was a small village situated there called Corwen, which consisted of a church, a few pubs and the omnipresent Spar shop. The remains of a country post office, which had been closed a few years before, stood between the pubs and the mini market. I decided that Corwen was the place to be to find out more about Max Blackman. Leaving my clothes in the guest house, I packed a few toiletries and drove to Corwen, hoping to get a room in one of the pubs. They advertised accommodation online but had no pre-booking facilities or information on availability. I decided to take the chance on booking in when I got there but kept my room in Llangollen too. I've discovered that staying in a pub and gassing with the local drinkers is the best way to find out about anything that you want to know associated with an area. Pretending to be interested in their locality can yield a plethora of information especially if you buy the orators a few pints.

I headed up the A5 and passed through the now infamous Carrog on the way. The temptation to take a closer look at the farmhouse was intense, but I knew that it would be ring-fenced by the ongoing investigation so I drove through the village and when I reached Corwen, I parked my vehicle on a side street near to the pubs. I took my bag, which contained a toothbrush, some deodorant and a razor and walked into the first pub that I came to. It was a typical Welsh pub, dark wood and polished brass and a slight smell of must mixed with damp. Every flat surface was covered with ornaments loosely attached to Wales. Welsh dragons made from slate and painted plates from all around the area cluttered the shelves and window ledges. A chalkboard displayed the day's specials and the polished tables were decorated with laminated menus, Heinz ketchup and ceramic salt and pepper pots. Three men were sitting on leather topped stools at the bar, passing the afternoon with a few pints of real ale and a good moan about life in general. As I walked in, their conversation stopped for a few seconds while they decided if I was Welsh or another pesky tourist. Their sour expressions told me that they'd decided on the latter and they turned back to their chitchat.

The landlord was a little more welcoming, greeting me with a smile as he eyed my bag. Filling an empty guest room upstairs was top of mind for him, no matter where I was from. After a brief exchange, I swapped twenty-five pounds for the key to room number 3, turning down the offer to view it first. I thanked him in Welsh, which turned the heads of the three men at the bar and their demeanour towards me changed instantly. One of them asked me where I was from and I told them that I was from Holyhead, Anglesey and that I was a writer looking for somewhere quiet to think about my next book. They were polite enough and we chatted while I drank my first beer. I purposely avoided asking about the murders in Carrog, waiting for them to bring the subject up. When they did, we made small talk about it with the landlord who was pissed off that none of the journalists had stayed in his pub for more than one night, opting for the much busier town of Llangollen.

Max Blackman's name was mentioned as he was connected to the story and from the village. A few more lunchtime customers from the village drifted in and out but I didn't learn too much new about Max Blackman until a man in a postal uniform at the end of the bar joined the conversation. This was the loose end that I'd been waiting for.

'I've known his family for years, but they all moved away after his dad died,' one of the men said. 'Max stayed here, but he has always been a strange one.' The comment at the end of his sentence rang a bell in my head that there wasn't much sympathy for Blackman.

'Everyone knows everyone here,' the landlord added almost apologetically.

'You don't have to explain that to me, Holyhead is a small town too.' I nodded.

'I used to go fishing with his father, nice man he was. I remember young Max being born but I don't even know where he lives now.' The man added. 'And I don't want to know either.'

'Not on your Christmas card list?' I tried to draw more information out him.

'No.'

'Must have been frightening for him though?'

'If you believe a word he says.'

'And you don't.'

'Not a word.'

I was struggling to get more than one-word answers and I didn't want to attract suspicion. Strangers asking questions in small villages are suspicious enough without any help. I felt that I was close to hearing the gossip, but they just didn't want to part with it yet.

'I know where he lives,' said the postman at the end of the bar. He didn't add any details and left the statement hanging in the air. Knowledge is power, especially in the pub. He stared straight ahead and waited for someone to bite.

'Where then?' The landlord asked almost as a challenge. He looked at me and rolled his eyes towards the ceiling. 'I remember his father lived up Bryn-y-Mor, but I've not seen young Max for years, wouldn't have a clue, but if you want to know where someone lives, ask a postman. Come on tell us, where then?'

'I'm not supposed to tell peoples' addresses, it's against the law, you know.' The postman rattled his empty glass on the bar and smiled like the village idiot. 'It's slipped my mind now.'

'I'll get that,' I offered and pushed my empty pint glass towards the landlord. I smiled at the postman and he grunted a suspicious thank you. 'Don't worry I'm not fishing for information; I just find the whole incident interesting in a morbid type of way.' The other men along the bar laughed and nodded that they understood my meaning. 'All part of being a writer.'

'Oh, I bet you'll get a few ideas from this Critchley nightmare.'

'We're all fascinated by bad news,' I smiled. 'Human nature.'

'Too true, that is,' one of them added. 'It's only human to be fascinated by other people's misfortune.'

'Other peoples' suffering is what we like,' the man continued. 'Look at how tourists queue up to see the dungeons and torture chambers at the castle. It's the busiest bit of the tour.'

'We're always more interested in bad news than good,' I smiled. 'Would anyone else like a drink?'

The landlord raised his eyebrows and shook his head as the others swallowed the pints that they'd been nursing for the last twenty minutes and offered them to be recharged. 'This lot will never say no to a free pint, tight buggers.' He laughed and his chubby cheeks wobbled as he spoke. 'Come on then, Dai,' he turned to the postman. 'Where is Max living now then?'

The postman leaned a little closer so that the other non-existent customers couldn't hear. 'He lives in the bedsits at the top of Caer-glas Road,' he said slowly. He nodded proudly and slurped a quarter of his pint in one go. 'He's a bit of a loner and I think he's on the other bus, if you know what I mean.' He added and waved a limp wrist over the bar. The other men reacted to the news that Blackman might be gay by shaking their heads in disgust and frowning appropriately.

'Bloody shirt-lifter,' one of the men muttered.

'Blackman a puff?' another added. 'His father would be spinning in his grave if he knew.'

'Can't understand bummers,' Dai added.

'Nice to know that my regulars are such an open-minded crowd,' the landlord said quietly in my direction. 'Trapped somewhere in the last century most of them.' He laughed.

'Cerris from the barbers told me that she'd heard that Blackman and others were often seen going to that farm,' Dai said in a hushed tone.

'Cerris is the oracle of all gossip around here,' the landlord explained. 'She's the local hairdresser, so she hears all the fresh news first.'

'Oracle?' the man to my left piped up. 'She's a bloody nuisance that woman. You can't fart without her knowing about it and telling the village.'

'You're right Tom,' said Dai 'She's been telling me for years that those bedsits are rife with skivers, drugs and bummers.'

The landlord rolled his eyes skyward and shook his head. 'I give up sometimes.'

'I wouldn't have thought a pretty village like this would have bedsits,' I said fishing for more details. 'Were they built as holiday flats?'

'God, no.' The postman nearly spat his beer out. 'There are loads of bedsits here and most of them are shit-holes built for the social to pay the rent.'

'You wouldn't think, would you?' I waited for him to bite on the bait.

'English developers bought most of the empty properties for holiday homes and now the youngsters can't get mortgages on them. A couple of property developers bought some of the three-storey houses and turned them into bedsits, knowing that the young ones would sign on and get the rent paid for them. Greedy bastards if you ask me.'

'Same thing happened in the tourist areas on Anglesey, especially around the Trearddur Bay area,' I sympathised with his opinion. 'The trouble with that is when they applied for planning permission the council forced them to build separate access to each floor in case of fires, so they had to fit fire escapes. Cost the developers a fortune.'

'Serves them right in my mind,' huffed one of them.

'Most of them had to have metal fire escapes fitted to the outside of the buildings, cost a fortune to make them to measure,' I added.

'Yes,' the postman took the bait. 'Same thing happened up at Caer-glas. They had to fit metal stairs to the bedsits too.'

That was my starting point. I had the name of the street and a description of the building. It was a three-storey house with a metal fire escape fitted to the outside. I didn't think that there would be too many of them in Corwen. I finished my pint and said my farewells politely, pretending that I was taking a stroll down to the river.

CHAPTER 2

Max Blackman

The Caer-glas neighbourhood was declining. Slate-built Victorian terraces mixed with taller apartment buildings and the occasional two-up-two-down stone-built house. I guessed that Max lived in the bedsit on the middle floor of the converted building. I couldn't be sure, but the curtains were closed tightly, and my instinct told me that he was hiding in there. The building was run down and in need of repair. The paint was chipped, the woodwork peeling, and a few broken windows were visible from the street. Paint flaked from the railings on the fire escape as they snaked up the deteriorated side wall of the house. I was staring at the middle floor window and obviously looked out of place on the quiet street when a voice disturbed my thoughts.

'Are you looking for Max Blackman?' The voice asked chirpily. An elderly man in a green tweed jacket and matching flat cap stood uncomfortably close to me. I hadn't heard him approach and his question startled me. 'I bet you're a reporter.'

'Something like that,' I winked at him. He seemed amiable enough.

'I get you, secret squirrel and all that,' he tapped his nose and smiled to reveal a full set of ageing yellow teeth. 'Not police, are you?'

'No.'

'There have been a lot of reporters looking for him lately although their numbers seem to have dwindled the last week or so. He's old news now.'

'The focus changes with a story like that,' I smiled. 'Do you know him?'

'I know of him.'

'Have you seen him around today?'

'No. The little creep is doing his best to hide,' said the man. There was an acidity to his tone. 'I haven't seen him out of his flat for days. Don't quote me on this but no one around here has got any time for him. He's a bit of a queer one, if you know what I mean.' The limp wrist was a clue to his message.

'Do you know if he's still around?' I asked. It wasn't lost on me that the male population of Corwen seemed to be a little on the homophobic side. 'I wouldn't mind having a chat with him.'

'Yeah, yeah, slow down, I'm getting to that.' He said secretly. He leaned closer and looked around before speaking. 'We all know of him around here but like I said, no one bothers with him. He hasn't told the whole truth.'

'Why is that?' I asked equally secretly.

'He's lived here about nine years already. That's a long time in this neighbourhood. We've all seen his picture in the papers and on television but it's nothing to be proud of is it?'

'Not at all,' I agreed, 'quite the opposite in fact.'

'Exactly,' he peered up and down the street again. 'Before all this came out, he was just a waster, now he's a big deal or he thinks that he is, anyway. He thinks that everybody's looking up to him because he almost got himself killed and eaten by some pervert weirdo from the next village. All I can say is, shame that he didn't.'

'It sounds to me like he isn't the most popular man in the village.' I laughed although I wanted to know why Blackman was disliked so much. It couldn't all be down to his sexuality.

'You could say that.'

'Why is he so disliked?' I got straight to the point. It was obvious that the man couldn't wait to have a gossip, so I didn't see the harm in asking for the dirt on him.

'Let's just say that there were allegations that he'd been messing about with a young boy a few years back.' He tapped his nose again.

'Was he arrested?'

'No and the family upped and moved away soon after, but the rumours stayed here with him.'

'I see,' I nodded. That would explain why the Press had dropped him so quickly.

'He's just after money with the Critchley thing,' the man tapped his nose again.

'What makes you think that?' I asked him with a straight face. 'Do people think that he's made his story up?'

'Word has it that he had been to Critchley's farm many a time before all this kicked off. He worked there through the summer holidays a few times when he was a teenager,' his voice was almost a whisper. 'He was no stranger to that place if you know what I mean.'

I nodded that I did. If the Press had heard whispers that Blackman knew Critchley, then that would explain why they'd backed off him so quickly. It would also explain why the police dropped his evidence from the investigation. An allegation made from a suspected paedophile would hardly stand up in court. It didn't matter now that Critchley was dead. 'I see that makes sense.' I replied offering a handshake. 'Maybe I'll leave it alone. Thanks for the information though, it's been nice talking to you.'

'And you,' he shook my hand with bony fingers. 'Which paper did you say you worked for?'

'I didn't,' I tapped my nose this time and his smile disappeared. As I turned to walk away, I saw the curtains twitching in the middle floor flat. Blackman was home. As I walked down the street, I dialled direct enquiries and asked for the landline number at Blackman's address. It was a long shot, but it paid off with his number. I rang it and eventually it clicked to a message service. I left Blackman a message offering him a thousand pounds for an interview and added my mobile number at the end. Less than five minutes later, Max Blackman called me back.

CHAPTER 3

The Meeting

At eight o'clock the next morning I knocked on Blackman's door. It was too early for the school runs to start; Caer-glas was quiet and as far as I could tell, no one had seen me arrive. I carried a holdall which I kept in the Land Rover. It held a number of items which had been useful when it came to dealing with Niners and I was convinced that Blackman had dabbled with the sinister at Critchley's farmhouse. One way or the other, I was about to find out if he was one of them or not. When he opened the door, I wasn't surprised by his appearance. He was short and slender. His blond hair was styled in a wavy bob, longer on one side than the other. His skin was smooth, almost feminine to look at and his mannerisms were camp, to say the least. There was no doubt in my mind that he was on the other bus as the postman had so eloquently pointed out. Blackman didn't ask to see any identification and he was well-mannered and surprisingly articulate. He didn't ask for any money up front which suited me. I had a thousand pounds in counterfeit twenty-pound notes in the holdall just in case he did ask.

His flat was untidy, and he pointed me towards a black leather settee while he took a matching armchair adjacent to it. We sat next to a coffee table in the middle of the living room. The table was littered with coffee cups, half-full ashtrays, old newspapers and a stack of fashion magazines. Another smaller table nearby held the spent spotless breakfast plate that Max had used earlier. In one corner of the room was a large plasma screened television which was muted and tuned to the BBC news channel. The developers had exposed the ceiling joists, both as a feature and to give the bedsit more height and a feeling of space. A teardrop shaped wicker chair was suspended by a chain from the joists above the smaller table. The flat was stylish but unkempt.

Max sat down in the chair and tucked his legs beneath him. Flicking his hair effeminately, he picked up his mobile phone and put it on silent, stuffing it in his pants pocket and then sat back nervously in his chair. He took a cigarette and lit it, blowing the smoke out of the side of his mouth. It was shaking in his hand. He closed his green eyes and concentrated. 'I suppose you want to know everything from the beginning?'

'I think that would be a good place to start,' I said. It was the first thing that I'd said to him. He had just assumed that I was who I said I was, and he guessed what I wanted to hear. It was a well-rehearsed routine for him.

'Are you going to record it or make notes?' he asked looking at my holdall. 'Your lot usually do one or the other.'

'I'll record it,' I said. I fiddled with my phone and pretended that I knew how to use it properly. 'Ready when you are.'

'It still knocks me sick when I think about it,' he shivered as the vivid memories flooded into words. I had to make my mind up whether they were memories, or a cleverly concocted story manufactured to make some money from the gory events in Carrog. 'I haven't slept in two weeks,' he began. 'I can't believe that this happened to me. There was no clue that he would turn on me like that. I swear to God that I looked into the eyes of the Devil and saw death in them. I'm lucky to be alive.'

'I can see that you're shaken by it,' I said. He was either a great actor or he really was traumatised by it all. It was a very dramatic performance either way.

'Believe me, God delivered me from Satan that day. I'm still in shock. I can't trust people anymore. I can't sleep and when I do try to sleep, I wake up in a panic, sitting straight up in bed, soaking wet with sweat. I'm still scared to death. I'm constantly looking over my shoulder.' Max paused, taking a few rapid puffs off his cigarette. His eyes flickered up now and then. He was gauging my reaction to his story. I tried to look shocked.

'Just start out with what happened that day,' I tried to get him to focus. He had mentioned both God and the Devil so far and that sent spikes of caution through me. I needed to know which one he favoured.

'I was in the Spar shop when Critchley showed up and asked if I wanted to have a party,' Max said exhaling a cloud of smoke. 'We all knew him from around the village. There was no way to guess he was a maniac. He was just an ordinary man. I didn't think too much about him either way.'

'Had you met him before that day?' I asked. I wanted to see if he would lie to me. I knew that he had worked on his farm. His opening account from the Spar shop sounded like a lie to me as if he was distancing himself from Critchley.

'I worked for him a couple of summers ago, just casual labour on the farm,' Max blushed red. He wasn't lying about knowing him but there was more to it than that. I could tell from the way he avoided eye contact that he was manufacturing parts of his story.

'So, you were friendly with him before then?'

'Well, sort of,' his eyes went teary and his lips quivered. He looked down at the floor as if he was watching an invisible screen down there. The memories were swilling about in his mind and he was choosing which ones to recount.

'What does 'sort of' mean?'

'Look, he was nice to me when I was in school,' Max shrugged but he still couldn't keep eye contact with me. 'He gave me a job for the summer, and he treated me well.'

'It sounds like you looked up to him then?'

'Well, sort of.' Max was uncomfortable with my questions.

'You're gay, right?' I asked. Better to let him know that I wasn't going to beat around the bush.

'Is that a problem?' he quipped and wrapped his arms around his knees, hugging them to his chest. He looked offended.

'Not for me but I could see it being a problem here in the village.'

'I'm bi-sexual,' he replied curtly.

'And Critchley?'

Max seemed to cast his mind back before he answered. 'I never thought he was gay or anything out of the ordinary at first, because the people in the village where he lived just never would have tolerated him. They don't like gays in this part of the world. If they'd thought that he was gay, the men in the village would have messed him up. They jump guys like that around here. It's just not accepted.'

'So, he was in the closet then?'

'I guess nobody really knew that he was gay, or into that kind of lifestyle. He just couldn't have survived if anybody knew about him,' Max emphasised that last sentence. I knew that he spoke from experience.

'He kept it hidden?'

'Yes,' Max sulked. 'Why are you going on about that, anyway?'

'I'm trying to establish what type of man he was.'

'I wish I had.'

'Sorry, go back to the day in the Spar shop,' I sat back to let him talk. I didn't want to spook him until I'd heard everything that he had to say.

"Let's get some of the guys and all go down to the river and have a few beers," he said to me in the shop. 'I've got a hundred quid here. I'll buy the beer."

'Which guys?' I stopped him.

'Well anyone we knew that liked to party and wasn't working,' Max frowned at me. 'Does it matter?'

'It depends which guys went with you,' I shrugged. 'Did anyone go with you?'

'No.'

'Did you invite anyone else?'

'No, we didn't bother in the end,' he snapped.

'So, he wanted to go to the river with you alone?'

'I don't know what he was thinking,' he sulked. 'Do you want me to make it up?'

'Not really, sorry,' I smiled. There were never any other guys going to the river. He was lying to me and I knew it. It was no wonder that the journalists had seen through his story. He was a bad liar.

'I was broke, and I hadn't been out for a while,' said Max, shrugging. 'It sounded like a good idea to me. It was hot and sticky that day and a few beers by the river would be good. We walked to the beer aisle and he got the beer. Critchley said he had to stop by the farmhouse to change clothes. He was still in his blue overalls and wellingtons.'

I now believed Blackman was lying about his motives to go with Critchley in the first place. I guessed that Max knew what was happening when he accepted Critchley's invitation to the farm. At least Max thought he knew what was happening. Maybe he didn't know about the twenty odd other victims that had proceeded him to Critchley's for a few beers. As it turned out, my instincts rang true.

Max had been around the block, but I was convinced that he was aware of what Critchley wanted that afternoon. At that point, my suspicion was that Max was bi-sexual and that he knew full well that Critchley's offer of free beer didn't include the company of any other guys. I wanted to ask who he thought the other guys were specifically but that could wait until later. The police had found thousands of photographic images on Critchley's computer and it was suspected that his modus operandi was to offer his victims money so he could take sexy photos of them. Most agreed to the deal, not realising where they would end up. And money was the major motivator with Max. He lived pretty much from day-to-day. I believed Max went to that farmhouse to play Critchley's games, but he was in for a surprise.

'It was really hot that day,' Max said lighting another cigarette from the packet which now nestled in the neck of his T-shirt. 'Everything seemed pretty normal. I'd never seen the inside of the farmhouse where he lived and when we first got there, it looked like a pretty nice place. We went in the door and the smell hit me right away,' said Max. 'What is that smell? I asked him but, Dewi just brushed it off. He said there was a problem with the sewers on the farm. As we walked down the hall, the stench made me want to gag.' Max wrinkled up his face. 'I said let's just grab a beer and get out of there and go to the river, and he said: 'That sounds good. I can barely stand the smell myself.' He said it was the sewer, and I've smelled some pretty raunchy sewers on farms before, so I just assumed he was telling the truth.'

Max leaned forward in his chair, his voice lowered dramatically. The droning monologue was hypnotic. He had told this story a dozen times. I concentrated on the gaps in his testimony and realised that we were on the portal, the point of no return. 'His living room was big but there was no air in there. A small fan unit buzzed near the sash window. The dark coloured curtains were drawn and the intense sun outside was locked out. We sat down on his couch and popped open a beer. He had a beautiful fish aquarium and the colours of the fish were stunning in the darkened room. They were so pretty.' Max let out a sigh.

I just nodded and listened.

'As I looked around and my eyes began to adjust. I could see the living room walls were covered with photos and drawings of men working out.' Max's demeanour suddenly changed. He became impatient, almost brisk. 'I hoped Critchley would hurry and change his clothes and we'd get out of there. It really stunk, and it was creepy somehow. I didn't feel right.'

Now there was no doubt in my mind that Max had gone there to have sex with Critchley and that he had been with him before. He was lying.

'Critchley told me he had all the drawings because he was a member of a health club. He was in pretty good shape; his arms were muscular and toned; he was strong and wiry from all the manual farm work. We were sitting on opposite ends of the couch, but it was a fairly small couch and there really wasn't much space between us. He said some of the fish were piranha, and he told me how they like to eat each other. We sat there for a while, making small talk about when I'd worked on the farm for him and stuff,' Max said, his voice falling again into that hypnotic drone and again abruptly breaking off, as if he were trying to shake off a bad memory. 'He was being heavy and boring and if it wasn't for that beer, I would have gone home. In fact, that's what I was thinking,' Max said his voice angry and hard. 'But he was way ahead of me. Before I knew what hit me, he had a handcuff on my wrist and a curved knife up against my armpit. Right up under my heart.' Max clasped his hands over his heart and twisted his body wildly in the chair.

I wasn't sure if I believed him or not at this stage. When a passing motorist found Max on the road, he was handcuffed so there was no doubting that they belonged to Critchley, but I thought that the handcuffs had been part of their sex game.

'He said, 'If you don't do what I say, I'm going to kill you.' He said, 'I've done this before. Don't make a move because I can kill you,' he snapped his fingers, 'just like that."

Although I was still debating what to do with Max, I was concerned for his well-being. His breathing was laboured, his eyes watering. I noticed Max's fingertips were stained yellow from the tobacco and I also noticed how his hands shook. I suggested he take a break, but Max waved me off with a better-to-get-this-over-with look. He seemed to be reliving the attack, but I was convinced that he was performing a well-rehearsed monologue which he had re-enacted for any reporter willing to listen.

'The knife in my side was black handled with a curved, double-edged blade.' I was impressed at Max's recall and his descriptive powers, although I had the impression that he had seen the blade before. 'It felt as if it had been sharpened to a point that would split hairs. I'll never forget what that blade looked or felt like.' He shook his curly hair and closed his eyes for dramatic effect.

'Was it a ritual knife?'

'What?' his face reddened, and he looked me in the eye but quickly looked away. 'I have no idea what you're talking about.'

'You said the knife was curved and double edged, so it wasn't your average kitchen knife or hunting knife was it?'

'No.' He shook his head effeminately and looked at the floor. He reminded me of a young girl being told off. 'I don't know if it was a ritual knife or not.'

'Okay it's not important,' I lied. 'Carry on.'

Max took another drag on his cigarette and swallowed hard. 'It was all so quick, he was experienced at snapping on the handcuffs, he must have had practice. It was all in one motion. I've got the beer in my hand and I'm talking about fish and in a flash the handcuff is on my wrist and the tip of the blade stuck in my side. I looked down and I could see through my shirt. I was bleeding.' Max caressed the bandage under his T-shirt.

'Then his eyes changed,' Max said. 'Maybe the sight of my blood did it. At first, I couldn't face him,' Max said, fervently, 'but God made me look right into his eyes. It was like confronting the Devil. He was pure and simple evil. Critchley looked nothing like when we first met in the summer holidays. He had changed completely. He had transformed somehow into evil. I could tell by the look in his eyes that he had killed before.' He paused as his eyes filled with tears and spilled over, running down his cheeks.

'You could tell that he had killed before?' I leaned forward to study his reaction. 'Just by the look in his eyes?'

'Yes.'

'That's quite some statement.'

'He had changed,' Max insisted. 'The look in his eyes had changed completely.'

'I get the feeling that something happened between you when you worked on the farm,' I needed to get the answer to that question because it made all the difference to his story. 'Did you have a relationship with him when you were at school?'

'Yes,' Max began sobbing uncontrollably. 'He was my first, you know?'

'Was it serious?'

'I thought so,' he sobbed. 'I loved him.'

'I understand.' I nodded. Now it all made sense. 'You obviously had feelings for him.'

'Back then when I was a teenager I did.' Max wiped his nose with the back of his hand. 'He was handsome and strong, and he sensed that I was the same as him, you know. I had a huge crush on him until…' He didn't finish the sentence.

'Until what?'

'He got all weird.'

'In what way?'

'I don't want to talk about it.'

'It's important to the story that you tell me the whole thing.'

'It's personal.'

'It's the truth and if you don't tell the truth—' I pointed a finger at him '—people will tell that you're lying.'

'Okay.' He whined.

'What did you mean when you said he got weird?'

'At first the sex got rougher and that was a shock, but I just thought he was experimenting, you know? I thought it was just fooling around but then he started hitting me,' Max squeezed his eyes together and tears spilled over, running down his cheeks. 'Then he asked me to do stuff with some other men too.'

'In the cellar?'

'Yes, it was horrible.' Max sobbed, and his shoulders heaved. 'They hurt me.'

'You said that you had never been inside the farmhouse.'

'I didn't want anyone to know that part of things.'

'Where you part of a ritual?'

'Yes.' Max tried to pull himself together. 'I was blindfolded but I could hear them doing stuff. Chanting stuff and then, well, I'm sure you can guess.'

'How many times did you go into that cellar?'

'A few.'

'How many times, Max?'

'I can't remember.'

'Did you ever see a pretty black woman called Fabienne Wilder?'

'Why are you asking me all this?' He snapped but his eyes told me that he had. 'I thought you wanted to know what happened to me that day. I don't want to talk about the other stuff. It's private.'

I sat back and took a deep breath. I needed him to finish the story before I decided whether he was a victim or a pervert. 'Sorry, I'll leave any questions until the end.' I bit my lip and listened. 'Carry on.'

'I knew that he had changed and that I was in trouble' he composed himself and began recounting his fairy tale. I could tell this was the concocted version he had used for the Press. 'A chill ran down my spine when I realised that the rankness in the farmhouse wasn't coming from any sewer. It was coming from the cellar. It was the smell of death.' Max's eyes were wide and staring at a point behind me. I looked over my shoulder just to make sure Critchley's ghost wasn't standing behind me.

'He kept telling me that he loved me and because of that, he was going to kill me so that I couldn't leave him. For an instant I felt incredibly stupid,' Max said, spitting out the last word. 'Then I realised I had no time to retrace my steps. I knew I'd been smelling death all along. And it was sitting right next to me.'

I frowned to show him that I was being sympathetic, but my mind was made up at that point.

'I know I'm only little, but I've had martial arts training and I know how to take care of myself. I'm stronger than I look but he was just so strong. It was so surreal. He couldn't quite force me to get my other arm around so that he could handcuff me. He didn't hit me. He kept telling me, "C'mon, babe, let me get your other arm." But I kept resisting, wrestling it away.' Max mimicked his panicked movements, twisting and pulling his arm close to his body. He stopped as a new, more macabre thought dawned on him. 'Critchley was trying to sweet talk me into my own murder.'

'Through all this time, you never once screamed for help? Didn't you ever consider screaming or fighting for your life?'

Max turned sullen. 'It's in the middle of nowhere. I was already bleeding from the cuts in my underarm,' he said. 'That knife seemed as sharp as a razor. They put eight stitches where he cut me. There was no doubt in my mind that if I'd raised my voice, he would have struck me dead right then.'

He had a point. The farmhouse was remote, and the area was unpopulated, but I think most men would have died fighting, rather than die easily.

'Critchley told me to stand up and he led me across the room by the handcuff. The knife was firmly stuck in my armpit. I told him, 'you don't have to try to hurt me. I'm not going to fight with you.' I tried to reason with him as he pulled me through the door into a scary scene. His bedroom was just off the living room; it was gloomy and foreboding. The dingy grey walls were plastered with nude pictures of men in all types of disgusting sexual poses. I'd never seen anything like it before and they weren't there when I worked for him.' He looked directly into my eyes as he spoke.

That was an admission that they'd had sexual relations in that house. 'But I didn't look at the pictures for very long,' Max said. 'I couldn't take my mind off the knife. The blade felt hot as fire. Every time I'd catch a glance of it, it was looking bigger and meaner. Meanwhile, Critchley was going through these wide mood swings. He'd whine a low moan over and over. One minute he'd be as cool as a cucumber and the next minute his face was screwed into the Devil's mask telling me how he would kill me and eat me. He kept telling me that you just can't trust anybody anymore, you can't believe people. I told him, "Dewi you can trust me." We had feelings for each other once, at least I thought we did. If I didn't trust you, I wouldn't have come here with you. You'll never leave here,' Critchley said. 'It won't be long, I'll show you. I'll show you things you won't believe. You'll stay here with me forever. You and the others."

Max's monologue broke off with a cough. He sipped his stone-cold coffee, grimacing at its temperature. Max looked up and I noticed his eyes seemed out of focus. But as long as the story was clear, it didn't matter.

'The bedroom was dark except for a lone light in the corner and a television set on the other end of his double bed,' Max recited the details. 'A video tape of The Exorcist was playing on the television. Critchley pointed at the television and told me,

'This was the best movie ever made.' I almost laughed. This nutter thinks he's a film critic,' Max said. 'The windows of the bedroom were blocked, and I could see that he had security alarms hooked to the windowsills. Nobody could get in or out of the place without an alarm going off. I was trapped. There was no escape from this room. I looked at the bed. There was a huge stain on the bed sheet. I guessed it was a bloodstain, but it had turned to a tarnished brown colour,' Max said, his face pale at the memory. 'I was beginning to lose it, the smell, the sounds of the television and Critchley. It was all getting to me. I felt dizzy and disoriented.'

But you still didn't fight for your life, I thought. I had to wonder how much of this was still a game to Max.

'Then I saw it – a hand was sticking out from under the bed.' Max's eyes were clenched shut so he didn't see my puzzled expression. Not one of the interviews with Max had mentioned a body under the bed. 'I could see the end of it. It was just a hand on the end of a small piece of arm. At first, I couldn't convince myself that it was real. It looked like something you might buy in a trick shop. But it was real.'

'Why haven't you mentioned this to anyone else?'

'I felt stupid for being there,' Max shrugged. 'It was my own fault. I just thought we'd have a few beers and a bit of fun, you know.'

'Carry on.'

'I wanted to throw up, but I couldn't. Just a dry retch was all I could manage. 'Don't be sick,' Critchley whispered wetly in my ear, 'I'll take care of you.' He pushed the knife harder and cut me with the blade a little deeper. He forced me to sit down on the filthy bed and sat down next to me.'

My eyes were riveted on Max as I listened to his bullshit. I didn't believe a word of it. 'Next to the bed Critchley had a small bedside cabinet. He reached over and pulled open one of the drawers. Inside the drawer was a human skull with the hair still attached.'

'Go on,' I urged Max.

Max blinked and rubbed his eyes. 'Critchley rubbed the top of the skull while he stared into my eyes. He said that I looked a lot like the men on the wall, but that I had a better body.' This was said almost proudly. 'He kept telling me I was very beautiful; it was as if he were talking to a woman. I was freaked out, but I kept focused on his eyes, looking for a chance to bolt out of the hellhole. I knew the man was possessed. 'I'll let you go if you just let me put your other hand in the handcuff so that I can take some nude pictures of you,' Critchley told me. 'Let me be more in control. Let me take some nude pictures of you then I'll let you go.' I guess I was in shock by this time. All the while he was stroking me slowly, my legs, my back and my head. I just kept talking – talking about anything to keep his mind off what he might have planned. He was holding on tight to the handcuff and once in a while he'd shove that huge knife further up into my armpit,' Max winced in memory of the blade.

'I said you've got to trust me; I'm not going to leave you. I'm going to stay with you.' I tried to reason with him, but I could see that he was going to do what he had to do. He wasn't buying it. He said, 'you're persistent, aren't you? You're real good – but you're going to stay with me forever.' I knew right then that he was going to kill me. He put the knife right in my groin and pushed steadily on it.'

I watched as Max started to cry again. He was a drama queen all right, but the tears and shaking were real. He had experienced genuine terror at the hands of his ex-lover. Even more horrifying was the realisation of what he had escaped from – how close he had come to his own end.

'Every so often, Critchley would open the cabinet drawer and rub the skull, then he'd look back into my eyes,' said Max, his voice breaking again. 'He was going through some type of ritual. He had done this before. Then he pulled some Polaroid pictures of dead men out of the cabinet. The bodies in the photos were decomposed and Critchley told me, 'You'll look really good this way. You'll look better than they did.' Then he put the knife deeply back into my armpit and ordered me to lay down on the bed. The pain was searing,' Max cried openly. 'I laid down on my back and he lowered himself slowly down on top of me with his ear to my chest. He said he wanted to hear my heartbeat. He told me he wanted to see how my heart looked. Then he said that he wanted to eat it.'

'Bollocks,' I muttered, but he just looked at me and carried on.

Max resumed. 'I told Critchley that I had to go to the bathroom. And, if he let me, I'd come back and take off all my clothes so he could take photos. I was trying to buy time, but I was already beginning to feel like a dead man. While I was going to the bathroom, he stood right there with me watching and keeping that knife in my armpit. When I finished, I unbuttoned my shirt all the way down, you know, to make him think I was going along with him. I said, "let's have another beer." He went to the refrigerator and got two, dragging me with him by the end of the handcuff. The kitchen was filthy. There were pots and pans with disgusting gunk in them everywhere. He wanted to go back into the bedroom. But I said, "It's cooler in the living room, let's have the beer in there." I noticed that he wasn't sticking the knife so close to me and I thought he might be getting drunk.' Max sounded hopeful for the first time in his narrative.

'He just kept telling me how pretty I was and how I had such a nice body. But he never tried anything sexual with me. I guess that came later. He told me he liked to keep bodies around. He said he liked it when they didn't move or struggle. We went back to the couch and I sat down. I made him think I was right at home, but I was watching his eyes every second.' Max sat forward in the chair, his hands resting on his knees and talked directly to me. 'Critchley said he'd soon show me things I'd never believe. He asked me if I was drunk and then told me he'd been drinking all day. I told him I was a bit tipsy. Then he started weaving back and forth, not saying anything, just humming in a low tone. It was like he was in a trance. I finally decided that this guy was going to have to kill me. I wasn't going to give in to him. I thought to myself, he's going to have to stab me or whatever, but I'm going to try to get out of here. I figured I was going to die either way.'

This bit gained my attention. It was about time the man thought about escaping.

'The fish tank was blocking the front window and there was no window in the bathroom. I wasn't going back in that bedroom. I couldn't see how I could get out. I told him that I had to go to the bathroom again and this time he let me get up from the couch by myself. I thought to myself, now's your chance. In an instant I grabbed the handcuff from his grip and ran for the door. He reacted like he was in slow motion. I got to the door and turned the dead bolt. It clicked open. Just then, Critchley grabbed hold of my arm. I turned and hit him flush in the face with my fist and kicked him backward. He reeled and I never looked back. He underestimated me and it was his undoing.' Max grinned proudly. 'I bounded at top speed down the hallway and I never even slowed down. I flew through the front door of that house and at last took a deep breath of sweet fresh air. I ran into the woods with the handcuff still dangling from my wrist and eventually spotted a car. They took me to the hospital, but I didn't want the police called. I was terrified of him coming after me.' Max attempted a pious mien as he moralised. 'I thank God I'm alive and I pray for all the poor souls that visited that farmhouse and never left. I know that God sent me to Dewi Critchley. It was my destiny to help put him away. I'd like you to quote me on that.' He smiled humbly.

For a few minutes it was quiet in the room as I digested what I'd just heard. 'But you didn't help to put him away, did you?'

'I didn't what?' Max looked shocked.

'You didn't help to put him away.'

'Of course, I did.' He sat up and put his hands on his hips. 'I came forward as soon as I felt safe. Once he'd been arrested, I told them everything. Haven't you listened to a word that I've said?'

'Yes,' I nodded. 'And I've listened to what you haven't said.'

'What do you mean?'

'You're a lying bastard, basically,' I reached into the holdall for my gun. The sawn-off shotgun looked ugly and dangerous and the colour drained from Blackman's face as he stared into both barrels. I grabbed a blue nylon rope from the bag and waved the gun towards the coffee table. I held up the noose and let it dangle in front of his face.

'Oh my God,' he cried. 'Who are you?'

'Stand on the table, Max, it's question time.'

CHAPTER 4

I made a tearful Max thread the nylon rope around the bolt which held the hanging wicker chair, I put the noose around his neck, then tossed the chair into the corner of the room. The slipknot was tight against Blackman's spinal column and he had to stand precariously on tiptoes to stop the rope strangling him. Tears ran down his face and he shook uncontrollably.

'Do you know who I am?' I asked him.

'No,' he squeezed his eyes shut and shook his head.

'Do you remember a policeman being murdered in Trearddur Bay last year by an author who had apparently gone on a murder spree?' I cocked my head and assessed his reaction. His eyes widened as the incident came back to him.

'Yes,' he grimaced.

'He was a member of the Order of Nine Angels,' I watched his face tighten at the name. 'So was your boyfriend Critchley.'

'I didn't know that,' Max whimpered.

'You're a liar.'

'I'm not.'

'A lot of Niners have lied to me before they died.'

'I've read about it,' he nodded and closed his eyes. 'I didn't know that he was one of them. Please don't hurt me.'

'Good, I can tell that you know who I am now.'

'I remember your face from the papers.'

'Do you know why I killed that policeman and the others?'

'Yes,' he whispered.

'Don't talk, just nod yes or no.'

Max bit his lip and nodded his head quickly. 'Please don't hurt me.'

'I killed them because they were members of a nexion,' I watched his face for a reaction. He understood the meaning of the word. 'You know what a nexion is don't you, Max?'

He nodded yes and a sob escaped his lips. He was going to speak again. 'Shut up and listen,' I held up my finger and put it to my lips. 'I'm going to ask you some questions. You will answer them quickly and you will answer truthfully, or I will kick that table away and leave you to hang. Do you understand?'

He nodded and tried to reply but I raised my finger again. 'Don't speak or you're dead. Just nod yes or no, understand?'

He nodded yes and closed his eyes again.

'You had a relationship with Critchley for a number of years, didn't you?'

He nodded yes.

'You went to the farmhouse that day for sex, didn't you?'

He nodded again.

'It was his thing, bondage and treating you rough wasn't it?'

He nodded yes.

'He didn't try to kill you, did he?'

No, this time.

'You went to the rituals in the cellar willingly, didn't you?'

He squeezed his eyes tightly and nodded yes.

'Were you a member?'

Max closed his eyes tightly to avoid the question, so I nudged the table with my foot. He wobbled and nodded yes in a panic.

'Did you go every full moon?'

Yes.

'The other men who attended the sinister,' I put my foot against the table and wobbled it. 'Do you know their names?'

Yes.

'Do you have their contact details?'

Yes.

'Are they in your mobile phone?'

Yes.

I reached into his jeans pocket and took out the phone. I scrolled through the list of contacts, thirty people in all and read out their names. He nodded yes to four of the men who were listed in his contacts.

'Are they local?'

Yes.

'Now think carefully,' I wobbled the table again. Tears were streaming from his face and a deep red welt was swelling on the soft skin beneath the noose. 'Did you ever meet a black woman called Fabienne Wilder or Baphomet?'

He tried to swallow but couldn't. He nodded yes.

'Recently?'

Yes.

'Was she pregnant?'

Yes.

'Was her face scarred?'

Yes.

'Did she visit this nexion often?'

No.

'Did Critchley invite her?'

No.

'Was it one of the other men on this list?'

Yes.

'So, Critchley wasn't the Temple Master?'

No.

'Which one of them is?' I flicked through the four names in turn. 'David Harris?'

No.

'Gwillam Hughes?'

No.

'Glynn Williams?'

Yes.

'And he is in touch with Fabienne Wilder?'

Yes.

I felt a knot tighten in my stomach. I'd found someone who knew where she was and how to contact her. I looked at Blackman with contempt and thought of one more question. 'Did you take the young boy you were accused of molesting to the cellar?'

He sobbed loudly and shook his head, no. 'Please.' he whined.

'Shut your face.' I snarled. All sympathy had gone from my being months ago. 'But you took him to Critchley, didn't you?'

Yes. Tears dripped from his chin onto the table.

'Were you there when he murdered the other men?'

'Please,' he whined. 'He was frightening.'

'Where you there when he killed them?'

He nodded yes.

'Were you involved in the abuse and murders?'

'Please,' he jabbered. Snot and dribble mixed with his tears now, dangling from his chin like jelly stalactites. 'He got so involved with it all that he became a monster. I was frightened of him.'

'So, you were scared?'

Yes.

'How do you think those men felt?'

He dribbled like a baby; his face twisted in self-loathing. He was as guilty as Critchley was.

'Have you got any porn films?'

He looked confused and nodded yes.

'Are any of them from the farm?'

Yes.

'Is there one in the DVD player now?'

Yes.

I grabbed the remote and pressed play with the butt of the gun, careful not to touch it with my hands. The sound of panting and moaning, mixed with the disturbing voice of a man begging for the torment to stop, drifted from the screen. I pushed the barrels of the gun under his chin with one hand and unfastened his trousers with the other, pulling his jeans and boxer shorts down to his knees with one tug.

'The police will love this DVD when they find you, Max.'

His face was a mask of confusion and fear. I stepped back and kicked the table from beneath him and watched his face turn purple as he choked to death. His eyes bulged and turned a deep red as the blood vessels burst. The slipknot hadn't worked. It didn't break his neck but to be honest, I didn't think that it mattered. Watching the little pervert swing, his legs kicking out in thin air was more satisfying than hearing his neck snap. When the twitching had stopped, I picked up my holdall and headed back onto Caer-glas Road. Max Blackman was on his way to hell, where he belonged.

CHAPTER 5

Ironically, I was sitting in a café in Wales eating a full English breakfast when the first reports of Blackman's death hit the news. The police had forced entry when his friend had reported that he wasn't opening his front door or answering his phone. The initial investigation revealed that he had committed suicide or died during some kind of sexual activity and that no one else was being looked for in connection with his death. By lunchtime that day, speculation that Blackman had been Critchley's lover and possibly his accomplice in the murders at the farmhouse was rife. Details of the DVD collection were being leaked by the police. The Press ripped his initial accounts of the alleged assault by Critchley to shreds and by teatime the following day, he was being painted to be as evil as the cannibal killer himself.

I felt satisfied with the way Blackman had been dispatched. I took out his mobile phone and texted a message to four names in his contacts list. It was time to ask Glynn Williams where Fabienne Wilder was.

CHAPTER 6

Max Blackman had been dead for over a week when I decided on my next move. I was sure that the police were calling it a suicide or misadventure and they'd gone quiet on his death. The DVDs had yielded enough evidence to implicate him in the murders and irrefutable evidence to connect him to the rituals held at the farm. No one had a clue that I was involved in his death, so for now I was in the clear. As long as I didn't do anything to connect his death to the remaining Niners then I couldn't see any reason why the police would re-open the inquest into his death. Going straight for Glynn Williams was my first instinct, but I was worried that if I did that, the others would scurry under a rock and Fabienne Wilder may disappear again. I wanted to make sure that the men in Dewi Critchley's nexion were either exposed to the public and the police as accomplices or exterminated without alerting Jenifer that I was close. One way or the other it suited me. Once I've identified a Niner, I never leave them behind.

The Press reporters were becoming tired of smearing Blackman's character and most of the big named reporters were returning to the cities. The television crews had moved onto the next big story, wherever that was, reporting on someone else's misery. Llangollen was morphing back to a picturesque market town and the tourist trade was bracing itself to go into hibernation for the oncoming lean winter months. Some reporters were digging up local stories from the last few years and trying to find tenuous links to the temple beneath the farmhouse. They focused on one incident, which had happened a few years ago and it was replayed on all the television stations worldwide.

Teenager guilty of pensioner's 'vampire ritual' killing.

(Taken from the BBC News online*)*

A teenager from Anglesey was today found guilty of murdering his elderly neighbour and drinking her blood in a vampire ritual. An art student aged seventeen, was jailed for a minimum of twelve years after being found guilty of butchering the woman at her home in Llanfairpwll, Anglesey, last November. The ninety-year-old widow's heart was cut out and her blood appeared to have been drunk from a saucepan. The teenager was obsessed by vampires and killed the old lady in a bid to become one of the creatures.

He denied any involvement in the murder and claimed his alleged fascination with vampires was no more than a 'subtle interest'.

After the verdict was reached, Mr Justice Richards lifted an order banning his identification. Hardman was convicted by a unanimous verdict. The seventeen-year-old wept when the male foreman read out the verdict and his mother shrieked and sobbed in the public gallery.

Judge Mr Justice Richards said all the evidence pointed to the fact that Hardman believed he could achieve immortality by killing the woman and drinking her blood.

Mr Justice Richards said, 'You have been convicted by the jury on the strength of the most compelling evidence. The horrific nature of this murder was plain to all. It was a vicious and sustained attack on a vulnerable old lady in her own home, aggravated by the mutilation of her body after she'd been killed.

'It was planned and carefully calculated. Why you should have acted in this way is difficult to comprehend but I'm drawn to the conclusion that vampirism had indeed become a near obsession with you, that you really did believe that this myth may be true, that you did think that you would achieve immortality by the drinking of another person's blood and you found this an irresistible attraction. I can make an allowance for a degree of confused thinking and immaturity, for some childish fantasy, but the fact remains, this was an act of great wickedness and one that you have not faced up to and one for which you have not shown any remorse. You hoped for immortality but all you have achieved is the brutal ending of another person's life and the bringing of a life sentence upon yourself.'

Hardman – who had lived just a few yards away and had been the woman's paper boy – mutilated her body before placing pokers at her feet in the shape of a cross. Her heart had been removed, wrapped in newspaper and placed in a saucepan on a silver platter next to her body. The prosecution said her killer drank her blood in a 'macabre ritual'. They also said that the teenager – who denied the charge – was obsessed with vampires and the occult and had told others he wanted to kill someone, in order to become immortal. You can google the murder to find the entire details.

The prosecution also outlined how Hardman had scoured the Internet for vampire websites and had read a magazine which featured an article on how to conduct a black mass. Although the case had all the markings of a satanic ritual murderer acting alone, I had the feeling that Williams's influence may have spread across North Wales. It would be an uncanny coincidence if it wasn't connected. The teenager could have been an 'initiate' trying to progress himself into the sinister by the act of murder. It's difficult to understand what goes through someone's mind when they select a victim to slay. The poor old lady was right on his doorstep, so how he expected to get away with it would be beyond anyone with average intelligence. I was convinced that the four men on my list would have been breathing a sigh of relief as the focus moved away from their immediate area and zoned in on Anglesey. That was perfect for me, as when I started hunting Angels, I wanted them to be off guard.

CHAPTER 7

Harris was relatively easy to find. I had his mobile number, but I didn't want to use it just yet, until I had a solid plan. A direct call from a stranger would spook him. Until I was fully prepared to capture him, I had to keep my powder dry. I needed to research my prey. I wanted to see him in the flesh and analyse his basic movements. I needed to know if he travelled alone and how much of a handful he would be when we met. I didn't know what he looked like, or what he did for a living. He could be a policeman for all I knew about him. He could be the only gay in the village, or he could be the heavyweight champion of somewhere random. Confronting a giant or a man who was a trained fighter was a dangerous gamble to take and the odds would be against me unless I studied him first. If he was always in the company of other males, at work and socially, then it would be more difficult still. It was not the type of surprise I wanted. Making sure that it would be simple to take him out was uppermost in my mind.

I couldn't leave a trail of dead occultists across North Wales without pinpointing my whereabouts to the police. I was still high up on their wanted list and I knew that I wouldn't last five minutes in jail. I just don't have the temperament to be incarcerated. I freak out if I have to stay indoors all day, let alone be locked inside a six-foot cell with just another criminal for company. If captured and convicted, I would be a high risk to the public and sent to a category 'A' prison for a long time, probably life. Prison would be full of the Niners' affiliates too. I would be silenced within days. Although there had been some sympathy for my position, especially after Constance was recovered unhurt, I didn't think that there was any guarantee a judge would see it that way. There was a swell of public support following her release and the ensuing flurry of nasty facts that was unveiled about her captors. The surviving Niner was sent down for fifteen years, which didn't seem long enough to me. I may get some consideration for extenuating circumstances, but I doubted it. I always hope for the best but plan for the worst.

If you're looking for a target's whereabouts, then the easiest way to find them is via their telephone number. Electoral lists are useful but if you're looking for someone with a common name, the telephone directory is the best way to narrow it down. When I looked through the telephone book, there were hundreds of listings with the surname Harris and the initial 'D' was common too. I decided to take the direct route to narrow the search and came up with a ruse. I called his mobile number from a telephone box. It took me twenty minutes to find a phone box in working order. I opened the door and the smell of stale urine hit me in the face. A dark stain flowed out of the booth and snaked across the pavement, still damp and sticky from the night before. I dialed his number.

'Hello,' he sounded cautious because the number that I'd rung from wasn't listed in his phone. The fact it was a local number would work in my favour.

'Is this David Harris?' I asked.

'Yes, who is this?'

'Have you still got the van for sale?'

'No, I'm not selling a van.'

'Have you sold it?'

'No, I've never had a van for sale. You've got the wrong number.'

'Bloody hell, sorry I was told there was a van for sale in Corwen.' I was taking a gamble on where he was. 'Are you in Corwen?'

'Yes, but I haven't got a van.'

'I must have the wrong David Harris then, sorry to bother you,' I lied. 'I don't suppose you know a David Harris who has a garage there do you?'

He hung up, but I'd narrowed it down to the same village as the one that Max Blackman was from. There were three D. Harris listed in the directory for Corwen. I stuffed another pound coin into the phone and dialed the first one on the list. It rang three times before the call was answered by a woman.

'Hello?'

'Hi, is David in please?'

'There's no David here, doll,' she replied politely.

'Sorry I 've been given this number about a van for sale and was told to ask for David Harris,' I lied again.

'No. I'm sorry, doll, there's no one here by that name. My name is Harris, but it's not David, doll, it's Diane,' she chuckled.

'Sorry to bother you,' I hung up and dialed the next number. This time a man's voice answered. 'Hi is that David?'

'Derek speaking, who is this?'

'Sorry, wrong number.' I hung up again and wrote down the last remaining address. If he was the D Harris listed in the directory, then he lived at 16 Williams St, Corwen. I needed to be sure that the Harris listed was a David. I dialed the landline number from the directory and after a few rings a woman's voice came onto the line.

'Hello?'

'Hello, is David there please?' I asked.

'No, he's out at work at the moment, sorry,' she said chirpily. 'Can I help?'

'It's not important, thanks. What time is he back?'

'They usually finish on the farm about five-ish,' she answered. He worked on a farm which linked him to Critchley. The farming communities are tight. Everyone knows everyone.

'No problem, I'll call him later on.'

'Shall I say who called,' her curiosity got the better of her, but I didn't want to get into any conversations with her. Making a mistake would be too easy so I hung up and thought about my next move. I typed the address into my phone and searched Google Maps for the position. It was a small side street not far away from the pub where I'd stayed when I hunted Blackman. The house was halfway down the street which consisted of two rows of small terraced houses. I would be noticed if I parked anywhere on that street but there was a street adjacent to it with a newsagent and a fish and chip shop. I could buy chips and a newspaper and sit there for a while without being noticed. I pushed my way out of the stinking phone box and enjoyed the taste of fresh mountain air again. I'd located my prey and the hunt was on.

CHAPTER 8

I reached Corwen in twenty minutes or so and when I passed the pub where I'd stayed, I turned left down the hill towards the river. The houses there were built on a steep gradient and the roofs of the buildings at the bottom of the hill were at eye level as I steered the Landy down the narrow road. I could see the shops halfway down the street. The newsagents had an awning above the window. The red and white stripes were faded and dirty, years of weathering had taken their toll. The chip shop was next door and there was a queue of people outside waiting to order their supper. As I drew nearer, the smell of chips and vinegar drifted into the Landy making my mouth water. I hadn't eaten all day and my stomach was telling me to give it something to digest. As I pulled up near the curb, I saw Williams Street on the left. The odd numbers were on the left and the even on the right. Number 16 was too far away for me to identify from the numerals on the door. The houses were uniform from the front although the odd one or two looked freshly painted and stood out from the rest.

I turned off the engine and climbed out of the Landy. I stretched and focused on the houses in Williams St. There wasn't a soul about. The queue outside the chip shop was dwindling, but I decided to let it go down while I bought a newspaper. I walked into the shop and a bell above the door alerted the owner that they had a customer. A woman in her sixties half smiled and eyed me suspiciously. Tourists were a novelty this far from the main roads. I scanned the rack of red-top newspapers, taking in the headlines.

A knot squeezed my guts when I saw my picture looking straight back at me. The Sun had linked the satanic cult in Carrog to my plight a year before and although they were speculating that it may be the same cult that had forced me into hiding and that the murders could have been self-defence, the photograph was the last thing that I needed now. The article read, 'Author still on the run-in connection with three murders, could have been targeted by a cult connected to the Cannibal Killer.' It read on to describe briefly the events of twelve months ago and was almost sympathetic to my situation. They highlighted the fact that there was irrefutable evidence that the dead policeman found at my house was a member of the Order of Nine Angles. My appearance in the photograph was much heavier with a fuller face. I was slimmer now and disguised enough not be identified easily from the photo but raising the profile of my disappearance didn't help me one bit. The last line made me smile as it warned the public not to approach me as I was considered dangerous. They were spot on, hunted men are dangerous but in my case the only danger I presented was to the Niners. I'd decided a long time ago that if the police came for me, I would give myself up and take my chances with the judicial system. Despite hating confined spaces, being gunned down in the street didn't appeal to me either.

I picked up the newspaper when the woman behind the counter coughed into her hand. I must have taken too long reading the headlines without making a purchase. I folded the paper into my jacket and dropped a fifty pence piece onto the counter without speaking to her. She grunted something as I turned and walked away but I didn't respond. I could feel her eyes following me as I walked past the window into the chip shop. Maybe I was being paranoid or maybe she'd recognised me. Either way, I didn't want to stand and chitchat with the miserable cow while my photograph was splashed over the front pages.

I ordered chips, fish and mushy peas on a tray and drenched them in vinegar, before climbing back into the Landy to eat them while I watched out for Harris. I scanned the headlines but couldn't concentrate on anything outside of the front pages. The food tasted as good as it smelled, and I demolished the fish and left half of the chips uneaten. My appetite was not as keen as it once was. As I screwed up the wrapping paper, a heavy-set man stepped out of a doorway roughly where number 16 would have been. I grabbed my mobile and dialed the number for David Harris which I'd taken from Blackman's contact list. As the number that I'd dialed began to ring, the big man reached into his jeans and took out his mobile. He looked at the screen with a confused look on his face. Bingo, I'd found him.

CHAPTER 9

David Harris looked to be over fifty years of age and he was wide at the shoulders, almost bursting the seams of his tartan shirt and had a beer belly which hung over the top of his chino trousers by about six inches. His well-worn pair of Caterpillar work boots looked to be about a size eleven. He was a big man. As he climbed into an old Ford Mondeo, I guessed he was about six feet tall and weighed eighteen stones or more. Lifting him up or squaring up to him in a fist fight were not options that I wanted to consider. I needed to lure him somewhere remote and entrap him. If I couldn't think of a way to incriminate him or link him to Critchley, then I would have to kill him and let nature help me out in disposing of his bloated body.

He started the engine, indicated and pulled the Ford away from the curb, before turning around at the end of the street and driving back towards me. I hid my face behind my newspaper as he drove up the hill, starting the engine as soon as he had gone and then followed him up to the main road. He turned right and headed up the A5 towards the Snowdonia area which gave me an idea. I needed somewhere remote; somewhere dangerous where nature could take a man's life.

I was frustrated when two hundred yards on, he slowed down and pulled the Mondeo into a parking bay outside the Spar shop. It was a total journey of about 300 yards, but the lazy bastard had chosen to drive to the shop rather than walking up the hill. I parked across the road and watched as he walked back to his car with eight tins of strong lager and a family sized bag of crisps. Obviously, his physique had been built on a mixture of poor diet, alcohol, and no exercise. As he turned his car around and drove back down the hill towards his house, I lit a menthol and pulled the Landy back onto the A5, driving north in the opposite direction. I knew exactly where I was going.

All I had to do was convince Harris to follow me. It was a thirty-mile drive to Betws-y-Coed and the sunlight was fading. I needed to wait awhile, so that Harris had drunk enough lager to impair his judgment but couldn't wait until he was incapable of driving. I'd never met the man, but I've met enough Niners to know what makes them tick. Once he was comfortable in his armchair munching on his crisps and drinking beer, it would be difficult to tempt him to get into his car and drive north. There was one person for who he would drive under the influence, no matter what the time was and so I sent him a text message from her on the way.

'Be at the Miners' Bridge, Betws at 9 p.m. I need to talk to you, Fabienne W x.'

The 'message sent' alert appeared on my screen. My phone vibrated almost immediately. 'How do I know it's you?' the text reply said.

'I am Baphomet Sekhemet, your high priestess and you will come to me, or I'll come to you,' I replied.

'Okay, sorry, just making sure. Do I need my stuff?' He replied.

'You know what to bring, you fool.' I replied. I had no idea what 'his stuff' would be, but it didn't matter. The bait had been taken, but I'd made a silly mistake; one that I would live to regret.

CHAPTER 10

Betws-y-Coed is a pretty village which lies in the Snowdonia National Park and is one of the most visited tourist spots in Wales. The name meaning 'Prayer house in the wood' links the origins of the village to a Christian place of worship. Betws was built around a monastery by the Anglo-Saxons in the late sixth century. Situated in a valley where the River Conwy is joined by the River Llugwy and the River Lledr, its waterfalls and forests are renowned the world over for their beauty. They're also known for their treacherous ravines and the powerful currents, chutes, siphons and whirlpools. Many walkers, climbers and canoeists die in the mountains and rivers every year.

When I reached the village, I parked the Landy next to the slate-built railway station and put four-pound coins into the parking meter. I grimaced at the price to park for two hours and then stuck the ticket to the inside of the windscreen. As I looked around, the souvenir shops which lined the station building were illuminated by their interior lights as dusk settled into the valley. It was as pretty as a picture and the village had calmness to it that evening and I could hear the roar of the Llugwy in the distance as it thundered down the falls.

I felt a terrible pang of loneliness as I watched couples walking arm in arm across the village green. My normal life was gone. I wished that I was parking up and booking into a bed-and-breakfast with my partner for the night. I wished that we could stroll along in search of a romantic restaurant to eat and drink wine and chat about the world but there was no partner for me anymore and no woman in her right mind would want to chat to me about the world in which I was living.

'What did you do this week babe?'

'Oh, I tracked down a little nonce in Corwen and strung him up from the rafters. It was such a hectic week but worthwhile seeing him dangle. You should have seen his eyes bulging out of his head. I thought they were going to pop out at one point.'

My imaginary conversation dragged me down to the lowest point that I'd been for months. I was alone in my terrible quest and the pain of loneliness bit deep into me that night as I watched the normal people strolling along enjoying the peace and tranquillity of the village. There were a few dozen tourists, mostly climbers and ramblers, milling around the outdoor pursuit shops, while couples and families browsed the souvenir shops and café bars. I wondered how things would be if I'd never stumbled across Fabienne Wilder. My life had become an existence outside of normal society. I was no longer a civilised human being who could feel the warmth and tenderness gifted by others. I was a predator, cold as ice when confronted with a Niner and focused on killing, yet inside there was still the man that I used to be, and he was afraid and alone sometimes. Loneliness and desperation wrapped itself around me like a living thing and I felt stinging tears welling up in my eyes. I wiped them away with the back of my hand and headed across the village green. It was darker there and no one would see me sobbing as I walked. I let the tears run freely down my cheeks and felt bitterly alone. It wasn't the first time that I'd cried, and it wouldn't be the last. When Evie Jones was with me, it didn't seem so bad. Her undying affection carried me through the bad days but in the end, she was a giveaway to who I was. The police were looking for a bald man with tattoos and a Staffie. I'd taken her to my ex-partner's new home and tied her to the gate. Driving away and leaving her there broke my heart, but she'd be safer there than with me and it was easier to blend in when I was alone. There have been good days and bad days since I left her, but I'm not in the position to crumble emotionally, the alternatives are far worse.

When the tears had stopped, I walked across the village green and crossed the Pont-y-Pair Bridge, which is pictured on hundreds of postcards. Recent rains had flooded the three rivers to bursting point and the water of the Llugwy roared through all three arches that supported the ancient, bluish stones. That day, even the bravest canoeists deemed the water too high to venture onto.

On the other side of the bridge was the shop that I wanted to visit. I had no idea if it was still in business as it had been several years since I'd visited it previously. The section of road leading to it had no street lights illuminating it and the trees which overhung the pavements turned into dark silhouettes as the sunlight dissipated into darkness. The branches looked like skeletal fingers reaching for me. A shiver ran through my soul and chilled me to the bone. My loneliness was eating away at my inner strength. I had to get a grip before it wore me down and made me weak. I thought about the victims at the Critchley farm and how their mothers, fathers, brothers and sisters would be feeling, knowing what their kin suffered before they died. Their bodies were desecrated, and their flesh devoured by sick animals like Harris. I steeled myself with the anguish that the families would be feeling and felt the passion and the anger returning to me. Anger was good. It made me focused again.

The shop that I wanted stood alone a hundred yards away from its nearest neighbor, tucked away beneath the trees at the bottom of a cliff face. A solitary strip light burned inside the front of the shop. The top attic window, directly above the main entrance, was blanked out completely. The doorway was virtually blocked by a display of kitbags, army issue camouflage jackets, military cocoon sleeping bags, and an array of baskets overflowing with boots, gloves and hats. The sign above the door read 'military surplus' and the shop did exactly what it said on the tin. I'd bought some army issue desert boots and a jacket years before and they were still going strong. The shop was an Aladdin's cave for climbers and walkers who dared to take on the elements in the mountains. I needed something a little more dangerous than a sturdy pair of boots this time and I was hoping that the owner might have a stash of stuff which he sold under the counter. I remembered that he sold some pretty dodgy weapons at the back of the shop. Sheath knives of every shape and size and knuckle-dusters with evil spikes and barbs welded to them. You have to wonder how they got away with selling them, but I hoped that they were just the tip of the iceberg.

The sound of a thrash-metal band drifted from the doorway, the lyrics unidentifiable and the guitars deafening. I was sure that the same track was playing years ago when I bought my boots. I decided that all that heavy stuff sounded the same to me as I ducked beneath a rucksack and entered the building. The walls on the left were hidden beneath an avalanche of military kitbags of every shape, size and colour. To the right was a glass counter which contained an array of Swiss Army knives and camping tools, Mag-lights and GPS devices. Sat behind the counter was the owner of the shop; a man-mountain called Bren who stared out through a thicket of black hair and whiskers. His Motorhead T-shirt was riddled with burn holes, obviously caused by years of smoking cannabis. There was a strong smell of incense sticks, probably employed to hide the smell of dope. They were failing miserably.

'all right,' Bren growled as I walked in.

'all right.' I scanned the wall behind him. There were twenty or more high-powered air rifles displayed there and a range of hunting crossbows which fired tungsten bolts.

'Are you just looking, or can I help you with anything specific?' Bren stood up and turned the music off; his full height was nearer the 7 feet mark than 6. I figured he weighed twenty-five stones or thereabouts. He followed my eyes as I checked over the array of weapons.

'I need a lantern, but one with a timer fitted,' I decided to start with the non-lethal items first.

'Walk this way; I've got a few over here.' Bren lumbered between shelves crammed with mess tins and camping stoves. He had to duck beneath a beam which had a dozen pairs of highly polished infantry boots hanging from it. 'Do you want battery or self-winding?'

'Battery.'

'Disposable batteries or rechargeable?'

'Disposable.'

'This one has a timer which switches the lamp off only, or this one can be set to go on and off three times in a twelve-hour period.'

'I'll take the one which can be set three times.'

'Do you want the batteries too?' Bren seemed to be staring at my face intently.

'Yes, give me two sets, please.' I smiled and walked away. His closer inspection of my face was making me nervous. 'Have you got any ponchos?'

'On the wall over there,' he grunted. 'They're all one size just the camo pattern that's different.'

'I'll take two, the black one and the green camo one please.'

'Are you doing some hunting?' Bren eyed me suspiciously but there was a glint in his eyes. 'Rabbits, badgers?'

'Something like that,' I smiled thinly and walked towards the back of the shop.

'16th Air Assault Brigade.' Bren wagged a finger.

'What?' I had no idea what he was talking about.

'Paratrooper regiment—' he shrugged his huge shoulders as if I should know what he was talking about '—they wear these ponchos when they're in the field. I got a couple of dozen at an auction the last time they went out to Afghanistan.'

'Sorry, I get you now.' I laughed. I browsed the walls and shelves as I neared the glass display cabinets which were fitted to the back wall of the shop. Steel blades of varying lengths glinted from inside, some serrated some saw-toothed and all razor sharp. 'Nice collection of blades here.'

'You looking for anything special?' He towered above me. The knowing glint was still in his eyes. 'This double-edged stiletto is still the weapon of choice for taking somebody out quickly. If you know what I mean?' He made a huge fist and placed it beneath his bushy beard. 'Push it straight up into the windpipe through the roof of the mouth and into the brain. Dead in seconds.'

'Do you get many commandos in here?' I smiled but Bren didn't find my sarcasm funny. 'I suppose one of those would be handy if it all kicks off at the gift shop down the road, eh?'

'Are you looking for a blade or not, smart-arse?' His face darkened and his huge hands twitched.

'No, not today but I could use a snare or garrote wire if you have any stashed away somewhere,' it was my turn to stop smiling. I looked straight into his eyes and despite his size, he stepped back an inch. 'I need something big enough to snare a deer. A big one.'

'Deer, my fat arse.' He laughed. 'Metal snares are illegal. Now what makes you think that I would sell something like that?'

'I'm guessing that I'm not the first poacher to come sniffing around in here.'

'Poacher?' He scoffed and lowered his face to within six inches of mine. He put his finger to his lips and smiled, 'I know who you are, Mr Jones. I've seen your picture in the papers. You're all over the net.'

I nodded and shrugged. He was between me and the door and I had no weapons on me. My emotions were at an all-time low and I simply didn't care that he had recognised me. 'Okay, so you know who I am,' I kept eye contact with him, and I could sense that he was nervous. 'What are you going to do about it?'

'I'm going to shake your hand and donate a lantern and a couple of ponchos to your cause,' he held out a hand the size of a shovel. 'I've been following all the stuff on the Internet for months. You got shafted big time by those fucking perverts eh?' I shook his hand although I wasn't convinced that Bren was an ally. His grip was strong but not painful. 'Did what happened with that bastard Critchley bring you down here? I bet it did. I bet you're looking for them, aren't you?'

'Yes, I'm looking for them.' I nodded and pulled my hand from his grip. 'Look it's best if you don't ask questions. I just need some stuff and then I'm gone.'

'Bollocks to that.' He grabbed my shoulders and rubbed them patronisingly. 'I want to know all about it. How the fuck have you stayed hidden all this time? Let's have a beer and you can tell me everything. I could help you out. Me and the missus have been following it all since day one. I've told her a thousand times that if I ever meet that bloke, I'm going to shake his hand.'

'Listen, Bren,' I said sternly. His enthusiasm was almost childlike. 'I have to be somewhere tonight. If it all goes to plan, I'll come back and visit and tell you everything but right now, I need a wire snare and I need to go, okay?'

'You could stay with us for a while. The missus would be made up with that.' He patted me on the back which felt like being hit with a minibus. 'Listen, I've got some stuff upstairs. Traps, snares, tasers, mace, body armour; you know, all the shit I can't sell in here but can move on the Internet.'

'Well I was hoping that you might have.' I smiled. 'But I need to hurry.'

He turned and walked toward a dummy which was dressed in a full NBC suit including a gas mask. Behind it was a 6X8 foot piece of chipboard, fitted with brackets displaying a colourful selection of Samurai swords. He slid the dummy to one side and then moved the chipboard as if it was made from paper, to uncover a doorway and a staircase which led up to the attic rooms. 'I'll need to lock the front door, give me a minute,' Bren said ambling across the shop.

Just as he approached the doorway, a woman stepped into the shop. The smile on her face told me that she was 'the missus'. She was dwarfed by the man she shared her life with, although her dress sense explained why they were together. Her hair was purple and backcombed into a mane which surrounded her face and finished halfway down her back. A diamond stud glinted from her nose and her eye make-up gave her the look of an Egyptian Queen. She wore an ancient black leather biker's jacket and faded blue jeans. The wrinkles around her eyes told me that she was pushing forty, but she looked good for it.

'Hey, how's the day been?' She reached up and flung her arms around his massive neck. 'Has it been busy?'

'So, let me shut the door,' he chuckled. 'Boy, have I got a surprise for you.' He took the haversacks down from the doorway and tossed them to one side before pulling the door closed and bolting it at the top and bottom. She watched him with a confused look on her face and then sensing that someone else was there, her eyes settled on me. The smile disappeared from her face, replaced by a frown. 'You won't believe who is here.' Bren said excitedly.

'Who?' She half smiled and walked towards me. 'Sorry, do I know you or is my husband tripping again?' Bren walked behind her with a wide grin on his face. She was confused but there was also a vague recognition in her eyes. 'I know your face, but I can't think where I know you from.'

I smiled uncomfortably and shifted my feet. I wanted to grab some stuff and be gone. 'If I said his name is Jones and he killed some of those sickos like that farmer from Carrog, would you get it then?' Bren chuckled again.

'Oh my God.' She clicked on. Her face showed both surprise and muted horror. 'Bren, what the hell are you doing?'

'What do you mean?' he looked offended. 'He walked in here to buy some stuff and I recognised him straight away. He's been all over the papers again today, haven't you?' he said smiling at me. Bren couldn't see that his missus wasn't as pleased to see me as he was. 'I'm going to show him my special stuff and help him out. He said he'll come and stay with us afterwards and tell us all about it.'

'Stay with us? Are you mad?' she asked incredulously. 'He's a wanted criminal. If you don't call the police, then I will.' She realised what she'd said and stepped back away from me a pace. Her eyes told me that she was scared.

'You don't need to call the police, I'll leave now.' I shrugged and smiled. I couldn't blame her for her reaction. 'Can I pay you for the stuff first?'

'Don't listen to her.' Bren frowned. 'We're not calling the police. This bloke has been running for his life and I'm going to help him.'

'And when did we start sheltering criminals?'

'We haven't. I just said he could crash with us after, that's all.'

'After what exactly?' she said quietly looking at me through piercing green eyes. 'Whatever he's about to do, we're having no part in this. He's wanted by the police for murder. Bren, have you gone mad?'

'You said that you felt sorry for him.' Bren frowned. 'I'm just helping him out that's all.'

'I think it would be best if I just go.' I took thirty pounds out of my wallet and offered it to Bren. 'This should cover the ponchos and the lantern; that's all I need.'

'Are you in danger?' she asked. There was pity in her eyes as well as fear. 'I'm Sade, by the way.' She offered her hand and I shook it briefly.

'I'm always in danger, Sade but that isn't your problem. I need that stuff and then I'm gone.' I forced the notes into Bren's hand and walked by them. 'No one will know that I've been here and I'm sorry if being here has disturbed you, Sade.'

'they'll know that you have been here.' Sade raised her voice. 'Are you stupid? How many places around here do you think sell that garbage?'

'Garbage?' Bren snapped.

'It's all shit, Bren.' She turned on him. 'Who the fuck buys ex-military clothing except grown men who want to play soldiers up the mountains? Oh, apart from the odd wanted murderer of course.'

'It keeps us going.' Bren looked mortally wounded.

'My job keeps us going, Bren,' she corrected him. 'This place barely breaks even. If he gets caught with that stuff on him anywhere within a fifty-mile radius of here, the police will be knocking on that door and if they search upstairs and find your 'special stuff' then you'll be going down for a long time, you retard.'

'That's enough.' Bren growled. 'Right, I'm not having this. Take your money back and follow me.' He passed me the ponchos and the lantern and stuck the notes into my coat pocket. He nodded and then marched off up the stairs turning almost sideways to fit his huge bulk up the narrow staircase. 'What else do you need?'

I glanced at Sade before following him. She'd flushed red with anger. The urge to walk out of the door was trumped by the need for some equipment. I followed the big man up the stairs. 'I need a snare and some mace, that's all.'

The staircase was unlit, and my eyes couldn't adjust to the darkness until Bren turned a key in the lock at the top and opened the door. A dull light permeated the stairwell and the smell of gun oil and cordite drifted to me. The attic room was long, and the ceiling vaulted. The roof trusses were exposed, and the black slate tiles were crooked in places. The floorboards were dark and dusty with age. At the far end of the attic was a target shaped like a soldier aiming a weapon. It was riddled with bullet holes as were the bricks behind it. That explained the smell of cordite. Bren must have had a pistol or a rifle which he fired up there. The attic was a firing range as well as his storeroom. He unlocked a storage cupboard and rummaged inside. His massive shape disappeared for a moment before he returned holding a canister of mace and a coiled wire trap. 'Here, take them and if you ever need anything else, call me.' He handed me a business card with his contact details. 'Take no notice of Sade she must have the painters in, the moody cow.'

I was about to thank him when a creaking floorboard alerted me to the fact that someone was right behind me. Blinding light flashed in my brain like a huge camera flash and then thudding pain shot through my head. My skull felt like it was about to implode, and the world turned dark.

CHAPTER 11

I woke up in total darkness and my head throbbed in pain. I reached for the back of my skull where the epicentre of the pain was situated and felt my blood congealing around a two-inch gash in the skin. Someone had coshed me from behind and I could only guess that it was Sade. Bren had locked the front door before we climbed the stairs, so it had to be her. I sat up and pulled my knees to my chest resting my head on my arms. I almost gave up at that point. The urge to lie down, curl up and wait for whoever to open the door was overwhelming. I almost resigned myself to a life behind bars until an image of Evie Jones came into my head. Her tenacity and fearlessness had saved my life several times and I couldn't let her down by giving up.

I shook my head and gave myself a mental slap. The pain was a dulling ache, but my senses were returning quickly. As my eyes adjusted, shafts of light formed a rectangle behind me. It was a closed door with the light from the other side filtering through the frame, so I presumed that I'd been dragged into the storage cupboard that Bren had unlocked. I could hear raised voices on the other side of the door. Bren and Sade were bickering about what they should do. Sade repeatedly told him to call the police and if he didn't, then she was going to. Bren was adamant that he didn't want the police in the shop and that he wanted to help me, not turn me into the law. I listened for a few minutes and their voices faded as they took the argument down the stairs into the shop. When I heard Sade mentioning a reward for information leading to my arrest, I knew that I had to move quickly. I wasn't going to let them take me so that she could buy a new pair of jeans. Cringing in a cupboard feeling sorry for myself was not how I was going to go down.

I reached into my pocket and took out my cigarettes and lighter. I lit one of the menthols and inhaled deeply and then used the flame to find my bearings. The cupboard was made from partitioned wood and the ceiling was the underside of the slate roof. I looked around at the shelves and rifled through the contents. I grabbed a camouflage rucksack and looked inside it. There were a dozen or so large flares crammed into cellophane wrapping with Chinese writing on the label. I stuffed the ponchos, the mace and the snare into the bag and slipped my arms through the straps. The lantern was lying on the floor near the door, so I picked it up and switched it on. Scanning the cupboard quickly, I saw my means of escape leaning against the wall. An ornate sledgehammer stood in the corner. The handle and shaft were wrapped with plaited leather and the head was moulded from polished steel. It was a replica of Thor's hammer or an imitation of a weapon from a fantasy war game. Whatever its origin, it would help me to escape.

I grabbed the lowest shelf and wedged my foot against the wall. Reaching up, I started to climb the shelves with the hammer in one hand. Standing on the second shelf, I could reach the slate roof tiles. There was no room to swing the hammer, so I stabbed at the tiles with the heavy steel head. Three strikes and the tiles splintered and tumbled into the cupboard. A fourth blow sent an avalanche of broken tiles skidding down the roof. I could hear them smashing on the road below. The clattering alerted Bren and his wife to my escape and I heard his footsteps thundering up the stairs. Sade's high-pitched voice followed him.

'Lock the door, you idiot.' She wailed. 'The police are on their way.'

'What do you think I'm doing, silly cow,' Bren retorted. I heard the door at the top of the stairs being slammed and locked. That suited me fine as I was heading the other way, onto the roof.

'They said we're to get out of the building and lock all the doors, an armed unit has been dispatched from Colwyn Bay.'

'I'm not happy about this, Sade. You're well out of order.'

'Shut up and think of the money,' she mumbled.

Her voice was muffled behind the doors now, but it carried enough for me to hear her. I knew the local police station was a one-man operation. Two at best. They would be ordered to secure the location and wait for armed backup. Colwyn Bay was a thirty-minute drive away even for a police interceptor with its blue lights flashing. I reached up through the tiles and grabbed a roof truss, smashing the hole bigger with the hammer as I climbed. Slates rained down on me, but the gap was soon big enough for me to fit through. I dropped the hammer with a crash and swung my legs up to the top shelf, my head and shoulders protruding through the hole in the roof. The night air was cold on my skin, but it sharpened my senses. The feeling of freedom sent adrenalin racing through my bloodstream. I looked around and wondered if I'd chosen the best escape route. The roof was pitched steeply and there was nothing to grip on to. The eaves had an overhang on them making climbing down a drainpipe impossible. At the back of the shop, the cliff face climbed thirty feet above to a tree line. There was no way down through the shop as man-mountain Bren was down there waiting for the police. If I was going to escape, then I had to climb up.

I shimmied onto the tiles and pressed myself flat against the roof. My arms and legs were splayed apart, feet at ninety degrees to my body. I began to edge along the slate slowly. I couldn't see Bren or Sade and at that point, they hadn't seen me, but then I caught sight of a strobing blue light approaching from the bridge. The siren blared for a few seconds and then stopped as it turned the corner toward the shop. I remained still for a moment as the headlights illuminated the roof. As the vehicle veered right, the lights swept over me and pointed at the river leaving me in darkness again. With the veil of darkness over me, I edged along the roof again my breathing was shallow, and my fingers ached as I tried to grip the smooth stone tiles. I could hear words exchanged but I couldn't make them out. There was no more than five yards between me and the edge of the roof, when I slipped.

A slate tile dislodged beneath my right foot and some of its neighbours went with it. I slid towards the roof edge tearing skin from my fingertips and ripping my nails as I desperately tried to get a grip. My left foot found a hold in the gap which the tiles had left, and my body weight forced me to spin 180 degrees, head first, in a circle. The tiles smashed on the concrete below and I was left hanging precariously over the eaves, my head hanging over and my legs and arms spread-eagled across the slate. The blood was rushing to my head as my feet were elevated by the pitch of the roof. Torchlight dazzled my eyes, blinding me as I was left gasping for breath and clinging on for dear life.

'He's on the roof,' Sade shouted.

'She's sharp. She doesn't miss a trick, does she?' a voice commented sarcastically on her observation. 'Stay where you are Mr Jones, there's nowhere to go from there.'

'Take that torchlight out of my eyes, please,' I asked. The light moved from my eyes enough for them to see me clearly and I could plainly see a uniformed officer standing next to Bren and Sade. The blue light was still flashing on his vehicle and I could hear the engine running.

'There's an armed unit on the way, Mr Jones,' the officer said calmly. 'It's time to come in and put your side of the story. Nobody wants to hurt you, so stay put and I'll call a fire engine to get you down.'

His radio crackled as he requested assistance from the fire brigade and backup from all available officers. My brain was working at warp speed trying to fathom how to get out of the mess that I was in. I should have known better than to walk into a shop when my picture had been on the front pages. I settled my breathing down and pushed myself back from the edge. Another shower of slate slipped and fell from the roof, splintering into a thousand shards when they hit the floor.

'Best you stay still for now,' the officer shouted anxiously. 'The fire brigade is on the way. Best you stay put,' he repeated.

'Best for who? You?' I shouted. 'When the fire brigade get here, tell them that Bren's little collection of explosives and fireworks are about to go off.' I laughed ironically. 'If you want to know what is 'best' then I think it's 'best' if you fuck off as far away from here as you can before it blows the roof off,' I shouted. 'I set fire to his cache of illegal shit in the attic before I climbed up here. It seemed like a good idea at the time but now I'm not so sure. These tiles are getting a bit hot.'

The officer reached for his radio again and blurted out what I'd said to whoever was listening. Startled voices replied over the airwaves. Bren and Sade looked at each other and began moving backwards. The officer noted their concern and followed suit.

'Are there fireworks up there, Bren?' He growled.

'A few but nothing illegal, George,' Bren muttered. They were obviously on first-name terms, which was the norm in a small Welsh village.

'I've warned you about keeping shit up there,' the officer hissed. 'I'll ask you this once and once only and if you lie to me, Bren I'll not be able to help you. Understand?'

'Yes.'

I righted myself slowly while they bickered. My story about the fire would only last for so long when they realised that there was no smoke billowing out of the roof. The pressure in my skull eased as I repositioned myself. As I edged inch by inch towards the back of the shop, I could hear them arguing.

'Are there any explosives up there?'

'There are some fireworks and some gunpowder.'

'Gunpowder?'

'Yes, for making ammunition,' Bren shrugged. 'I've been pressing my own bullets for my .22.'

'You idiot.' the officer snapped.

'I've got a license for it, George,' Bren whined. 'I only use it for rabbits.'

'He's moving.' Sade pointed out.

'He's the least of your worries, Sade,' the officer said walking to his vehicle. 'Get back to the bridge now!' he shouted. He opened the car door and climbed in, gunning the engine as he reversed it toward the bridge. I decided that Bren's confession was a bonus ball for me. Reaching into the haversack, I took out a flare. I snapped the top and it ignited with an intense red flame. I heard Officer George shouting something as I tossed the flare into the hole in the tiles. When I looked inside the attic, the flare was fizzling away harmlessly on the floor, but the smoke would help my predicament. I dropped two more ignited flares and the loft was filling up with coloured smoke. I noticed that one of them had set fire to a cardboard carton the size of a large suitcase. The Chinese writing on the box made me suspect that it could be full of fireworks or flares or better still, gunpowder. Orange flames licked up the side of the box and spurred me into making a move. I kept my back to the tiles which was difficult with the haversack on and shimmied sideways across the roof to the rear of the building like a huge crab. The gap between the rock and the roof was less than five feet. I looked back and the smoke was pouring from the building. It was black and acrid, and it was beginning to choke me. A siren approached from the north and I knew that was where the fire station was situated. I contemplated climbing down, but it was futile. The police officer and Bren would be more than enough to restrain me. If I jumped for the rock face, I would grip and climb or fall and break my neck. The rock was criss-crossed with tree roots from the woods above and I had a good chance of gripping something. My decision-making process was interrupted when a huge bang deafened me.

It echoed across the village and along the valley. A section of roof simply exploded upwards in a shower of multicoloured sparks. Slate shards whistled skyward through the air like a thousand sharp daggers and as the old adage says, 'what goes up must come down'. I would be cut to ribbons or blown to bits if I stayed where I was. I had no choice. Despite my fear of heights, I jumped.

CHAPTER 12

I slammed against the cliff, my hands grasping desperately for a tree root to hold. My left hand found nothing but air, but my right clutched something solid. My feet kicked in the dark, looking for a toehold. I slipped three yards down the face before my left grabbed something of substance. I dangled against the wet rock and looked up. The summit seemed a long way away from this angle and the muscles in my arms were already feeling the strain of my weight. I didn't have the luxury of looking down. I knew that my stamina would only last for so long. I reached up and grabbed a thick root and then used my feet to take my weight, pushing myself a yard closer to the top. The police officer kept his torchlight on me as I climbed and, on several occasions, I swear that he illuminated hand holds above me. I would never have made that climb in the dark. I was amazed that Officer George held his torch on me all the way to the top. Whether he was keeping me in sight or helping me to find hand holds so that I didn't fall, I'll never know but there was no doubt that it helped me on the climb. Whatever his reason to help me, I was grateful yet confused. Maybe he didn't want me to fall and create a month of paperwork for him, or maybe he was sympathetic to my plight. I think that saving Constance touched a few hearts. Who knows? If I ever meet him, and there's a good chance I will the way things are going, I'll ask him.

Because of him, my climb up the rock face was not as traumatic as it could have been. Stone outcrops and tree roots acted as a natural ladder and I was safely in the tree line before the fire brigade arrived. When I reached the top, I took one last look back to see Bren dancing around like a lunatic with his head in his hands. Sade was closely behind him swinging well aimed kicks at his fat backside.

As I watched them, a series of small explosions launched another section of the roof hurtling through the air before a final enormous blast blew the top off the building. I chuckled to myself, 'that must be the gunpowder,' I thought. At least any evidence of Bren's illegal weapons would be incinerated, and he would be in the clear once the insurers paid out; as long as they didn't find out that he'd been storing fireworks. Still, they were his problems, not mine.

There were no roads behind the tree line. I knew the area well enough to know that the police couldn't drive up and cut me off. If I kept walking up the steep ridge through the trees to the north for two miles or so, I would reach Miners' Bridge. As long as I kept the river to my left, I would find it without any problems. I debated walking down the steep hill to the other side of the river and then crossing in the darkness at a shallow point to get the Landy, but the water level was too high and the village would soon be flooded with policemen and armed units looking for me. Going back for the Landy and my gun was not an option. I would have to head north and make the most of the equipment I had. The police would never guess that I was heading deeper into the forest. They would be expecting me to return to a vehicle in the village somewhere. I had to stick to the plan. There were two hours left before David Harris would turn up at the remote bridge across the Llugwy.

The sound of sirens echoed down the valley and I caught the odd flash of blue light through the dense forest every now and again, but their attention was centered in the village. The ground was boggy, and the going was slow until I found a tourist trail which ran parallel to the river and then my pace increased. Forty minutes on, I felt safe enough to turn on the lantern and it wasn't long before I stumbled across a weathered wooden signpost which pointed down the hill. 'Miners' Bridge' 500 yds.

I headed down the path to the top of the gorge where the wooden bridge spanned the river. The gushing water below was almost deafening as I neared the river. On the right of the path was a handrail fitted to fence posts, to help walkers navigate the steep incline to the bridge. The bridge is narrow and fixed at an acute angle making it difficult to use. It sways and the wood creaks when you walk on it. There is only room enough for one person at a time to cross and it's so steep that the user must hold both handrails as they climb or descend. Although I was twenty feet above the thundering river, spray was splashing my face making the wooden boards on the bridge treacherous to cross. Only an idiot, or someone with an urgent need to traverse the Llugwy, would try to cross the bridge in the darkness with the water level so high and that's what I was banking on.

I set the haversack down on the ground at the base of a tree and hung the lantern from a low branch. I took out the rolled ponchos and slipped the black one over my head, pulling up the hood and adjusting the face mask so that only my eyes were showing. Looking around, I found a branch at head height and hung the second poncho from it. I walked to the top of the bridge and looked back. With the lantern light behind it, it appeared as if someone was standing near the tree. It was far enough away for the viewer not to be certain if the form was real or not, and all I needed was for my prey to hesitate for a moment and my job would be done.

Taking the wire snare, I opened the noose and spread it on the forest floor where the bridge met the mountain. Rotting vegetation provided the perfect material to hide the wire, even the sharpest eyes would struggle to see it in the dark. I found a stick about three inches thick and wrapped the tail of the snare around it, making a sturdy handle with which to pull the noose tight when the victim stepped into the circle of steel. I slipped the mace into the pouch which was on the front of the poncho and then looked around for a makeshift weapon. My eyes fell on the metal handrail next to the path and after half a dozen kicks to one of the posts, a section broke free. A three feet section of metal pipe was no substitute for a sawn-off shotgun, but that was all that I had to hand. I took the flares from the haversack and placed them on the ground. I lit a cigarette, sat on the bag and waited for my prey to arrive. I didn't have to wait long but when he arrived, I had a nasty shock.

CHAPTER 13

From my elevated position, I could see the path which ran along the top of the gorge on the opposite bank. Half a mile to the left, the path snaked right through the forest and met the main A5 road that ran through the village. A stone-built style and a small footpath sign were the only indication that the bridge was there at all. Thousands of tourists must have driven by the path without ever knowing of the Miners' Bridge existence. To the right the gorge climbed steeply through a series of staircase waterfalls for a third of a mile before it met the enormous Swallow Falls.

The only safe way to the bridge was from the road to the left. Harris would have to use the path and he would need a torch. I would see him ten minutes before he got near to the bridge. I tossed my cigarette into the night and a beam of light caught my eye in the distance. I wasn't sure if it was a passing vehicle but then there it was again. At first, I thought the mist from the river may be blurring my vision, but it soon became apparent that there were two torches weaving along the path on the far side.

I thought for a moment that maybe it was the police, but they would send more than two officers down a secluded forest path if they were hunting a killer. It had to be Harris but who had he brought with him? It must be another Niner, or why else would he bring someone? I thought about the messages which I sent to him and remembered that I hadn't told him to come alone. That was a silly mistake. I'd taken it for granted that he would come alone, but I should have known better than to assume anything. They were pack animals drawing strength from the depravity of others. My mind raced as the torch lights flickered along the path. Could my plan work against two men or was it time to withdraw and wait for another day? They could only cross the bridge one at a time, but if they were armed, then I was as good as dead.

The river roared and my brain pounded against my skull as I weighed up the options. The torches were less than a hundred yards from the stone steps which led down to the foot of the bridge on the other bank. It was now or never. The noise of the water seemed to grow louder, and I thought it was a trick of my imagination until the humming noise grew clearer. A single beam in the sky above the village answered my question. It was a police helicopter. It hadn't crossed my mind that they would send up a search craft and that was another stupid mistake. If they widened the search from the village, their heat sensors would pick up my shape in the forest, no matter how dark it was. Turning back was no longer an option.

The torches were level with the steps and one of them began to descend. I darted to the lantern and set the timer, grabbing a flare as I ran. The forest floor softened my footsteps and my movements were masked by the roar of the water and the dense trees. I snapped the top off the flare and tossed it high into the trees. Running in the opposite direction, I hid behind a tree and gripped the handle of the snare. Harris and his associate saw the flare and they stopped on the steps and pointed to it. I heard his raised voice over the noise of the water and when his friend answered him, it sent a shiver through my body. It was the voice of a woman. She had a local accent and I had a terrible feeling that I recognised it. I thought it could belong to the woman who I'd spoken to on the telephone, his wife.

My heart was beating rapidly, and my hands began to shake. I didn't know if it was the aftereffects of the blow to my head earlier, or the fact that one of the Niners was a female. It wasn't such a shock to think that there would be females involved in their sick games, but killing a woman wasn't in my plan. I didn't have a clue how this was all going to pan out, but it was too late to think of a second option. One of them stepped onto the bridge and began to climb up the steep incline. Wooden struts were screwed to the planks to act as grips for passing tourists to plant their feet. I looked around the tree and saw that the woman was coming first, David Harris close behind her. The lantern switched on and the shadowy figure of the poncho appeared by the tree deep in the woods.

'Over there.' I heard her shout. She was nearly at the top of the bridge now.

'I can see, just keep moving will you,' Harris called back. Standing over the gushing torrent which was thundering down the gorge was making him nervous. She took two more steps and was on the mountain right in the middle of the snare. I needed her to move. The lantern switched off and she froze. I should have set it with more of a delay. It spooked her. 'Move will you, I want to get off this bridge,' Harris growled.

'Why have they switched the light off?' she asked nervously. 'I don't like this, David. I'm not coming again after this.'

'We can't just walk away, she won't let us, now move please.' He raised his voice at the end of the sentence, and she stepped out of the snare as Harris stepped into it. 'I don't like heights at the best of times… what the fuck?'

Harris shouted and cursed as I yanked the snare. The steel wire contracted quickly with a whistling sound, as it tightened around his ankles. I pulled hard, stepping back three paces and yanked him off his feet. He fell heavily onto his elbows and grabbed at the wire with both hands. Metal teeth in the steel made loosening it impossible and the wire cut painfully into his flesh. Mr and Mrs Harris screamed in unison as he thrashed about in the darkness. I ran over to him and sprayed mace in his face, disabling him further. A gurgling sound came from his throat as the stinging gas made its way into his airways and he clutched at his eyes trying to stop the pain.

Mrs Harris was frozen to the spot in terror, as I raised the canister and blasted her with the mace. She collapsed onto the floor in a crumpled heap, gasping for breath, saliva and snot running from her chin.

'You fuckingshsh basshtard.' Harris slurred. His speech was barely translatable as his larynx constricted. 'I'll fushking kill youshsh.'

'Shut up and listen to me,' I grabbed his hair and pulled his face up toward me. The gas on his skin made my eyes sting and I pulled away a little. 'What's in your bag, David?' I turned him over onto his front. A canvas haversack was laden with bulky items. 'Don't tell me, are they your toys when you play at worshipping Satan?' I pulled his hair back again and I could see the fear in his eyes. 'You silly, sad fuck. Do you know what happened to Max Blackman, David?' I used the straps on the haversack to heave him closer to the edge. His eyes widened in horror at the mention of the dead Niner's name. 'I strung him up in his own living room and watched him choke.'

'Pleaseshh don't kill messhhhh,' he hissed; mucus dribbled from his nose in thick rivulets. His fat cheeks wobbled, and his eyes streamed with tears.

'I won't kill you,' I said looking into his eyes as I took his mobile phone from his coat pocket. Relief crossed his face and he half smiled. 'When they find you, they'll think that your wife did it. Can you swim?' I reached for the metal pipe and brought it down hard on his face. His nose splattered and his front teeth splintered. His lower jaw hung at an awkward angle, shattered by the force of the blow. I lifted his feet up to my chest and heaved him over the edge. His bloated body hit an outcrop ten feet above the raging water and then bounced into the torrent of water, disappearing in seconds. The contents of his haversack would tell the police who he was and what he was.

Mrs Harris was sniffling on all fours. I don't think that she was even aware that her husband was drowning in the Llugwy. There was a dilemma here that I had to figure out. She had a rucksack too, which I thought was nice. His and hers, how quaint.

'Here, grab onto this,' I passed her the section of metal handrail. 'Hold it and get up.' She looked up and nervously grabbed the pipe. 'Both hands, it will be easier.' I ordered.

She was shaking as she tried to find the strength to stand. A huge flash of light deluged the bridge, illuminating the forest. I ran beneath a tree and looked up. The police helicopter was a few hundred feet above us and although I wasn't directly in the light, I knew that the thermal imaging cameras would have picked me up.

'This is the police, stay where you are.' The loudspeaker boomed. 'I repeat, stay where you are.' Torch lights pierced the night to my left where the stile met the road. I turned and looked up the mountain towards the village at the way I'd come, and a dozen beams pierced the trees in that direction too.

'Well I guess we're both fucked now eh, Mrs Harris,' I leaned against the tree and laughed aloud. 'I can't wait to see their faces when they look in your bag. They'll have you banged up for the Critchley farm murders by tomorrow morning.'

She looked at the pipe in her hands and then looked up at the helicopter. The torches on the far bank were moving quickly and I could hear their voices over the noise of the water. I took another look up the hill and the first silhouettes were visible through the trees. I was trapped for the second time that night.

'Did you hear David squealing like a bitch when I threw him over the edge?' I goaded her. I needed her to react. 'What was it like sharing a bed with a fat pedophile all those years?'

'Shut up.' she screamed. She watched the torches flickering in the trees.

'They'll be here in five minutes and when they search your bag, they'll love your little playthings.'

'Shut your mouth.'

'The other women in jail will love you when you get there. They'll eat you for breakfast.' I laughed and she swung the pipe at my head. I ducked and heard it thud against the tree. There were five yards between me and the edge of the gorge. I ran full pelt. I didn't want to be captured that night and the loneliness that I'd been feeling drove me to despair. I didn't care if I lived or died anymore, so I jumped.

CHAPTER 14

The feeling of weightlessness lasted for what felt like minutes and combined with the ice-cold spray and the deafening roar my, senses were overwhelmed. I didn't hit the water; it hit me like a locomotive travelling at ninety miles an hour. The freezing torrent took the breath from my body as I plunged beneath the icy waters. I was thrown about like a ping pong ball in a washing machine, gasping for a mouthful of air whenever the current pushed me to the surface. I was spinning around and lost all sense of direction. I couldn't tell if I was going up or down. Although I was using all my strength to stay on the surface, I was powerless against the force of the river and exhausted, I gave up fighting and let it take me where it would.

    I don't know how long I was in the river, but I know where I got out. It was a half-a-mile south of the railway station at Betws. I lay on the bank freezing and numb from the battering that my body had taken on the rocks. Fearing that I would die from hypothermia, I dragged myself up and staggered through the fields towards the village. I could see the helicopter in the air, two miles north above Miners' Bridge. Relieving a chestnut gelding of its horse-blanket; I trudged back towards the Land Rover. The car park was virtually empty, and the Land Rover looked like an oasis to me. I threw off the blanket and sprinted across to the Land Rover unhindered. Ten minutes later, I was heading south towards Llangollen with the heater blasting and the radio on. Being alive felt surreal, as I'd given up back at the bridge. I'd chosen to die there but God didn't want me dead yet. I think he knew that I had more of Satan's followers to kill before he would let me leave. The temple master, a man named Williams was next on my list and he would tell me where I could find Fabienne Wilder before he died.

CHAPTER 15

My limbs ached to the bone and although the heater was blowing hot air towards my hands and feet, my fingers and toes were painfully cold. I had brain-freeze behind my eyes, similar to the feeling when you eat ice-cream too quickly. I could have pushed a needle through my cheek painlessly, my skin was so numb. There were two directions to choose from, north up the Conwy Valley or south down the A5 towards Llangollen. I knew that any police backup would be coming from the coastal towns to the north, so I ruled it out immediately. I headed south and debated my next move. I had to act quickly. Max Blackman had told me that Glynn Williams was the master of the temple in Carrog and as such, he was my only link to Fabienne. I needed to find him and interrogate him as to her whereabouts. Both he and his remaining associate, Gwillam Hughes were still out there somewhere, although I wasn't convinced that Hughes was in possession of the information that I needed.

Williams was the head of the nexion. He was the one I needed to keep alive long enough for him to tell me how to find her. There was no doubt in my mind that I had to act quickly. If I'd chosen to wait until the morning, they may have followed the local news. I'd hoped that the police would be convinced that Harris and his wife were connected to the murders in Carrog, but they knew that I was there too. I wasn't sure if they would flood the news with my image, in the hope that the public would report any sightings of me. If they did, Hughes and Williams might connect what had happened to their nexion associates at Betws-y-Coed and realise that there was someone hunting them. If the police decided to focus on finding me, then I knew that my face would be all over the newspapers by morning which would make staying at liberty while I searched for them difficult.

I felt that I was running on borrowed time. Hate and loneliness were my only companions and while they were my driving forces, they demanded a heavy toll for their company. They fuelled my determination but sapped my will to live. I could see nothing but death before me, theirs and mine. As long as I killed Fabienne Wilder first, I didn't care what happened to me. My only objective in life was finding her and killing her.

The drive down the A5 towards Llangollen was surreal. My body was frozen to the bones and my hands were shaking from the cold. The adrenalin in my blood stream was waning and I felt weak and exhausted. The road follows the course of the river as it snakes its way south from Betws. The bends are so sharp it is difficult to reach higher than third gear for much of the first few miles. Blue flashing lights screamed towards me periodically, heading in the opposite direction to support the search operation I'd left behind. The thought that they were coming for me never crossed my mind. Somehow, I felt like I had a cloaking device which stopped them seeing me. Part of me wished they would and then it would be over but the other part of me, the angry part, the killer in me, wanted to carry on until I'd found them all.

As the blood began to circulate back into my fingers and toes, a burning hunger hit me. I needed food before I did anything else that night. Something else niggled in my mind too. I had to get to the other two men before the local news identified Harris as missing, or dead, with his wife as the main suspect for his death. I couldn't risk going back to my bed-and-breakfast. The chances of arrest were slim at this stage as the photographs which the television was broadcasting held only a passing resemblance to the man I saw in the mirror. However, the big man at the surplus shop had recognised me so I had to be cautious. I was more concerned that if I made it to my room, I would sleep for days and lose the element of surprise. Hughes and Williams wouldn't be aware that I was coming for them yet. With that in mind, I turned left at Pentrefoeles and headed up the road, through the moors, towards Denbigh. A few hundred yards on was the last fuel station for miles. I pulled in and stopped next to the diesel pump, checking out the CCTV cameras before climbing out of the Land Rover.

I pulled my hood up to hide my features a little and popped the fuel flap open. The wind made my damp clothes feel like they were frozen to my skin; the material stiff and heavy. The kiosk was empty as the pump clicked around to over £70.00. I placed the nozzle back into its holster and took a deep breath before heading towards the door, my hands pushed deep into damp pockets.

The overweight attendant buzzed the lock on the door, allowing me access. Her greasy brown hair hung lankly down each cheek hiding the arms of her thick black glasses. I grabbed a basket and an empty fuel canister, stuffing two packets of sandwiches, four bags of prawn cocktail crisps and a litre of semi-skimmed milk into the basket. The woman eyed me suspiciously as I moved quickly between the chilled counter and the aisles. I wanted to fill the canister with petrol but didn't want to take it outside before paying for it.

'Do you want to put fuel in that, love?' she asked in a chirpy voice.

'Is that okay?'

'Yes, no problem.' She smiled. 'Let me scan it first and then you can get your fuel.'

'Thanks,' I kept my head down. She studied my face as she scanned the item.

'You're not from around here, are you?' It wasn't a question.

'No, I've been camping but I'm heading back to London tonight.' I turned and walked towards the door. Her voice made me jump.

'Excuse me.'

'What?' I opened the door, ready to run to the Landy.

'Could you leave the fuel outside, love please,' she nodded seriously. 'You're not allowed to bring it back in here you see.'

'No problem.'

The wind bit through my clothes and my limbs were shaking as I filled the canister. The mountains were huge black silhouettes against a darker sky. Beams of light caught my eye. Headlights illuminated the hedgerows halfway up the mountain. I gauged that the vehicle was about a mile away, heading down the mountain road towards me. Quickly, I opened the back of the Landy and wedged the fuel canister against the wheel arch. I jogged back into the shop to settle my bill. The attendant was glued to portable flat screen TV. She pulled her eyes away from it as I approached.

'£95.62 please.' She smiled thinly. Her eyes gave her away. 'So, you're heading to London now, then?'

'Yes, I'm afraid so,' I looked her straight in the eyes. She looked away quickly and her face flushed red. 'I'm booked onto the Eurostar tomorrow. I should be in Paris by teatime.'

She frowned confused. 'United are playing in the European cup,' I picked up my supplies and scurried out of the shop without another word. I didn't know if she'd pass on the duff information or not and I didn't care. If she did recognise me and picked up the telephone to the police as soon as I left, I'd be long gone, anyway. I climbed into the driver's seat and threw the carrier bag of food onto the passenger side. The vehicle that I'd spotted weaving down the mountain was a few hundred yards away and indicating to turn into the petrol station. The headlights dazzled me, and I couldn't make out the shape of the vehicle behind them. My heartbeat quickened as I turned the ignition key and the engine roared to life. I steered the Landy in a wide arc and the tyres squealed as I accelerated onto the road heading back towards Betws. As the darkness swallowed up my Landy, I saw the approaching vehicle pulling onto the forecourt of the garage. Illuminated by the station's lights, it was clearly a traffic police car. My breath caught in my lungs and I cursed my luck. The attendant would get her chance to tell the police about her encounter with a fugitive much sooner than I'd hoped.

CHAPTER 15

I pushed the Landy as fast as I dared without looking too suspicious until I turned a bend in the road. Once the petrol station was out of sight in my rear-view mirror, I floored the accelerator. As I reached the A5, beams of light searched the night sky behind me. The traffic patrol was on to me. I could see their headlights in the near distance, but I knew they wouldn't be able to see the Land Rover until they reached the straighter sections of road on the A5. I turned off the lights, accelerated and turned left off the main road onto the Blaenau Ffestiniog road. The road was a narrow, single track with grass growing in a green stripe along the centre. Spiny fingers of hawthorn grabbed at the sides of the vehicle sounding like the fingernails of a giant scratching to gain access. Two minutes later, I rounded a sharp bend and the road descended at a steep gradient. There were no street lights for miles and my visibility was zero. I eased off the accelerator and slowed the Land Rover down to a crawl. If the traffic police realised that I'd turned off, then I couldn't outrun them, anyway. Wrapping myself around an oak tree didn't seem an attractive alternative to jail. I crawled along the track for a few hundred yards, my eyes straining against the blackness until it became obvious that the police had gone the wrong way. Probably south on the A5 looking for a fugitive who told the petrol station attendant that he was heading for London.

  I took a deep breath before turning on the headlights. A hundred yards ahead of me, green orbs of light seemed to float above the crumbling tarmac. My nerves were on edge as I locked my gaze with the animal, instinctively accelerating towards it. It held its position and stayed in the centre of the road. There was no stoop in its posture, no fear in its eyes. It didn't try to skulk away, nor did it look frozen in terror. It stared defiantly as the Land Rover hurtled towards it. I couldn't decide if it was a big cat or small badger and if I'm honest, I didn't care. Did I think it was a servant of Satan, or the eyes of Fabienne Wilder searching for me? Who knows what insane thoughts ran through my mind at that time? As the Land Rover neared, it seemed to grow in size as its fur stood on end. I felt more in fear of it than it did of me but as it thumped against the front bumper, realisation gripped me. There were no evil spirits tailing me, transmitting telepathic images of me to Fabienne and her master. There were no animals taking sides in the war of good against evil. There was only flesh and blood, life or death. The Niners I'd encountered so far had no magical powers to protect them. They breathed the same air as I did, and their bodies were as fragile as mine. Under the force of a heavy blow, their bones would splinter and snap. Their skin could be penetrated by a sharp object and their organs could be ruptured without much effort. They would bleed and die as easily as the animal beneath the Landy had. That's what I thought until I saw the rear lights of the Landy reflected in its eyes. It was very much alive, and it was watching. The rear-view mirror reflected two orbs of piercing red. I braked hard and looked again. The animal was gone.

'Bollocks.' I put my foot down and told myself that the pressure was getting to me, but my hands began to shake, nonetheless.

CHAPTER 16

I drove for a few miles, just to put some space between myself and the police search. I was worried that the helicopter would move away from the epicentre of the village and pass over me looking for the southbound Land Rover. I was heading west slowly, but the road was so narrow, it was dangerous to go over thirty miles an hour. I couldn't be seen from the A5, but from the air my headlights sweeping across the remote spaces between the redundant slate quarries above Blaenau would be clearly visible. I needed to get off the road and decide how I was going to get to Hughes and Williams. My intention was to use the mobile which I took from Harris to contact them. As I concentrated on finding somewhere to stop, a devastating thought hit me. I'd been in the water for ages. I hadn't come across a mobile, yet which could survive being submerged. If I had a pound for each time someone had told me about dropping their mobiles down the toilet, in the sink or in a puddle, I would have a pocket full of gold coins. I can't recall any happy endings to the stories. Hair driers, tumble driers, radiators, ovens, fan heaters and airing cupboards had all been tried, but I'd never heard of a successful resuscitation of a drowned mobile phone. My spirits crashed to an all-time low as I thought about the mobile in my pocket. It was probably as good as useless.

I switched on the radio and tried to find a local news broadcast, but a million tons of granite and slate blocked any signals. All I could hear was static. As I searched for a station, the strangest thing happened. There was a polyphonic ringtone piercing the silence which was joined by vibrations against my right thigh. Instinctively, I quickly touched it through the damp fabric of my jeans. I wasn't imagining it; the mobile was ringing. The road was too narrow and winding to allow me to take my hands from the steering wheel for more than a second. Struggling to remove the mobile from my pocket would end up with the Land Rover in a ditch. I cursed beneath my breath as the Landy trundled over the lumps and bumps. The road twisted sharply to the right and the answer to my problems loomed before me in the darkness.

Slate gateposts towered above adjoining walls which seemed to run endlessly in both directions until they were swallowed by the night. Rusted gates hung from ancient hinges at odd angles. A splintered sign on the left-hand post read 'Plas Craig Slate Works'. The lettering was blistered and peeling but it was readable. The wrought-iron gates were offset enough for me to navigate the Landy between them and the sound of shale crunching beneath the wheels joined me. I was surprised that the gates weren't secured but as I rounded a curve in the road, I understood why. The headlights illuminated three concrete blocks the size of a family saloon car. They completely blocked the access road and were far too big to move. The Land Rover had a tow bar fitted but the sheer size of the blocks made that irrelevant. The Landy would snap in half before it would pull such a weight. The sides of the access road were lined with slate piles so high that I couldn't see what was behind them.

    I pulled the Landy up to the blocks and killed the engine. The headlights went out plunging everything into inky blackness. I waited a few minutes until my eyes adjusted to the darkness. Beyond the blocks I could make out the silhouettes of two low buildings and a chimney stack. Behind them the ground rose almost vertically blotting out the night sky. I was nervous when I reached into my jeans to retrieve the mobile. There is something unnerving about sitting in the dark with the engine turned off. I felt much safer when the vehicle was moving. Alone in the pitch-dark I could only feel vulnerable and frightened. I gripped the phone and looked at it closely. The manufacturer was JCB, which explained how it had survived the icy water. I suppose you would have to live in the mountains to purchase a waterproof mobile phone, but I was grateful that he had. The screen displayed that there was one missed call. I clicked the menu button, but the caller had used a withheld number. Scrolling through the contacts list, I found two numbers listed as Glynn. One of them had the letter 'W' after the name. It had to be Glynn Williams.

CHAPTER 16

Everything that I did from that point onwards was purely to find Williams. Hughes was on my list; there was no doubt about that. If I could kill two birds with one stone, then it would be a bonus, but my one true goal was to find Fabienne. I sent a text message and then searched for Geraint Hughes in the contact list. The message was simple, and I knew it would depend on whether Williams was aware that the members of his nexion were dying. If he did, then he would realise that it was a trap. If he didn't, he may come to me. I couldn't pretend that Fabienne wanted him. If he was in direct contact with her, then he would simply phone her and ask her what she wanted. My message was meant to frighten him enough to provoke a reaction.

'We are in big trouble. The police know everything. Bring that bastard Geraint with you. He's a grass. Don't call me I think they're tapping my phone. I'm at the old quarry at Plas Craig on the Blaenau road, get here quickly'

I thought about moving the Landy but there was nowhere to hide it. I didn't think that it would matter either way. I climbed out of the Land Rover and opened the back door. Pulling the rear passenger seat forward, I took the Mossberg from its hiding place, before opening the boot and grabbing the petrol and my bag of shotgun cartridges. Holding the loaded shotgun made me feel much less vulnerable. The Mossberg had become my only true friend in recent months. It was always there when I needed protection and its power was undeniable. Those who threatened me to the point of me raising the gun invariably died. Its justice was brutal, swift, and deadly.

I locked the Landy and headed for a gap between the concrete blocks, walking towards the disused buildings. The wind was biting through my clothes and it carried the scent of pine trees with it. I shivered as I walked along the slate shingle track. I could hear the river in the distance as it made its way down the Conwy Valley to the sea. The rocks, waterfalls and whirlpools created a comforting splashing sound which travelled on the night air. The road widened into a huge rectangle the size of a football pitch, probably the turning space for articulated lorries many years ago as they ferried massive slate blocks away from the quarry to feed the construction industry after the war. To the left a mountain of slate rocks climbed towards the tree line and on my right the ground sloped away towards the tree-tops, which clung to the riverbanks. The buildings in front of me looked dark and foreboding. The windows looked like eyeless sockets daring me to approach them. Enter at your peril, rattled around my head. Keep out. Trespassers will be shot, sprung into my befuddled mind; both warnings which I read a thousand times in comic books from the '70s. Their meaning back then was almost hilarious, yet forty years on, alone in the dark, hunting Angels, it wasn't funny anymore. I looked up and the chimney stack seemed to grow in height as I neared the buildings, standing like a silent slate sentinel guarding the quarry from intruders. I held the Mossberg tightly, took a deep breath and walked towards them.

CHAPTER 17

When I reached the buildings, I looked at the main entrance and saw that the massive wooden doors were protected by a rusted metal grill secured to the brickwork with padlocks the size of a melon. I walked to the left and passed three arched windows which were shuttered and protected by similar metalwork grills. There was no access to the front of the building, so I walked on, stumbling over lumps of slate and clumps of weeds. I was beginning to think that winging it might not have been the best idea. My mindset was so mixed up that I didn't really have a plan, but I persevered and retraced my steps. As I passed the main doors, I heard the familiar humming of rotor blades coming from the north. The noise seemed to grow and then fade. The mountains and trees blocked my view of the helicopter, but I knew it was up there and would take just a few minutes for it to reach the skies above me.

The windows to the right of the door were fastened in the same fashion. I pushed on and reached the end of the building, before taking a path which led to the rear. A coil of rusted barbed wire blocked my progress and although it was dark, I could make out further rolls of razor wire beyond the first. If I tried to pick my way through, it would cut me to ribbons before I'd made more than a few yards. I couldn't risk an injury which would need stitching, or a rusty wound which would become infected later on. Hospitals and doctors were beyond my reach. I had to find another way. I walked back the way I'd come and decided to try the second smaller building on the left. It was an unusual shape and from my position, there appeared to be no doors or windows in the front elevation. As I neared the building, I understood why.

A road ran from the turning area to the side of the building, which was in fact a cutting shed and loading bay. There was a large opening on the far side which allowed articulated trailers to reverse into it, so that custom sized slate blocks could be loaded. From the side it looked like a low one-storey building. It was an illusion created by being built into the slope. The road snaked around the building and then dipped beneath it; hence it couldn't be seen from where I'd parked the Landy. It wasn't ideal, but it was the best shelter on offer. I had no idea how far away Williams lived, or if he would come at all, but I had to act on the premise that he would arrive sooner rather than later. Encouraged, I jogged towards the loading bay entrance, which was nothing more than a gaping black maw beneath the building. The road twisted in a sharp u-shape and dropped down steeply. I slowed my pace as I reached the incline, gravity pulled me down the slope where the darkness reached a new level. I literally couldn't see a thing. I had no choice but to try to use the light from the screen of the mobile. I took it out and pressed the menu button. When the screen illuminated, so did a button on the side of the device. The button read 'Torch'. I pressed the button a powerful beam of light illuminated the building. God bless JCB for making a mobile which was used by farmers, builders, and contractors the world over. Someone somewhere was throwing me a lifeline. Using the phone as a torch, I entered the loading bay with renewed hope.

The road stood a metre below the loading platforms which ran on either side from the front opening, all the way to the rear of the building. Stone steps cut into the platforms on both sides, allowing access for the Landy drivers to supervise their loads. I took the steps to my right and climbed up. On the platform, the torchlight revealed tracks which would once have guided an overhead crane. The crane itself had been stripped, along with all the other scrap metal left behind when the quarry closed. At the end of the platform, wooden stairs climbed up to another platform which supported a supervisor's office. The office spanned the loading bay, three wide windows, long devoid of glass, allowed a panoramic view of the operation below. Plywood hoardings covered the office windows now. If the stairs were intact and I could remove the hoardings, it was the perfect place to observe the Niners if they fell for my trap. From there I could see them and cover them with the Mossberg.

My first instinct was to position myself in the office and wait for them to arrive, but the more I thought about it, the more it looked like a dead end with no escape should things go wrong. With that thought in mind, I climbed the ancient wooden staircase. The smell of wet rot drifted to me and the steps had the spongy feel of decay. Each step brought a different creaking sound and the threat of plunging through the wood onto the concrete below hung heavily in my mind. I placed my feet carefully, testing the strength before transferring my weight. Progress was painfully slow but rushing now could end up with me lying helpless with a broken limb, a rat caught in my own trap. I counted thirteen steps to the landing. The door to the office was made from wood; three panels of plywood separated by thicker bars. The handle was missing, either broken off or removed on purpose to deter intruders. The floorboards on the landing groaned as I neared the door. I pushed it with the flat of my right hand and it moved slightly. A heavy barge with my right shoulder rattled the door in its frame and a second blow split the rotten frame near the lock. The door clattered against the wall as it flew open. The torchlight revealed an empty room, cobwebs hanging from the ceiling timbers. A strip light dangled, only one end attached, the wires exposed, and the smell of damp and decay pervaded the dank air inside. The right-hand side of the room was exposed brickwork; the left side was stud wall with the three boarded windows. I stepped inside towards the nearest window and instantly felt that the floorboards were different. I realised too late that decay had won the battle with the timbers and my right leg disappeared through the floor.

CHAPTER 18

My right leg went through the wood to the knee. I could feel warm blood trickling down my shin and there was a burning pain coming from a graze above the ankle. I lurched forward and had to let go of the gun and the petrol. The floorboards groaned beneath my weight and I could hear fragments of wood hitting the loading bay below. I held my breath and waited for the noise to abate before trying to pull my leg free. I placed my hands palms down on the floor and pushed upwards. The wood cracked beneath me and I dropped through the widening hole to my chest. Debris clattered into the loading bay and I grabbed at thin air as I came to a painful stop; only my arms and shoulders preventing me from following it. My legs dangled freely as I desperately tried to find purchase on something underneath me.

My breath came in gasps, fear and adrenalin forcing my body to fight my predicament. I looked over my shoulder and twisted my body around slowly. Grabbing the door frame with my left hand, I nudged the shotgun and petrol gently through the doorway onto the landing and then tried to pull myself up. I needed both hands to budge a few inches. A loud crack from behind me stopped me struggling and a low groan followed as the tortured wood settled again. Seconds felt like hours as I held onto the door frame. I took a deep breath and pulled with all my strength. My chest came free of the rent in the floor and with a few kicks of the legs, I was lying breathless face down in the doorway. The office floor creaked loudly, and a fifteen feet section simply dropped away from the structure. With the support gone, the front wall snapped and followed the floor into the loading bay, crashing and splintering into dozens of pieces. I got to my knees, grabbed my gun and the petrol and sprinted for the staircase. As I reached the third step, the remaining sections of the office gave up the struggle to stay intact. Gravity proved to be stronger than the rusted screws and corroded nails and it ripped free of the walls, hurtling onto the loading bay below. A choking cloud of dust and debris filled the cutting shed and the clatter of timber against concrete deafened me.

I jumped three steps and then leaped the last three, landing in a bruised heap on the platform. I sat up, tired and aching all over, as the clamour quietened. Giving up and walking away into anonymity suddenly became attractive; more attractive than anything before. I'd had enough. As I got to my feet, resigned to making it to the Landy and driving over the mountains away from this madness, I heard engines approaching. Tyres crunched the slate shingle near the quarry gates, at least two vehicles, maybe three. I listened in the darkness as the engines laboured and then fell silent. I couldn't see if it was the police or the Niners but something inside told me that it was the latter. They were here and I didn't have a clue what I was going to do next.

CHAPTER 19

I ran to the entrance and peered around the edge. Three sets of headlights illuminated the main building and the chimney stack. I could hear voices on the wind, three men, probably four. Their silhouettes shifted from one vehicle to another. One walked over to my Land Rover and peered into the driver's window. There were more words exchanged, some in Welsh, but not all. Then there was an angry exchange, raised voices, finger pointing, angry aggressive tones and then a punch was thrown. As one man fell onto the shingle, another made to help him while the others tried to kick him while he was down. More angry voices and finger pointing and then the two attackers seemed to calm down momentarily. They chatted and argued for a few seconds and then they looked towards the buildings. I needed them in the cutting shed. I wasn't sure what I would do when they were there, but I knew something would come to me. I took the lid off the petrol canister and poured half the contents onto the huge pile of rotten wood which only minutes ago was the office. Taking a disposable lighter from the bag of shotgun cartridges, I set fire to the wood. The flames jumped quickly from one piece to the next and as the fire met a petrol-soaked section, it ignited it with a resounding whoosh. The wood crackled and pieces of burning embers shot into the air. Smoke began to fill the vaulted roof space as the flames climbed higher towards the ancient roof beams.

I ran back to the arched entrance and looked over the loading platform. The Niners were three hundred yards away and I knew that they couldn't see the entrance to the cutting shed from their position, but they would see the glow from the flames. They turned and ran to their vehicles. I could hear some of their words drifting to me. I heard 'bat' and 'hammer' and then their headlights were switched off. They were coming; four men carrying weapons of varying descriptions. I ducked low and ran up the incline away from the cutting shed. Crouching as I ran, I hid behind the side of the building where I could see them approach, but they couldn't see me. As I watched them, something important sprang into my messed-up brain. How would I know which one was Williams?

As I watched them walking across the shingle turning space, I tried to decipher as much information as I could. Two of them held torches. One of them was much taller than the others and he was well built. He was carrying a baseball bat. The man next to him had a screwdriver; a very big one and his nose was bleeding. He didn't look comfortable at all, in fact, he looked like he was shitting his pants. One held a claw hammer in his right hand and a carving knife in his left. They all had beer bellies that pushed against the material of their coats. I envisioned their guts hanging over their pants like droopy muffin tops. I guessed that the man with the nosebleed was Hughes, purely because I'd told Williams he was a grass, but I didn't see which one had hit him and to be honest it didn't matter. I couldn't afford to kill anyone until

I knew who Williams was. The four men walked in silence and rounded the bend at the top of the incline. They looked at each other as they saw the flames inside the cutting shed.

'Harris.' The tall man shouted. The others looked at him again for guidance. 'Harris.' He called again.

'Let's take a look inside,' nosebleed man suggested. 'He might be hurt.'

'Shut your mouth, Hughes,' the tall man snarled. He waved the bat close to his face. 'If he's right and you have blabbed to the police, I'll shove this bat up your arse and set fire to it. Do you understand?'

'I haven't told the police anything,' Hughes replied angrily although he looked very frightened. 'Harris is a fucking liar. He always has been.'

Bingo. Now I knew who was who. Or so I thought. It wasn't the first time I'd been wrong.

CHAPTER 20

Geraint Hughes was fuming as he stormed down the incline towards the entrance. An orange glow illuminated the approach road and the interior of the cutting shed and thick grey smoke poured beneath the top of the arch. The accusations against him had infuriated him and had already cost him a bloody nose. Much worse would follow if he didn't clear things up.

'Harris, you gobshite,' he bellowed as he entered the loading bay. 'What the fuck are you playing at?' A moment's hesitation and he disappeared into the building.

'What do you think?' The tall man asked the man to his left. 'Do you think Geraint is a grass?'

'I don't know what to think yet,' the smaller man stepped into the light. Holding just a torch, he seemed the least dangerous of the men, yet he had an aura about him. He wasn't armed and he didn't look nervous or scared like the others. 'Follow him and see what's going on. Bring Harris and Geraint out here.'

'Bollocks,' the tall man hissed. 'I'm not going in there.'

The smaller man just glanced at him but there was malevolence in his eyes. Whatever silent message passed between them, the taller man lowered his gaze and walked towards the building. 'You too, Rob.' He turned to the remaining Niner. The man didn't argue or question the command. He followed the others into the cutting shed. As I watched him from the shadows, his eyes scanned the area. He seemed suspicious as he looked around him one way and then the other. His focus passed over me twice, but I knew he couldn't penetrate the darkness. He shuffled his feet and for a moment, I thought he was going to about turn and leave, but he headed into the shed instead. There was only one way in and one way out. I had them where I wanted them.

Breaking cover, I ran for the top of the incline and bent double to see what they were doing. The fire at the rear of the building was radiating heat and light and the glow warmed me as I approached the entrance. The four men stood peering beneath the fragmented wood, looking for signs of their friend underneath. They looked at each other, confusion and anger etched into their faces.

'Your fat friend is dead,' I shouted to get their attention. The men spun around to face me; weapons raised instinctively. They had fear and surprise in their eyes. All except one. 'His pervert of a wife will be spilling her guts to the police by now, but Harris is fish food.' They eyed the shotgun and backed away as I approached. 'Harris told me that Geraint Hughes is the master of your sinister tribe,' I lied. They looked from one to the other nervously. Hughes looked especially nervous. 'That's you, right?' I pointed the gun at the man with the bloody nose.

'I don't know what you're talking about.' He shook his head and his fat jowls wobbled, making him look like a turkey. 'I'm not in any sinister tribe.'

'Why would you call it that then?'

'Call it what?' Hughes looked confused.

'A sinister tribe.'

'That's what you called it,' he mumbled but his face told me that he'd realised his slip up.

'Your average man on the street wouldn't know that the word 'sinister' isn't a description, but we know that, don't we?'

'I don't know what you're talking about,' he looked at the floor as he spoke.

'Well that's a shame.' I took another two steps towards them. They edged backwards but the heat from the fire was too intense for them to move much further. 'I only want Geraint Hughes, so which one of you is Hughes?'

Three of the men looked at Hughes. Hughes looked shocked that they would give him away so easily. I couldn't fathom why he was so surprised. They were all lying paedophile scum, so in my mind expecting them to be trustworthy was ludicrous. 'I'm Geraint but I'm not the temple master,' his face drained of colour as he spoke. He knew that Williams and the others would despise him for his treachery, despite the fact that they'd just betrayed him. 'I'm no one.'

'I'm the temple master,' the tall man lied. I suppose he thought there would be some devilish reward for sacrificing himself. 'Who the fuck are you, anyway?' He sneered. 'What do you want?' The expression on his face changed, but it registered with me a second too late.

'He knows Geraint Hughes isn't the master,' a voice came from behind me. 'Put the shotgun down or I'll blow your brains out.'

I kept the gun trained on the four men in front of me while I stole a glance behind. A tall man in a long-waxed jacket was aiming a double-barrelled Laurona at the back of my head. 'If I was you, I'd have already pulled the trigger,' I said. I didn't care if he did or not and desperate men with no fear are dangerous. His curiosity had kept me alive.

'Are you the writer who has been on the news?' He walked to my right-hand side; the gun trained on my head. 'You set fire to the farmhouse at Brunt Boggart, didn't you?'

'I'll take it that you're Glynn Williams.'

'Clever man here, boys,' Williams chuckled. 'Drop the weapon.'

'Not a chance.'

'Then you will die here tonight.'

'So, be it, but who's coming with me?' I aimed the Mossberg between Williams and the others.

'I know all about you, Conrad Jones.' He smiled thinly. His thin lips barely twitched at the corners. Watery blue eyes narrowed as he spoke. 'She's got a thing for you. She wants you to suffer really badly and you will. Do you know how many of us there are?'

'Too many.'

'Clever and funny, eh?' He frowned. 'If you lived another fifty years, you wouldn't make a dent in our numbers, you, stupid bastard.'

'Shoot him and have done with this,' the tall man with the bat growled.

I squeezed the trigger and the Mossberg roared. The gunshot was deafening in the enclosed space and none of the men were expecting it. The tall man was knocked off his feet as the blast hit him square in the chest. He lay on his back, staring at the ceiling. His lips moved silently, and crimson bubbles came from his mouth. I couldn't help but notice the irony in the way his arms were splayed, like Jesus on the cross. Williams tightened his finger on the triggers, but nothing happened. His eyes widened in horror as I turned the gun towards him.

'Safety catch, dick-head,' I fired again. Williams was sent into a spin as the blast punched into his right shoulder. The shotgun clattered across the concrete. 'Who is stupid now?'

He slumped against the loading bay wall; his shoulder socket exposed; the white of the bone exaggerated by the dark ragged hole around it. All three remaining men covered their ears and turned away, staring over their shoulders at me in disbelief. 'Where is Fabienne Wilder?'

'Fuck you.' He spat blood onto the floor. Thick mucus mixed with it as the globule landed near my foot. I leant over him and smashed the butt of the Mossberg into the bridge of his nose. There was an audible crack as the bones in his face disintegrated. His eyes rolled into the back of his head.

'I haven't got the time to fuck about.' I patted his pockets and took out his wallet. Flicking it open with one hand it revealed that I'd been wrong again. 'Dale Robinson?'

I took his mobile and stepped back. There was a tear running from his eye down his right cheek as I shouldered the shotgun and squeezed the trigger. The close proximity of the blast blew the front of his face off. Jawbone and splintered teeth splattered the others. Blood and grey goo clung to their faces and clothes. There were bubbles appearing where his oesophagus once joined his throat; his dying breath leaving his ruined body.

'Fucking hell.' Hughes began to cry. His face twisted as if in agony. 'He's the temple master.' He pointed to the man I'd originally identified as Williams with a shaking finger. 'I've only been a few times. I didn't fully understand what the fuck was going on.' He blubbered. 'I didn't want anything to do with them, but they threatened me.'

'Shut your mouth.' Williams snarled at him. 'Pull yourself together.'

'What exactly do you want?' The man with the hammer and carving knife asked. His voice quavered with fear. I hadn't heard him speak until now. He was of no consequence to me or my objectives. I aimed the gun low and squeezed the trigger again. The maelstrom of shot ripped through his right leg tearing chunks of thigh muscle and knee ligaments from the bone. He screamed and grabbed at the wound, a thick jet of blood spurted between his fingers, the femoral artery severed. 'Agh. My leg, you bastard.'

Hughes buckled at the knees; fear stripped any resolve he had left. He cowered on the floor with his hands covering his head. 'Please don't hurt me; I'll tell you whatever you want.' His eyes pleaded for mercy. I thought about the innocents who were killed at the farm. I thought about how they must have pleaded for their lives while they were being raped, tortured, and murdered. Any shred of sympathy disappeared. There was no mercy left in me. Not for them anyway.

'I'm bleeding to death.'

'Shut him up,' I shouted at Hughes.

'Get an ambulance.'

'Where can I find Fabienne Wilder?' I ignored the screams and pointed the gun at Williams.

'I don't know what you're talking about.'

'Everyone thought Dewi Critchley was the temple master, didn't they?'

Silence but their eyes belied the truth.

'Max Blackman blabbed before I kicked the chair from underneath him.'

Silence again. They exchanged a nervous glance.

'Did you believe that he killed himself?'

Only the moaning of the injured man and the crackling of burning wood answered me. The flames were tickling the rafters and I knew it wouldn't be long before the roof started to burn. I stepped closer and gestured with the gun. 'Kneel down,' I picked up the petrol and held the canister against my thigh, twisting the lid from it with one hand while I kept the gun aimed at him with the other. His face was ashen as I poured the stinging fluid over his legs and feet. I spilled the rest over Hughes, which pushed his wailing to a new pitch. 'If you think that I'm fucking around here, then I suggest you take a look at your sicko friends. He's dead and he's bleeding to death. Geraint here is about to feel what hell will be like before he actually gets there, aren't you, Geraint?'

'Oh Jesus, please don't burn me.' He blubbered. Snot ran from his nostrils and saliva dribbled from his chin. He looked like a giant baby with a cold. 'Tell him where she is, you, stupid bastard.'

'Shut up, Geraint.' Williams hissed. 'I don't know what you're talking about.'

'Fabienne Wilder?' I spoke slowly and pronounced every syllable. 'How do you keep in touch with her?' I replaced two shells into the Mossberg. Williams held my gaze. There was still no fear in his eyes. That shook me a little. Most men would be crapping themselves, but he seemed completely calm. I had to make him realise that his knowledge was the only thing keeping him alive. The man with the injured leg was screaming incoherently. I turned the gun towards him and fired. The blast ripped the top of his skull off. His body twitched violently as his brain spilled onto the concrete. Hughes retched and his vomit splattered across the floor. 'Last chance, where is the bitch?'

'What do you think you can achieve by finding her?' A thin smile crossed his lips. His eyes had a glint in them. 'Do you have any idea what she is?'

'Yes, I know what she is,' I shrugged and pulled the lighter from my pocket. I knelt down near to where Hughes was cowering. He was still trying to empty the contents of his guts onto the concrete. His face twisted by terror as the flame neared him. His mouth opened and closed in a silent prayer. 'She's a sick fucker just like you.'

'What you call 'sick' we embrace. What you loath, we love. Do you think I fear death?' He smiled again. 'I know what awaits me when this mortal shell has finished breathing. I also know what she has planned for you. You don't need to find her; she's coming for you, anyway.' He rocked his head backwards and laughed like a lunatic. 'You can do whatever you want to me. I'll never tell you where she is.'

'Empty your pockets.' I had to regain control. His lack of concern for his own life knocked my confidence.

'What?' He frowned. His eyes flickered. It was the first sign of weakness.

'Empty your pockets.'

'Fuck off.' He sneered. His eyes dared me to near him. 'Come and empty them yourself.'

He didn't want me to get my hands on something which he had. I guessed it was a mobile or a notebook PC of some kind. 'Empty his pockets, Geraint and throw it all here in front of me. Do it now and I'll let you walk out of here.'

Hughes looked at me trying to gauge if I was telling the truth. 'Why don't you just tell him, for fuck's sake?' he muttered as he stood up. 'He's obviously fucking mad and I'm not prepared to die for her.' He walked over to Williams and began to dig into his jacket pockets. 'Just tell him where she is.'

'You always were a spineless bastard.' Williams smiled.

Hughes shook his head, scoffed and removed a wallet and mobile phone from his left-hand pocket. He tossed them onto the floor. Williams reached into the other pocket and held something up in Hughes's face. 'Do you need a light, Geraint?' He flicked his Zippo and Geraint Hughes turned into a human torch. His clothes and hair blackened quickly, and he flailed around like a burning windmill, staggering towards the inferno at the rear of the cutting shed. His screams were cut short as he inhaled the flames and the delicate tissue of his mouth and windpipe frazzled. Williams laughed as his fellow Niner stumbled headlong into the flames. A cloud of sparks and burning embers erupted into the air as he crashed into the fire. His limbs flapped for long seconds before death took him. I was tempted to put him out of his misery using the shotgun but part of me wanted them all to suffer before they died. 'Sorry, but I couldn't resist that.' Williams snorted. 'And to be fair, I think you were about to set fire to him, anyway. Why have you only put petrol onto my legs?' He shrugged. 'You're going to set fire to me too and hope that the pain is so bad that I tell you where she is. Well go ahead and see what happens.' He really had no fear of me. I had to accept that he wasn't going to be frightened into parting with Fabienne's whereabouts. That left me few or no alternatives.

'Maybe killing you is the wrong thing to do,' it was my turn to smile. 'But I need to make sure you don't get to molest any more children.'

I aimed the Mossberg at his groin and squeezed the trigger. For the first time, fear flashed in his eyes. He tried to cover his genital area with his hands, but he was too slow. The shot ripped two fingers from his left hand before it shredded the soft flesh of his penis. A second blast ripped the remaining tissue away leaving a ragged bleeding maw where his reproductive organs once lived. His screams still echo around my mind today. They all do, but the screams of their victims drown them out sometimes. I didn't choose this path, they forced me down it.

'How does that feel?'

'She'll tear your heart out and make you eat it.' He wailed and writhed across the concrete on his back as if he could outrun the pain between his legs.

'Maybe she will and maybe she won't, but she had her chance and she blew it. This time will be different.' I knelt beside him and frisked his clothes. There was a second mobile in his jeans. He weakly tried to stop me taking it but there was no strength in his efforts. His fingers searched for something beneath him. I grabbed the mobile and stepped back as he raised his Zippo. He smiled at me again and the twinkle in his eyes was back.

'I'll see you in hell,' he said, laughing as he ignited the petrol on his clothing. His laugh seemed to reach an unbearable pitch as the flames took hold and seared his flesh. The lower half of his body was alight; from the waist up, his clothes were untouched. His eyes widened in horror and his face was set in a permanent grimace as he watched his legs frazzle, blister and burn. 'Shoot me.' He screamed.

'Give me your hand.' I held out my left hand and gripped his right. Pulling him roughly away from the other bodies, I dragged him burning to the incline. I let go and walked up the incline away from the cutting shed. The roof was alight; flames leaped and jumped through the slate tiles. A billowing tower of white smoke climbed hundreds of feet into the night air. The helicopter would spot the flames within minutes now that the roof had caught fire. I turned to walk back to the Landy.

'Where are you going?' Williams screamed. His burning legs smelled like a drunken barbecue late in the evening when the only food left is charcoaled. 'Shoot me.'

'Fuck you,' I shouted as I jogged away across the slate shale. 'Burn; the police will be here soon, they'll put you out.'

'Don't leave me like this please....'

His words turned into a sickening wail. He had a good chance of surviving his wounds although life without legs and a penis wouldn't be much fun for him. Fabienne Wilder might even go and see him some day, although I didn't think she'd be too pleased with her flock in Carrog. Her contact details were in the second mobile. I didn't know how I knew but I did. I climbed into the Landy, feeling tired but motivated. I had a direct link to her. If I could find somewhere safe to rest up, I could use the Internet to trace her mobile number. There were plenty of sites offering to 'ping' mobile numbers to gain a location. Some of them even hacked the number for you. I'd had a successful night. Six members of the Order of Nine Angels were dead, or in custody. I had a direct route to find Fabienne Wilder. I wasn't sure what I was going to do once I'd cut her head off. Life wouldn't have the same purpose after that. At least that's what I thought then. The cutting shed was totally ablaze as I pulled out of the slate works and headed towards the mountains; thousands of burning embers spiralled skywards. The world seemed like a safer place for a while – it wasn't a feeling which lasted very long.

CHAPTER 21

After leaving Glynn Williams and his cronies, I drove west all night until eventually I reached the coast. The sun was climbing fast as I reached the sea. Barmouth is one of those places whose name belies its beauty. Craggy mountains and rolling hills descend to some of the widest beaches I've ever seen. The sand dunes are almost white, spotted with razor sharp, lime green grasses. The sea is crystal clear and the three-storey Victorian façades which line the promenade are painted in pastels, giving it a postcard quality. As I arrived, the piercing whistle of a vintage steam train echoed across the bay. Plumes of smoke and steam gave its position away. I watched its progress across a cast iron bridge, a mile wide, which spanned the mouth of the river Mawddach. The old town is raised, and I could see a mixture of steep steps and slate-roofed cottages on the side of a mountain. Couples walked hand in hand enjoying the morning sunshine. The harbour looked beautiful and I wished I could walk across the Barmouth Bridge holding hands with a woman who loved me. I thought of the women who had shared my life and wondered how different things would be if I hadn't been so selfish most of my life. My determination to become a successful writer had landed me where I was. I'd ignored their feelings and ploughed on, regardless of how my blind and stubborn determination affected them. I wanted to stop running. I wanted to stop hiding. I wanted to go back in time to when my life was normal, but the truth was none of them would look at me sideways anymore. I was but a shadow of the man I was then. The killing didn't worry me, but the loneliness was crippling my soul; whatever soul I had left, I mean.

As I reached the coast road, the resort was waking up. Tourists walked along the seafront and shopkeepers were setting out their wares on the pavements. Little cafés were filling up with hungry holidaymakers looking for the cheapest fry-ups in town. The clear skies promised that a perfect day by the seaside was on its way, although anyone familiar with Snowdonia knows better than to take the weather for granted. It could be warm and sunny one minute and monsoon-like the next. The close proximity of the mountains next to sea creates its own unique weather patterns.

The smell of bacon mingled with the salty air was stimulating the hunger receptors in my brain. There is nothing on this planet that makes my hunger neurons jump like the smell of bacon. Except maybe the vinegar aroma outside a fish and chip shop. The cafés used chalk boards of various shapes and sizes, listing all the ingredients of their 'special' breakfasts which added to the discomfort of my empty stomach. Bacon, eggs, sausages, black pudding, beans, toast, hash browns, and mushrooms, every syllable teased me. The sight of a man with a newspaper tucked beneath his arm as he entered a little café, which had a faded blue and white awning, made me think that risking breakfast could be suicide. I envisaged my face on the front page of every newspaper. The thought of getting halfway through a belly-buster breakfast, before being surrounded by armed police almost seemed worth it.

I pulled the Land Rover into a parking space outside a camping shop on the seafront. The owner was pulling wire bins full of flip-flops onto the pavement. Had it been raining; I guessed the bins would have been full of plastic-macs and collapsible umbrellas. Today it would be beach balls and buckets and spades. I turned off the engine and climbed out of the Landy, checking both ways for any sign of the police. The sound of seagulls calling above me settled my nerves. Even back then when I heard the flying scavengers on the air and smelled the sea, I felt like I'd arrived home. I still do.

I walked quickly into the shop and grabbed a tweed flat cap and a pair of £1.99 imitation designer shades. Putting them on, I scanned the shelves and came up with an idea. The smell of rubber Wellington boots and Gortex reminded me of the many camping trips that I used to go on with friends from my local pub. We used to pull up, pitch up, then get pissed up. I grabbed a four-man dome tent and a cocoon sleeping bag, a Calor gas stove and some mess tins. There were plenty of remote campsites along the coast. I could mingle into the woods and trees for a few nights while I selected my next targets. The owner coughed nervously behind me distracting me from my thoughts.

'The hat fits you okay then?' He said sarcastically. His features were angular as if his face had been chiselled from granite.

'Yes, and the glasses fit too,' I replied in a whisper. I put my finger to my lips. 'It's my idea of a disguise. I came down here to get away from the missus, but I've heard she's coming down to try to find me.'

'Oh, I get it, disguise it is then,' he tapped his nose and nodded conspiratorially. 'I split up with my missus five years ago. The bugger took everything, and she still haunts me now. You can have the glasses on me.'

'Thanks,' I smiled.

'The hat is £9.99.'

'Absolute bargain,' it was my turn to be sarcastic. 'Like I said, thanks.' I couldn't help but chuckle to myself. 'I'll take this lot too please.'

'Right you are,' he rubbed his hands together before keying it into the till. I noticed his hands were strong. They looked scarred around the knuckles. The total increased as each item was added. Each addition seemed to lift his demeanour. He looked out of place working in a camping shop. 'Seventy-five, ninety-nine; where are you thinking of heading for?'

'What?' I asked suspiciously.

'I assume you're going to a campsite?' he nodded towards the tent and accessories and smiled. 'I just wondered which one.'

'South, I think I'll see the west coast,' I lied. I wanted to head north towards Harlech. I handed him four twenty-pound notes. 'Where's the best place for breakfast around here?'

'If you want to stay out of the way, there's a greasy spoon down the next street,' he smirked. 'It's not the best, but it's cheap and cheerful.'

'I'll give it a try.'

'Have you seen the news at all this morning?' His eyes narrowed.

'No,' I picked up my purchases nervously. Maybe I'd pushed my luck too far.

'You might want to have a look at it.'

'Why is that?' I could feel my face tensing up and although I couldn't see myself, I knew that I'd gone red.

'You might have a little more than your ex-wife to worry about.' He shut the till drawer and stepped back slightly. 'According to the television, more members of that cult from Carrog were found dead near Betws-y-Coed last night. Papers said there was a 'Massacre in the mountains.' Sounds like they got what they deserved to me.'

'I'm not sure what you mean, but thanks for the glasses.' I turned to walk out of the shop. Obviously, the events of the night before were public knowledge.

'It probably doesn't mean much but I'm right behind you,' he half smiled. 'The police are linking the murders to all that shit that went on in Carrog. They're nothing but paedophile scum. Whoever killed them should get a medal. Paedophile scum and nothing more than that.'

I looked at him and nodded but I couldn't think of anything to say. He knew who I was, hat and shades or not. Any thoughts I'd had about breakfast evaporated. I needed to get away from populated areas quickly while I planned my next steps. 'Nothing more than that,' I agreed quietly.

'What I think of it might not mean much to you,' he nodded gravely, 'but here's my card. If you ever need anything and you can't risk going to a town, call me or email me.' He handed me a business card from the till. 'My name is Joseph.' He held out his hand and I took it. 'I mean it, any time.'

'Thanks, but I wouldn't want to get anyone else into trouble,' I turned and walked away. I was strangely touched by the gesture but doubted very much, his offer of support would ever be tested. I opened the door and checked outside. 'Thanks, though,' I said as I left.

'They found one of them alive,' he called after me.

Obviously, Williams had survived. That pleased me. The quality of life he would have would be no more than he deserved. I jogged from the shop to the Landy. I bundled the tent and supplies into the back before climbing into the driver's seat. The shopkeeper stood in the doorway and saluted as I drove away. A strange gesture but his solidarity with my actions lifted me somewhat. As his image grew smaller in the mirror, I searched for a local radio station. Sure enough, when the news came on, the lead story was about two fires and a number of suspicious deaths in the Betws-y-Coed area of Snowdonia. The report said that four men had been found dead, one was missing and that a local woman and man were helping the police with their enquiries. The follow up report stated that the police were searching for another man in connection with the case, the author Conrad Jones. They directed listeners to the pictures which were on their website and warned the public not to approach me, as I was armed and dangerous. There was a soundbite, from the lead detective. 'We're appealing to Mr Jones to turn himself in. We know that his life was threatened, and things have got out of hand. Turn yourself in before things get worse. We know that you're a frightened man and if you cooperate with us, we can help you at this stage.'

Help me to do what? Secure a life sentence maybe. I didn't think things could get any worse. Yet again, I underestimated just how low rock bottom really was.

CHAPTER 22

I stayed on the coast road for six miles. The road climbs onto the headlands above the sandy beaches. The views were stunning. Sunlight glinted off the sea making the rock pools look like puddles of molten silver. When I reached the tiny village of Nant-y-Col, I turned right onto a single-track road. A brown signpost directed me to a campsite situated high above the village. Driving over a series of bone shaking cattle grids, I entered the campsite and trundled around until I found a pitch well away from the other campers. There was a single storey shower block with a slate roof and a small camp shop attached. The arrival of a new vehicle attracted the attention of a few random campers. Some of them waved hello, others just glanced and looked away, returning to whatever they were doing. I kept my head down and ignored the well-meaning greetings. Campsites are traditionally friendly places to be but the last thing that I needed now was attention. New friends were not a commodity that I could risk having.

Parking next to a dry-stone wall, which separated the campsite from a copse at the base of the mountain, I used the Landy as both a windbreak and a shield from curious eyes. The wall had deteriorated in places where campers had stolen the stones to make camp-fire rims. I picked a spot next to a section of wall with a deep 'v' in it and pitched the tent a yard from the break in the wall. It took me twenty minutes to pitch the tent and set up my stove. Hunger was still stalking me and my newfound jubilation at being ready to cook a meal was snatched from me by the realisation that I had nothing to cook. The camp shop was my only option. I looked across two hundred yards of open grass which was teardrop shaped; tents and camper vans lined the edge at regular intervals. The sound of children playing blended with the rumble of the Nant-y-col waterfalls. The bleating of sheep, which looked like tiny balls of cotton wool on the surrounding green slopes, echoed across the camp. This was heaven for those seeking to escape their mundane nine-to-five routines. The peace and tranquillity soothed my jangling nerves. It was a peaceful place far away from the nightmare of the previous night.

Trade at the shop looked steady, campers drifting in and out. I pulled my cap down tightly and pushed the shades up to the bridge of my nose. I took a deep breath and headed across the field towards the shop. The smell of bacon cooking on camping stoves drifted to me from nearby. My mouth was watering and my stomach rumbling. The closer to the shop I got, the more campers I encountered. I nodded silent greetings to those who said hello. Every glance was a stare, every look an accusation. Hunger drove me on, and I kept my head low as I entered the building.

To my left was a magazine rack. Everything from archaeology to zoology had a periodical dedicated to it. The shelves were crammed three publications deep, floor to ceiling. Daily newspapers lay face-up on the floor next to them. I scanned the front pages nervously. Thankfully the red tops were all leading with the breaking news that a leading Tory MP and two Labour Peers were being linked to the Order of Nine Angels. There was also mention of a flurry of senior police officers resigning under a cloud of disinformation. Dozens of people had come forward to make complaints of abuse at the hands of members of the cult. It appeared that my hunt was bearing fruit. The deaths at Brunt Boggart had blown the roof off the Angels and a detailed widespread investigation began into the cult and its network of paedophile rings. It seemed that the investigation was gathering pace. Police analysis of computer hard drives and mobile phone bills had revealed an insidious web of cult members and affiliates, reaching from the poorest suburbs to the halls of power at Westminster and beyond. International links were being found. Maybe the world wouldn't think that I was a crazy after all. There was sympathy with my plight, but it wouldn't extend to a courtroom. Of that, I was sure.

Directly in front of me was a chilled shelf. Packets of farm killed smoked bacon screamed at me to eat them. I walked to the chiller and picked up three packets of bacon, a black pudding and six pork and apple sausages. My mouth was watering at the thought of them sizzling in a pan.

'All bred, slaughtered and cured on our farm,' a voice informed me proudly. A gentle nudge in the ribs reinforced the claim. The farmer piled fresh packets of lamb chops into the chiller as he spoke. His smile faded as he looked at me. 'Have you booked to camp on here?'

'I booked online in January.' I lied. I'd camped there years before and remembered that Nant-y-Col was booked solid most of the year. Although it was remote, it was oversubscribed through the summer months. It was one of a few camps, which actively encouraged campfires and sold sawn logs to facilitate it. I'd spent many an evening watching the burning embers floating towards a star filled sky with a beer in one hand and a frazzled sausage in the other. The memories of happier days tugged at my heart strings. I also remembered that the camp's website was archaic, and their administration had holes that you could drive a bus through. 'I booked three nights, one adult a tent and a Landy.'

'Just checking.' The farmer smiled but his bushy grey beard masked it. Yellowed teeth hid deep behind the bristles. 'We're booked three months in advance, all year round here, you know?'

'That's because it's such an idyllic spot,' I smiled. 'I've been here for the last five years running with the family, wouldn't go anywhere else.' I hoped that my flannel would avoid him looking for my booking. 'I've come on my own this time. I want to get some walking done.'

'I thought your face looked familiar,' he nodded his massive head. Wispy white curls quivered above his ears. He had a look of Santa without the jolliness. He nodded towards the counter, 'my son does all the checking in and out now.' A sly wink and a whispered, 'right clever bastard he is, but they all think they are at that age, eh?'

'Don't they just.'

'Not as clever as he thinks he is though.'

'I remember him selling logs from his quad bike in the evenings,' I reinforced the fact that I'd been there many times. 'He was always a very polite lad.'

'He's not a bad one.'

'Keep that to yourself.' I laughed nervously as I walked to the back of a queue, four campers long. The shelves around me contained tins and bottles of every description and colour. It was a Tesco store crammed into a double garage with prices that you would choke at anywhere else, but halfway up a Welsh mountain you can pretty much charge what you like, I guess. The young man behind the counter didn't bear any resemblance to his father. Three decades of waking with the sunrise and weathering the mountain winds had taken their toll on the farmer. It felt like an age for it to be my turn, but it was probably a few minutes in the real world.

'Morning, have you booked in yet?' The teenager asked abruptly without looking at me.

'No, not yet,' I tried to smile, but it probably looked like I had wind. 'I'll take these and pay for my pitch if that's okay.'

'Name?'

'Jones.'

'Initial?'

'J for John.'

'We haven't got a booking for a John Jones, sorry.'

'I booked it online months ago,' my smile was now more of a grimace. I wanted to give the kid a slap and then go and cook my bacon. 'Every time I book a pitch online here, I have problems when I arrive.'

An icy glare met my comments but at least he was looking at me now. 'There's nothing wrong with our new website.' He challenged. 'It works perfectly if the users are Internet-savvy.'

'I'm a programmer for Apple, so I know a bit about websites,' I lied, 'my booking was made and confirmed.'

'Apple,' he stuttered. 'Are you really?'

'God's honest truth,' I lied. I was a murderer so being a liar seemed to be a step in the right direction, as far as redeeming my soul went. 'So, I know my way around computers somewhat.'

The kid didn't know how to take me. 'Well we don't have a booking in that name and we're full all week.'

'Check it again.'

'We're fully booked.'

I looked behind me. There were four campers waiting patiently. The farmer had stopped loading the chiller with meat and was eyeing the situation coolly. 'You said that your new website was perfect?'

'It is.'

'What about the old one?'

'What do you mean?'

'Is it still online?'

'It is, but it directs customers to the new site.' He smiled sarcastically.

'The direct links to the old booking page are still active and there is no notice of a change of site on the booking page. The home page might direct them to the new site, but your contents pages don't come up with the link.'

'What?' His face reddened. His lips were tight together.

'Your regular customers, like me will just use the links direct to the booking page of the old website. Why would I need to use the home page when I come every year?'

'Well…'

'Well nothing, Einstein,' I slapped sixty pounds onto the counter. The noise made him flinch visibly. 'Take the old site down or disable the booking pages or link it to your new site. Do whatever you need to do to correct your mistake and while you're online, look up some customer care courses because your attitude stinks. There's my money so give me my docket and my shower room key, and I'll be on my way, shall I?'

'Best to do just that, Bryn,' the farmer stepped behind the counter. 'I told you to get someone proper who knows what they're doing to change that website.' he scolded. 'I'm sorry for your inconvenience. Three nights you said?'

'It's no problem. Like you said, they know it all at that age.' I grinned at the red-faced kid and felt a little sorry for him, but I needed to eat and then sleep in peace. The farmer grinned and seemed to revel in his son's discomfort.

'Enjoy your stay and the bacon.' He placed four-pound coins on the counter. The youth glared at me angrily. 'Home reared and home killed.'

'Yes, you said.' I smiled. 'I will. Thank you.' I turned and walked past the growing queue. The campers avoided looking at me as I walked out. The sunlight warmed me as I trudged back to my camp. Ten minutes later, I was forking my sizzling breakfast straight from the pan into my mouth as fast as I could. The flavours were intensified by my hunger, every taste receptor tingled as the cooked meat caressed them. It was probably the best breakfast I'd ever had, listening to the gentle roar of the falls and the sound of children playing in the river. Peace seeped through my soul and I realised just how shattered I was. I desperately needed sleep. My body ached, every muscle sore and every joint creaked. I grabbed the Mossberg and wrapped it with the sleeping bag. Crawling into the tent, I instantly fell into a troubled slumber, holding the shotgun as if it was the most beautiful woman in the world.

In my dreams, I could hear the gentle roar of the waterfalls upstream and all was well with the world, until a different roar joined the first. I heard the helicopter blades initially and then the first siren pierced the tranquillity, swiftly followed by another. I sat up and rubbed the sleep from my eyes. My watch told me that I'd been sleeping for eight hours. I was in a panic, confused and fuzzy headed. You know what it's like when you awaken from a deep sleep with a start. It took me minutes to work out where I was, never mind what was happening to me. I could hear sirens, but they were neither approaching nor dissipating; they were static. I held the Mossberg tightly and crawled on my knees to the door. I grasped the zip and pulled it up six inches, peeping through the gap with bleary eyes.

The camp was silent. The sound of children was gone. There was no sound apart from the sirens and the waterfalls in the distance, which blurred with the deep hum of the helicopter above.

'Conrad Jones,' a metallic voice boomed, startling me. 'Armed police. You're surrounded. Come out of the tent with your hands up.'

There was a sick feeling in my guts as I realised that the camp had been evacuated while I'd slept, and the police had moved in quietly. They'd used the sirens to alert me to their presence. I instinctively knew the farmer's son had bubbled me. I unzipped the door flap to the top and looked around.

'Armed police.' the voice boomed again. 'Come out now and lie face down on the ground.'

Fifty yards across the field, three marked police cars were side on to me. Each had two or three armed officers behind them. They were all pointing standard issue Glock-19 automatics at the tent and more specifically, at me.

'Do it now or we will shoot.'

I looked to the right. A dry-stone wall snaked up the valley as far as I could see. There was a sniper perched behind it to cover my flank. The sheep in the field behind him grazed oblivious to my predicament.

'Come out of the tent with your hands up now,' the voice was more urgent now. He was becoming more aggressive in an attempt to shock me into action. 'This is your last warning.'

It's funny, but I wasn't feeling the same urgency as he was. Looking back, I was remarkably calm, almost glad that they'd found me. I had no intention of shooting anyone, except Niners of course, so I didn't see the reason to panic. If I couldn't see a way out, then it was all over and something inside me took comfort in that. I looked at the officer with the loudspeaker and our eyes met for a few long seconds. The evening air was cool but there was sweat running from beneath his peaked cap and he looked far more scared than I felt. I suppose they knew that I was armed with a shotgun and that I'd left a trail of bodies behind me. Fugitives like me usually went out in a blaze of glory, guns blazing, or they turned their own weapon on themselves. I had no desire to do either of those things. It might sound weird, but I actually smiled at him. The confused look on his face was priceless. I caught surprised glances passing from his officers as they trained their weapons on me.

'Do it now, Conrad,' he encouraged me. 'We don't want to shoot you, but we will if you don't comply.'

I heard him but still didn't feel the urge to respond or react. I looked left at the Landy. It would take me three steps at the most to reach the driver's door. The keys were in the ignition and she was pointing towards the copse of trees, which formed the natural border between the camp and the mountain. Jumping into the Landy, driving through the wall and into the trees might be an option in a movie but this was no Hollywood production. There wasn't enough space to build up speed to breach the wall, notwithstanding that the damage incurred to the front of the Landy would probably render it useless. Add to that the denseness of the copse, and it was a non-starter.

'Last chance.' Desperation tainted his voice this time. He could see that I was contemplating my options. As if reading my mind, he waved an arm towards the sniper. 'There's no way out of here.'

There was a loud retort as the sniper rifle spat. It echoed up the valley and into the trees. Sheep bolted across the field bleating in alarm as they ran from the alien noise. A loud bang made me jump, as a high-powered bullet ripped the rear tire of my Landy into shreds. I had zero options to begin with and they were becoming slimmer by the minute. The helicopter swooped low, prompted to enforce its presence by the rifle shot. The downdraught flattened the long grasses which grew next to the wall and the tent flapped noisily. It was crunch time, leave in a body bag or leave breathing and take my chances with the justice system. I stood up and stepped clear of the tent, ready to face the music but I made a mistake.

'Drop the weapon, now.'

The armed men tensed and readied themselves to shoot. I had the Mossberg in my right hand, and I stared at it as if I'd never seen it before. I hadn't realised that I was holding it. The shotgun had been my only friend for weeks and letting go of it seemed wrong.

'Drop it now or we'll shoot.' He signalled to the sniper again and a shot rang out. The front wheel of the Landy exploded and something in my mind snapped.

I dived back into the tent and closed the zip.

'Move in.' I heard the order to close in on the tent.

I scurried across the groundsheet, grabbed my bag and slashed the back-wall material with my blade. There was only a metre between the tent and the 'v' in the wall and the breach was out of sight to the police. I jumped onto the wall and scrambled over it in seconds. It crossed my mind that they may have a sniper in the trees, but I doubted it and didn't care, anyway. Ducking low, I sprinted into the trees and didn't look back.

'Come out of the tent, now.'

I heard the command repeated over and over as I ran for my life. The ground beneath me was spongy and the sound of twigs cracking, and leaves rustling seemed almost deafening. The scent of spruce and pine filled my nostrils as I bolted through the trees; their lower branches scratched and whipped my skin as if they were conspiring to slow me down.

'Throw the weapon out of the tent now.'

They hadn't seen me escape through the back. My choice of pitch had been the right one although it had been more luck than judgement. The trees became denser as I ran, and blood mingled with the sweat running down my face as I ploughed blindly through the foliage. The ground began to climb steeply the further I ran. I could hear the waterfalls becoming louder and the voices of the police faded as I began to climb the lower slopes of the mountain. The helicopter hovered over the camp, unaware that I was putting distance between us. I knew it would be minutes before they realised that I'd slipped through the net and then the helicopter would scour the mountain with heat seeking cameras. I had to put as much space between them and myself as I could before they began hunting me. My lungs were screaming at me, every breath burning my insides. The muscles in my thighs felt like concrete had been injected into the veins as my legs pumped wildly up the steep incline. Saliva sprayed from my lips with every pounding step and the sweat stung my eyes making focusing impossible. Dodging the tree trunks was difficult enough but avoiding the whip like lower branches was nigh on impossible. I headed towards the sound of the falls, knowing that following its path up the mountain would be easier than climbing blindly. I ran and ran for what felt like hours until my body decided that it wouldn't or couldn't carry on without rest. As I reached the river below the falls, I collapsed into a bloodied sweaty heap and then I heard a mobile phone ringing in the bag.

CHAPTER 23

I rooted through the bag searching for the ringing phone. I had five belonging to dead Niners. It was the waterproof JCB phone, which I'd acquired at the Miner's Bridge episode. I stared at the screen and felt the blood running cold in my veins.

'Hello,' I answered trying not to sound exhausted.

'Conrad,' her voice sent shivers down my spine. 'I take it they haven't shot you yet.' She giggled like a teenage girl. 'I really wouldn't want that to happen.'

'Fabienne,' my voice rasped. I didn't have a clue what to say. This was the woman who had caused all my pain, all my despair, all my loneliness, all the murders, all the fear and here she was calling me on a dead Niner's mobile. 'How did you know it would be me that answered?'

'Oh, I just know things like that.' The giggle sounded more disturbing this time. 'I knew you would have their phones. You're a clever man.'

'Not that clever, or I wouldn't be in the shit I'm in now.'

'It wasn't your choice,' the words almost whispered. 'Don't kick yourself. I would have got to you one way or the other.'

'All this because of a book.' I sighed. My breathing was settling down and as I lay looking at the evening sky listening to the water falling over the rocks, I could have stayed there forever. 'I guess I'll never learn when to leave something alone, eh?'

'I guess so.'

'Someone would have exposed you sooner or later.' I sighed. I felt remarkably calm as I talked to her. 'People just won't tolerate child abuse.'

'There you go again,' she sounded like a slightly pissed off girlfriend. 'You just can't get your head around it all, can you?'

'No one normal would.'

'I don't make anybody do what they do,' she lowered her voice again. "Do as thou shalt", is the code we live by. Some want to hurt and abuse, rape and torture, while others find it repugnant. They do what they want to do, you know, really want to, deep deep down in their black hearts,' she giggled again. 'You're as dark as my darkest followers, Conrad. You're a killer, a murderer, a torturer. You're no better than them.'

'They're sick, like you,' I snapped. I sat up and scanned the woods for my pursuers but there was nothing but birds in the trees. 'I hurt those people because they're evil. They don't deserve to live.'

'You are the man to decide that, are you?'

'For now, yes.' I sighed. 'The spotlight is on your cult, Fabienne. The police and the Security Services are trawling the country for your kind and they'll find some of you too. I don't give a fuck how many of you die before they catch me.'

'You've proved that already.'

'What do you want, Fabienne?'

'Your head on a stick, your heart in a bowl alongside your other organs and oh, did I mention that I want you to watch while I feed your child to my priests?'

'There is no child, you lunatic.'

'You know what happens when a man puts his little sperms into a woman, babies are made.'

'I don't know what happened,' I argued. I wasn't lying. To this day I don't know if it was all a bad dream brought on by some kind of telepathy or if it did actually happen. She'd done something to my mind. That was for certain.

'You loved it.'

'You're sick.'

'You wanted to fuck me the first time you laid your eyes on me.'

'I felt sorry for you.'

'You were infatuated.'

'Don't flatter yourself.'

'Oh, I've been around enough men in my time to see it their eyes,' she giggled again. 'But you know that I didn't just see it in your eyes, I read your mind.'

'Whatever.'

'You wanted me the minute you saw me, and you still do.'

'I really want to see you again, Fabienne,' I chuckled to myself. 'So, I can blow your fucking brains out.'

'She's three weeks old.'

'Who is?'

'Our daughter.'

'Bollocks.'

'You know it's true.'

'I don't and I don't care,' I clenched my teeth. 'Anything that has come from you is pure evil. You can try to put my head on a stick with pleasure but trust me, I'll take some of your scum-bag followers with me. Just tell me where you are, and I'll come to you.'

'That's why I'm ringing you, silly boy,' she whispered again.

'What?'

'You heard me.'

'What game are you playing now?'

'No games.'

'What then?'

'I'm going to tell you where I am.'

'Why?'

'Because I don't want the police getting hold of those mobile phones which you're carrying, or listening to you ranting about our order,' she hissed. 'I need you dead, Conrad and if you're determined to find me, then I'll tell you where I am, and we can put an end to this once and for all.'

'Suits me fine.' I took a deep breath. 'Where and when?'

'Trefignath.'

'Where?' The name rang a bell in my head, but I was so tired and confused that it didn't sink in properly. The name seemed to echo inside my head. I'd read about it but I couldn't remember when or why.

'You know it, Conrad,' she giggled again.

'It sounds familiar, but I can't place it.'

'You've been there many times.'

'Just tell me where it is.'

'It lies at the centre of the source of our power.'

'What power?' was all I could think to say. I was searching my memory banks for the name. 'You're nothing special; you're deluded.'

'Charming.' She chuckled. 'The night after next is the Lammas Day and the full moon. I'll be there then.'

'Are you talking about the standing stones?' It clicked. 'On Holy Island?'

'Clever boy.'

'Are you having one of your demented little gatherings there?'

'Something like that,' she whispered. 'But this is a special one, just for you. You'll be the guest of honour.'

'There's nothing special about it. Just a bunch of perverts bumming each other in a field,' I said. The more distance there was between myself and Fabienne Wilder, the less I believed that she was anything but a sick woman. 'I don't think you'll be there; you're too scared. You're lying.'

'I could be.'

'Why play games?'

'I don't want you telephoning the police and spoiling everything.' She sighed. 'I've planned this for so long.'

'So where will you be?'

'Go to Trefignath and someone will meet you there,' she went into impatient girlfriend mode again. 'They will bring you to me, if the others don't get to you first.'

'What others?'

'There are many hunting you, Conrad,' she snapped. 'The police are the least of your problems.'

'I've done okay so far.'

'Granted,' she said. 'Be at the stones and my people will meet you.'

'Good,' I didn't like the plan one bit. 'Then they'll die just before you do.'

'Do you really believe that you can kill me?' She sounded irritated now. 'After all you've been through, do you really think that you can?'

'You bleed just like I do,' I said looking at the blood and sweat smeared on the back of my hands. 'If you bleed, then you die; simples.'

'You're boring me now,' she snapped. 'Be there, you fool.'

'Fuck you.'

'Poor boy,' she said sarcastically. 'I'll see you on Friday.'

The line went dead as she hung up. I stared at the blank screen and thought about the call. Trefignath was situated on Holy Island. It's an island separated from Anglesey by the 'Inland Sea'. Tourists visiting Trearddur Bay or travelling by ferry from Holyhead to Ireland rarely realise that it's a separate landmass. There are standing stones dotted all over North Wales, which are aligned with those on Anglesey and Holy Island. Many believe they're sited along 'ley lines' where spiritual or mystical energy can be accessed. I'd read many theories about the ley lines but remembered one specifically, which mentioned sites where the lines intersected. The author had called them 'ley gates' and Trefignath was the one he theorised as the most significant as it was at an intersection of not one, but four ley lines. The theory is that the ancient Druids used the ley gates for ceremonies because that was where the mystical energy was the most potent. Mumbo-jumbo or not, the stones are there and are dated to 3500 BC. Who knows why they were erected or who did it, but it seemed that Fabienne Wilder and the Order of Nine Angels believed that they could tap into this mystical energy? If it's there, then I suppose it can be used by evil doers just as easily as it can for good. Trefignath is a stone circle with a plinth across two of the stones. There's a chamber beneath. I knew it well as I'd spent many years on Anglesey and it was somewhere, I used to walk the dog back then.

I knew where it was, however, I had no vehicle and it was sixty miles away on the other side of the Snowdonia range and across the Straits. Add to that several armed police units, a helicopter and any number of Niners and reaching Anglesey was as simple as flying to Mars on a push-bike. I felt like giving up at that point. Suddenly, an engine noise pierced the air. I rolled over and searched the trees with my eyes. I was expecting police, but the sound wasn't right. It wasn't a car engine or motorbike; it was petrol driven; I could tell that. Another loud burst from my left confirmed my thoughts. It was a chainsaw and it was nearby, and I had a feeling that I knew who it was too. I hoped that I was correct in my assumptions.

I grabbed the bag and picked my way up the riverbank towards the falls. The chainsaw was deeper into the trees to my left. Stooping low, I set off in that direction. I could hear the throaty buzz growing louder as I approached a firebreak in the tree line, and the smell of petrol exhaust fumes wafted in the air. I caught a glimpse of yellow moving in the trees. It was a high viz jacket. I could see the figure fetching and carrying logs and I could only hope that he was working alone. As I neared, I recognised him. It was Bryn, the farmer's son. I felt hope rising in my guts. Bryn went everywhere on the campsite selling his logs, riding on a 400cc quad. I doubted he would have come this far up the mountain on foot. His quad would give me a slim chance of getting off the mountain without being arrested or shot.

I skirted the firebreak so that I could approach him from behind. Sure enough, he was alone, and he was wearing industrial earmuffs to protect his hearing. He wouldn't hear me coming until it was too late. I picked up a small log and threw it into his line of sight, wary of the deadly chainsaw in his hands. He turned to see who had thrown the log. When our eyes met, he saw the shotgun immediately and he placed the chainsaw on the damp earth. I signalled for him to take off the muffs.

'They didn't catch you, then,' he said.

'Doesn't look like it.'

'I told him not to phone the police.'

'Who?'

'My dad.' He half smiled. 'He's an arsehole sometimes.'

'I figured that you'd called them.'

'Not me. I didn't recognise you,' he sounded sincere. 'I think what you've done is pretty cool. I was friendly at school with one of the boys they found in Carrog. Gwillam his name was. They only found his skull.'

'I'm sorry about your friend.'

'That's why I told him not to call them, but he wasn't having any of it.' He shrugged again. 'How did you get away?'

'I ran very quickly,' I said sourly.

'Are they coming after you?'

'I think they're under the impression that I'm still in my tent but as soon as they realise I'm not, they'll be after me.'

'Take my quad,' he gestured towards the big, green machine.

'That was the plan.'

'Oh.' he smiled. 'I hadn't thought that's why you stopped here.' He blushed, embarrassed by his naivety. 'Where will you go?'

'Up the mountain.'

'Have you ridden one before?'

'Only on holiday,' I thought back to a trip to Morocco years before. Two friends and I booked a four-hour quad ride through the Blue Mountains. It's not as easy as it looks. 'It was a long time ago.'

'If you don't know how to handle a quad and you go up the mountain, you'll get caught,' he pointed towards the sheer rocks of the summit which were just visible through the tree canopy. 'I've been up that track thousands of times and I've never got across the mountain. It's too steep at the top, even for an experienced rider.'

'Is there a way around the mountain?' I asked tiredly.

'Not without crossing the falls and you can't do that on a quad,' he shook his head thoughtfully, 'you could go down the mountain to the coast road.'

'No, they'll have roadblocks everywhere within an hour.'

'The only other trail leads back to the campsite'

'I guess I'll just have to take my chances at the top then,' I moved towards the quad. 'Where's the keys?'

'The keys are in it.'

'How much fuel is there?'

'Not much,' he shook his head. 'I normally fill it up at night when I've done my log runs. It'll get you ten miles or so, but you won't make it that far going up.'

'Bollocks.' I sighed beneath my breath.

'Listen,' he stepped closer as if not to let the trees hear us. 'My nan's place is only a few miles away down the firebreak She's been dead for a while, but my dad uses it for feeding the sheep in the winter, so he won't get rid of the place. I could take you there and you could hide out for a while.'

'Sounds too good to be true.'

'Her car is still in the barn too.'

'Hallelujah,' I said. Maybe someone upstairs was on my side after all. 'If they find me, tell them that I forced you at gunpoint.'

'I will,' he said. 'Get on; we need to move.'

Bryn fired up the quad and with a throaty growl, the machine moved off quickly down the firebreak.

CHAPTER 24

As we reached the lower slopes, the trees gave way to rolling green fields, criss-crossed by grey stone walls which seemed to go on forever. In the distance, I could see Barmouth, the buildings like miniatures against the startling blue of the sea. A darker blue line on the horizon told me where the sea met the sky. The sun was falling towards the sea and as the breeze blew in my face, it was hard to think that I was the subject of a manhunt. My thoughts ran away with me as the quad made easy going of the tracks and trails.

'This is it,' Bryn shouted over the engine noise.

A slate-built farmhouse was nestled into a grassy knoll; two barns and a tall silo to the right of the ivy-covered building. The firebreak ran onto a dirt track which scythed a crescent shaped path from the track to the farm. Although it was an idyllic setting, the dark windows filled me with a sense of foreboding. I'd been living on my instincts for years and had my situation not been so dire, I would never have gone near the abandoned farmhouse. If I was surrounded there, it was a dead end with no way out. That aside, there was something about the farm that worried me. The breeze, which had been refreshing, now chilled me to the bone.

'Does your dad still use this place regularly?' I shouted.

'We use the silo for sheep food in the winter if it snows and he uses one of the barns to slaughter the odd sheep. Most of the animals go to market but he kills some for meat in the camp shop.'

'What about the house?'

'Still the same as when my nan was alive, although it's a bit dusty inside now,' he pointed to a barn. 'Her car is in there. My dad started it up a few weeks ago. There's a generator in the cellar for electric. It's not too noisy so you should be able to use it.'

'When is he next due here?' I asked over the engine noise.

'I can't see him coming down here with all that shit going on at the site,' he shouted as he steered the quad towards the farmhouse. 'You could take your chances riding across the fields towards Barmouth. No police roadblocks up here.'

The idea appealed to me much more than holing up in the farm, but I would be out in the open and easy to spot from the helicopter. It would take at least an hour to cross the patchwork of fields. If the helicopter climbed to a decent altitude, they would be able to see for miles. I wouldn't get far before they spotted me. At least in the house they wouldn't know which direction I'd taken. After forty-eight hours they would have to widen the net so far that I might be able to slip through it. 'They'd see me before I crossed the first field,' I looked towards the sea and longed to be there. 'I'll hole up here for a while. Tomorrow at least and then I'll slip away.'

'I'll bring you some food later,' Bryn said. He slowed the quad down and guided it to the rear of the farmhouse. The barns were wooden structures with curved tin roofs. Nettles, thistles, and tall grasses formed a waist high, green border around them.

'No don't,' I replied as we came to a stop near the back door. It had a wooden porch with a sloping slate roof on it. The dark blue gloss was cracked and curled away from the timber revealing the grey undercoat which had been applied decades before. Discoloured net curtains hung in the windows behind grimy glass panes and the gossamer of spiders' webs glinted from every corner. I didn't want to look through the glass let alone enter the place. 'You might be seen, and I need to know that if anyone comes near, they're looking for me. Best if you just go home and forget that you've seen me.'

'I just wanted to help you,' he complained. He turned off the engine and waited for me to dismount the quad.

'You have,' I said, scanning the mountain behind us for signs of pursuit. Nothing moved, which struck me as strange and there were no birds tweeting. I remembered reading about a new housing estate in Southport where the homeowners noticed that no birds flew into their gardens. The developers had demolished a chicken factory to build the houses and for whatever reason no birds came to the site where millions of their feathered cousins had been slaughtered. Maybe the slaughter of sheep in the barn had the same effect. Whatever it was, it made me shiver inside. 'You don't want to be arrested for aiding and abetting a known criminal. That won't look good on your website.'

'I suppose.' He grinned. 'The keys are under that plant pot. I'll put the quad in the barn and show you where everything is.'

'Okay,' I agreed somewhat reluctantly. I'd been travelling alone for so long that I was uncomfortable having company. On the flipside, I really didn't want to enter the farmhouse alone. I couldn't put any rationality behind my concerns; it was just a feeling. I stepped into the porch and moved the terracotta pot which Bryn had pointed to. A filthy swathe of a spider's webs stretched from the pot to the wall, its maker long since dead. A single mortice lock key lay in the dust. I took one last look around before picking it up. The cold metal felt almost frozen against my skin. A tingle ran through my fingers. I felt that my mind was playing tricks on me, fear and panic conspiring to muddle my thought process. A breeze blew and tugged at my jeans, further adding to the chill which I felt inside.

'I've put the quad out of sight,' Bryn's voice made me jump, 'are you okay?'

'Yes.' I nodded and looked for the keyhole. The paint on the door was the same shade of blue as the porch; it was blistered and peeling above the brass footplate. I put the key into the lock and twisted it; it clicked easily without a sound and I pushed the door open and let Bryn go in first. 'All those police and guns have made me jumpy, that's all.' I half joked.

'You'll be fine here,' he said from inside. 'Proper little home from home. Like I said, it's not changed a bit since Nan died. I'll go and switch the generator on.'

Bryn opened a door which I assumed led down to the cellar. I stepped into a long kitchen which had dusty red tiles on the floor, a pine table with four chairs and a wood-burning stove fixed into a brick fireplace. The porcelain sink was yellowed with age and dust particles drifted through the beams of light which managed to penetrate the grimy window. The smell of damp and decay drifted up from the cellar. A new kettle stood next to a box of PG teabags and a jar of nondescript coffee. Their newness looked out of place in the museum like setting. I heard the generator kick into action and then footsteps rising from the blackness. I don't know why, but I pointed the Mossberg at the cellar doorway. I wasn't sure what was climbing the stairs and the muscles in my chest constricted trapping the breath in my body.

'Let there be light.' Bryn joked. He saw me pointing the gun and the blood drained from his face. He held up his hands, frightened and startled at the same time. 'What's up?'

'Nothing,' I lowered the weapon. 'I'm sorry. Like I said, I'm just jumpy.'

'I think I've shit my pants,' he swallowed hard but managed a smile.

'Sorry.'

'No worries,' he pointed to a small white fridge beneath a beige Formica worktop. 'There's some long-life milk in there if you want a brew. Cups are in there.' He nodded towards a Welsh dresser which was fixed to the far wall. Decorative china plates lined the top shelf. 'You'll find the keys to her car in the top drawer.'

'Thanks,' I said walking over to the dresser. I opened the top drawer and took a key fob which was marked with the VW logo. 'Best if I keep these on me.' I glanced at the contents of the drawer. There was a rainbow of cotton bobbins, a card wrapped with fuse wire and an assortment of buttons, pins and needles and strangely, a shotgun cartridge. I picked it up and studied it before closing the drawer.

'Farmer's wife,' Bryn said brightly.

'What?'

'Farmer's wife,' he gestured to the cartridge. 'They could shoot the tail off a rabbit if they needed to, but they don't like loaded guns in the house. Nan always used to unload Granddad's gun when he came back from shooting and she'd put the shells in the bobbin drawer. It used to drive him demented but she wouldn't have a loaded gun around.'

I felt embarrassed by his disclosure of life in his grandparents' home. There was fondness in his voice when he spoke about them. The daylight was fading, and I switched on a light. A low-wattage bulb fizzled into life. Worried by the thought of attracting my pursuers with the light, I walked to the window and pulled a pair of soiled pink curtains closed. I thought about how the day had unfolded and tried to take stock of what I needed to do if I was to maintain my liberty long enough to kill Fabienne Wilder. I had to stay free until Friday. As my pulse rate settled down, I was becoming painfully aware that running blindly into Fabienne's trap, and I knew that's what it was, would result in my slow and painful death and nothing more. I had to make a plan. I had to think about my options and then make a rock solid, foolproof, inventive plan, a plan that would end this nightmare and rid the world of Fabienne Wilder.

'Come on, I'll show you around.' Bryn disturbed my thoughts. 'There's a spare room still made up at the back of the house. Dad lets the shearers stay here when it's shearing time. He stays here himself sometimes, misses my nan I think, and it gives him a break from my mum too.'

Bryn walked out of the kitchen into a short hallway. There were two doors on the left, both glossed white which had aged yellow with time. I figured that they were the living room and dining room, a pattern of architecture from yesteryear. I stopped next to each door momentarily, listening and sensing what was on the other side. I could imagine highly patterned floral carpets, velvet curtains, velour suite, and a mishmash of rugs. The mantelpiece above the open coal fires would be cluttered with knick-knacks and memorabilia, brass ornaments and china plates; images taken from the memory of my own grandparents' homes. I wanted to look at them, but Bryn was already halfway up the stairs. There would be time to explore once he had gone home. I glanced at the pictures, which lined the staircase and hallway, pastel drawings of Conwy, Beaumaris, Chester, York, and various other castles. The carpet was faded and threadbare at the middle of each stair, the fibres at the edges thicker and brighter in colour. A thick layer of dust and grey hair clung to the gaps where the carpet met the skirting boards.

'Bathroom is there, toilet in there and this is the spare room,' Bryn gave the guided tour. The spare bedroom had two single beds; both covered in brown satin quilts. Lace trimming decorated the pillow seams, another throwback to a lost generation. The room smelled used and slightly damp, but it was better than the alternatives. It had a claustrophobic feel to it, almost coffin like. I didn't envisage sleeping like a baby in there, although I appreciated his good intentions.

'Use anything you need. If you do take her car, leave the keys in it when you've finished with it—' he shrugged '—at least I can get it back when they find it. Oh, and will you lock the back door when you leave?'

'Of course,' I replied gratefully, 'we wouldn't want any criminal types getting in, would we?'

'You don't know who is hiding in the woods these days.'

'Could be murderers on the run,' I added ironically. 'Don't want anyone like that wandering in the back door.'

'Definitely not.' He laughed. 'Nan would go mad if she knew.'

'I'm very grateful to you,' I said.

'I was good mates with Gwillam,' he lowered his eyes. 'I don't care how many of the bastards you shoot.'

'They'll get me in the end.'

'Probably.'

'No doubt about it.' I was getting impatient with the chitchat. 'I don't want to sound ungrateful, but can you get a mobile phone signal here?'

'Yes, why?'

'I'm going to find their leader and I need to do a bit of research on the net before I set off. I need to connect my phone to the net.' I guessed that at least one of the mobile phones I had would have a browser.

'I can do better than that,' he frowned, 'Nan used to keep in touch with my uncle in Australia on the net. She had a computer in the dining room. Granddad didn't know how to switch it on, but Nan was all over Facebook to keep tabs on the family.'

'How come it's still connected?'

'You know what it's like up here when it snows,' Bryn looked out of the window as he spoke as if imagining the fields covered in a blanket of white powder. 'If it gets really deep, it's easier to stay here than risk crossing the mountain. Dad has left it on for convenience's sake. I know the code.'

'That's perfect.' I smiled. My trepidation about the farm seemed to be melting away slightly. I tried to summon every positive cell in my body to lift me. I had everything that I needed to plan my next move so what could go wrong?

CHAPTER 25

'The password has been changed.' He frowned as he tried to enter the login details for the sixth time. He looked confused and a little embarrassed. 'God knows why he would have changed it.'

'I'm assuming your dad would be the only one who would change it?' I looked around the dining room as if the password would jump out at me from somewhere. A drop-leaf table dominated the room, its walnut veneer scarred in places by cup rings. I imagined the argument that the first cup burn would have caused. As predicted, every flat surface was covered in cheap souvenirs. Mementos of a handful of days away from the farm, mixed with tacky presents bought by family and friends returning from their holidays. Holidays for hill farmers of Bryn's grandparents' generation were pipe dreams, which only non-farming folk achieved. Still, I suppose receiving a conch seashell from Benidorm was almost as good as being there. A walnut display cabinet held yet more precious tat. 'Maybe he changed provider or something.'

'He didn't mention anything,' Bryn tried again in vain.

'Does he make a note of anything?' I asked, opening a drawer in the roll-top desk that the computer was set up on. The teak desk was a throwback to another time. In contrast, the Dell was a cutting-edge home computer; old and new working in harmony but appearing abhorrent to the eye. I rummaged through pastel coloured pads of post-it notes and pencils but didn't see anything of use. 'Check the other drawer.'

'Sorry about this.' He sighed as he opened the drawer on the other side.

'What was it before?'

'What?'

'The password.'

'Password.'

'That figures.' I nodded. 'Easy for your nan to remember.'

'Yes.'

'What's on that pad?'

Bryn pulled an A5 pad from the drawer. The front page was covered in a scrawl that made no obvious sense. He flicked through a couple of pages, which contained various dates written in black pen but nothing that looked like a password. I scanned the dates which meant nothing to me and turned another page; the rest of the pad was blank all the way through.

'Does he have a password for the campsite computer?'

'Cantona-2468.' He shrugged apologetically. 'He's a United fan.'

'You sure?' I asked sarcastically.

'He's always used that password.' Bryn smiled.

'Try it.'

'He's always been a big United fan, but I don't ever recall him going to see a game live, armchair fan,' Bryn said typing. 'No, it doesn't work.'

'Try Oli with the same numbers.' I took a stab in the dark with the new Manchester United manager.

'Nope.' He shook his head.

'What about Pogba?'

'Nope.'

'Marcus Rashford?'

'Nope.'

'RVP?'

'Nope.'

'Rooney?'

'Nope.'

'I give up.' I was becoming impatient. 'Unless you can think of something else, I'll use one of the phones.'

Bryn typed in three or four names in succession, his mother's name, his sister's name, his granddad's name and then his grandmother's. 'We're in.' He held out his hand to high five. I reluctantly slapped it. 'Now then, what do you need to look at?'

'It's really best if you don't know that, Bryn,' I grimaced. 'If the police do realise that I've been here, then I can guarantee that the Niners will find out and they'll both want to know where I'm heading. If you don't know, then you can't tell them.'

'I wouldn't tell them.' He sounded offended.

'When you've been on the run as long as I have, you learn not to trust anything to other people or fate.' I tried to soften the blow. 'Trust me, it's for the best.'

'I understand.'

'I owe you one, but I doubt that I'll ever get the chance to pay you back.' I offered my hand. 'You should leave now and let me get on with what I have to do.'

'Can you hear that?'

'The helicopter is over the mountain,' I said.

'It's dark now,' he said looking through the curtains. 'I can see a searchlight.'

'They'll be combing the trees. You should leave now.'

'I'll take the quad back through the trees with the headlights on,' he said, 'they might think it's you and follow me.'

'Wait until that searchlight is on the other side of the woods,' I didn't want him to draw attention to the farm.

'It might be better if I stay here with you,' he said.

'Bryn, trust me when I tell you that you don't want to be around me for too long,' I said firmly. It took me another twenty minutes to cajole Bryn into going home. His face was a picture of disappointment as he closed the back door. I thought about making a brew before getting onto the computer, but I didn't have time to rest with a cup of tea. A small army was hunting the mountain and the woods for me. I had to make the most of whatever time I had left.

Locking the back door behind Bryn, I went back to the dining room, the smell of mothballs replacing the dank smell in the hallway. The computer was displaying a screen saver of various waterfalls on a slideshow. I typed in 'standing stones on Anglesey' and waited for the search to complete. You can imagine my surprise when the computer showed me the recent 'related' searches and it became obvious that someone else was interested in them too. I looked at the web destinations which the last user had visited, and my heart sank. Someone had been surfing for information about the ley lines on Anglesey, which was too much of a coincidence to ignore. They'd been searching significantly darker sites too.

One of them was a site explaining the Satanic calendar. I've included a copy of it in the back of this book, read it and then tell me these people are a figment of my imagination. Can you believe that's online for anyone to access? If that isn't incitement to kidnap, rape, and murder then what is?

I grabbed the pad and studied the scrawl. The dates scribbled on the pad corresponded to some of the key dates in the Satanic year. Bryn's father was either a Niner or he was investigating their websites out of curiosity. I doubted that. I was beginning to believe that he'd recognised me as soon as I walked into his shop. No wonder he'd been so keen to allow me to book in without a confirmed reservation. The nerves in my spine tingled and the apprehension, which I'd felt approaching the farm, seemed justified. It seemed that I'd developed a sixth sense about them, similar to the way Evie Jones had. I missed her every minute of the day. My instincts had told me not to go into the farmhouse, yet I hadn't listened to them. I felt vindicated for feeling anxious, yet vindication had given me no comfort. I was incredibly aware of the danger I was in. Was Bryn's father one of them or was he just curious?

I had to distinguish which it was. It didn't take me long to find some evidence. I clicked on the 'downloads' file and then 'pictures' and waited for the images to appear in tiles. Images of women and children of both sexes being sexually abused appeared in the hundreds, possibly thousands if I'd trawled through the filth he'd downloaded. Having those images saved to the computer was concrete proof that he wasn't just investigating the dark side, he had stepped into it. It couldn't be an accident. Stumbling across unsavoury images can happen when you're surfing occult sites but downloading them to your computer is no mistake. I wondered now if he was an active member of a nexion, or just a curious pervert with a similar taste in non-consensual sexual activity. The news coverage, which my plight had attracted, had sparked interest and even curiosity from those appalled by the Niners and it would also interest those of a similar twisted mindset. The scandals uncovered by the police investigations would expose many members, but it would attract new ones too. Bryn's father was obviously interested in joining them, or he was already a follower of the sinister way.

    I searched for the Order of Nine Angels and sure enough his historical searches for them appeared. I clicked on the most recent site, which was simply named *ONA.org*. The homepage appeared and the usual Satanic shite loaded up on the screen. The site asked me for a password. I typed in Gwen-2468, which Bryn had used to access the computer. It didn't work. Maybe he wasn't a member after all. Then a thought crossed my mind. Maybe he'd been a member for a while. I typed in Cantona-2468, which was a much older password and unsurprisingly, I gained access. I clicked on news feed and felt my hands starting to shake. The forum was rife with recent posts about my whereabouts. One post mentioned the stones of Trefignarth as my final destination. Another explained that there are only two bridges onto Anglesey, which meant it would be easy to watch for me driving onto the island, while a post uploaded only thirty minutes earlier gave my position as in the area of the Nant-y-Col waterfalls and predicted which route I would have to take to reach the stones. I felt very frightened and alone and as I sat there with my head in my hands, I heard a key rattling in the back door. I knew that I'd left the key in the lock. I always did as a precaution, twisted slightly off centre so that it couldn't be pushed out from the other side. It would never stop a determined assassin from breaching the door, but it was an effective early warning sign. I grabbed my bag and my gun and headed for the front door, killing the lights as I went.

CHAPTER 26

You might think it odd that I chose the front door but under the circumstances, I had to assume that whoever was trying to get in, meant to harm me. Why did I think that? A number of things occurred to me when I heard the key rattling in the lock. First, the police wouldn't attempt an entry like that when an armed killer was inside. They would surround the building, create a siege situation and then when they decided that forced entry was the only option remaining, they would use smoke bombs and stun grenades first, to disorientate the gunman, namely me. I knew it wasn't the police. Bryn didn't have a key, or he would have used it when we first arrived. He told me where the key was and asked me to leave it safe when I left, therefore it wasn't Bryn trying to get in. Whoever it was had a key, so I had to assume it was his father, who I'd just discovered was an affiliate, at the very least, to the cult that was hunting me.

He was trying to gain entry through the back door with a key. I didn't know if he was aware that I was hiding in the house or not, but I had to assume that he did, which would mean that he wouldn't have come alone. No one in their right mind would attempt to take on an armed man who had demonstrated that he was willing to kill to survive. An average man planning to drive his target out of a building would use the tactics that he'd seen many times on the television, which was basically a load of crap made up by researchers and script writers. If he was trying to gain entry to the back of the house, then he would have ordered someone to guard the front of the house to act as an ambush, to kill the escaping target as they desperately fled the building. Grouse hunters use unarmed beaters to drive the birds towards an impenetrable line of double-barrelled shotguns where they're blown to smithereens. The safest thing for a smart grouse to do is to fly towards the beaters.

I knew that they couldn't get in without breaking a window or door and they wouldn't want to do that as a first option. They'd banked on the key opening the door, so now they would need another plan of action. I had a few minutes and no more to react. I ran from the dining room into the kitchen, down the cellar stairs and looked for the generator. I hoped that there would be spare fuel down there. Sure enough, a five-gallon jerrycan stood near the rattling machine. I snatched it and bolted up the stairs. As I ran and planned my next vital steps, something in the cellar registered in my brain but it would have to be shelved until another time. I sprinted to the Welsh dresser and grabbed a reel of cotton from the drawer, skidding across the tiles and banging into the kitchen door frame, I ducked low and moved quickly along the hallway. I reached the front door and slid a brass bolt open, twisting the Yale lock at the same time, leaving it on the latch. I tied the end of the cotton around the handle and headed back to the kitchen, switching on the hallway light as I went, signalling to those outside that I was moving towards the front door.

When I was safely in the kitchen, I tugged the cotton opening the front door. Shotguns roared, shattering the leaded glass and long splinters of wood became deadly shrapnel as they were blasted from the door frame. The front door was decimated as shot after shot exploded around it. The light bulb at the base of the stairs shattered into a million particles and a split second before the light went out, I saw one of the pastel drawings disintegrate into pieces. As the shooters reloaded, I heard two sets of footsteps running away from the back door, passing the kitchen window and heading towards the front of the house. I ran to the cooker and switched on the electric rings, placing the petrol drum flat on top of them so that all four came into contact with it.

Another volley of shotgun blasts ripped chunks from the front door and the hallway walls, but this time there were more guns firing. I opened the back door and peered through the gap. The barns stood like inky black silhouettes against a darker backdrop. There could have been a shooter there, but I doubted it. They were all at the front of the house, blowing the shit out of shadows. Happy that it was safe, I bolted for the barn. Every muscle in my body was tensed and I took shallow breaths as I ran, waiting for a shotgun blast to knock me off my feet. None came. As I reached the barn wall, I hid in the long weeds and scanned the farmyard behind me. Nothing moved. The shotgun blasts had become less intense and more sporadic. They sounded muffled and there were flashes of light in the windows that looked as if they were coming from inside the house.

I figured that they'd reached the kitchen when I heard raised voices, some of them panicked and then the windows at the rear of the farm exploded. Glass clattered and smashed against the walls of the barn and pinged off the metal silo. Towers of flame erupted through the window frames, spiralling across the farmyard and into the air. Muffled screams were cut short by the explosion. A single figure staggered from the back door burning from head to foot. The mouth was open in a silent scream; a gaping black maw surrounded by orange flames. I could see the shape of a pair of Wellington boots bubbling and sizzling, the flames below the knee a different hue of orange to the rest. The figure dropped to its hands and knees and crawled a few yards before collapsing completely, the limbs twitching violently as life left the body and floated skyward with the smoke. I was mesmerised for a moment but then another scream came from the burning building. I realised that some of them may have survived. I sprang up and ran between the huge wooden doors into the barn. As my eyes adjusted to the gloom, the scene before me stopped me in my tracks.

I took a flashlight from my bag and scanned the scene quickly, fearing that the light would attract my pursuers. The quad bike was still parked there, the keys in the ignition. A Volkswagen Polo from the 1990s was behind it, the tires slashed. The bonnet was raised, and all the spark plug leads had been cut, along with the hoses and the fan-belt. The damage was recent. My first thought was that Bryn was part of the cult too and that he'd pretended to leave while he waited for backup. It wasn't beyond reason that he was the Niner, not his father. I played the torchlight around the entire barn and there was the answer to my question, Bryn right in front of me. He had been there all the time. As I looked into his eyes, I knew that he wasn't a Niner.

Bryn's lifeless body was crucified to the wall; a pitchfork had been driven through one arm deep into the wood and two chisels drilled through the other. His throat had been slashed just below the chin and his tongue had been pulled through the wound so that it hung like a short pink tie against his neck. A piercing pang of guilt stabbed my guts, but I had no time to feel sorry for him. I knew the gunshots and the explosion would bring the police down on top of me. They would see the flames from miles away. I had to get out of there quickly. It was difficult to ignore the butchered body of the young man who had helped me to get off the mountain, but I had to act if I was to escape the carnage.

Placing the Mossberg across the seat, I pushed the quad next to the VW and scanned the barn for a length of pipe. There was a green hosepipe rolled up and hung on a rusty nail. I cut a length and ran to the petrol flap. It was locked. I used my blade to pop the flap and then fumbled for the keys to open the cap. My hands were shaking, and my breathing became laboured. Thick black smoke was drifting into the barn and the flames cast an orange glow over the farmyard. I threaded the pipe into the tank and sucked hard. The stinging liquid hit my lips and I spat it out and shoved the pipe into the bike's tank. The fumes were acrid and began stinging my eyes as I siphoned the fuel from the car into the quad. The tank was full within minutes although it felt like an age, standing there staring at Bryn's crucified corpse. His eyes watched me accusingly. I'd made him leave for his own safety but all I'd achieved was his brutal death. Looking at the amount of blood, I guessed that he'd be pinned up while his heart was still beating. I wondered if his death was at his father's hands or those of another.

'You bastard.' The voice sent my heart into my mouth. Torchlight illuminated Bryn's body and then blinded my eyes. I grabbed the gun and crouched behind the quad, my own torch now pointing at the man. His face was blistered and raw on one side, the hair gone and the ear nothing more than a smouldering lump. Smoke drifted from his charred clothes and his right hand looked like a blackened claw. 'You bastard.'

'I didn't kill Bryn,' I said. 'Put your gun down and move out of my way.'

'You animal,' the charred figure stepped forward. The grey curly hair and beard which remained on one side of his face, told me it was Bryn's father. He looked like a character from Batman only far more sinister. His shotgun hung uselessly from a smouldering hand. He tried to raise it but the effort was too much. His knees buckled and he went down heavily. I climbed onto the quad and pressed the ignition button. The engine growled into life. 'She'll get you and you'll burn in hell.' he shouted over the noise.

'You're already there, arsehole.' I engaged first gear and steered around him, heading into the farmyard. What the police would make of the scene, I had no idea and didn't really care, but I had a feeling that they would blame me. If his father hadn't killed him, then one of his sicko friends must have. I could only hope that the killer had been barbecued in the farmhouse. The building was completely ablaze now, and I could hear the helicopter moving closer. In the dark, I had a slim chance of making it across the fields to Barmouth, if I could find the gates which linked connecting the fields and avoid any rocks and ditches. Once there, I could circumnavigate the back streets avoiding the main roads and search for an opportunity to escape. The threads of a plan were beginning to form. If I could reach the coast, I could get to Anglesey avoiding the bridges and the roads which the Niners and the police would be watching. All I needed was a boat and someone who knew how to pilot it.

CHAPTER 27

I steered the quad through the farmyard and into the field, purposely avoiding the track which led to the coast road. Once the fire was spotted, the police and fire brigade would be swarming up that track. I guessed that no one at the farm would place an emergency call, if of course they'd survived the explosion, and it was so secluded that there would be no passing traffic. My greatest concern was the helicopter. I steered the machine as fast as I dared in the darkness. The quad had headlights, but I couldn't risk using them. I could hear the helicopter in the distance, and it didn't appear to be any closer yet. After ten minutes of bouncing around on the padded seat and hanging on to the handlebars for dear life, the first of a series of dry-stone walls loomed out of the night. I knew there would be a gate into the next field, but I didn't know if would be to the left or to the right. I had a 50/50 chance of fucking it up. As I contemplated which direction to take, the engine noise from the sky changed tone.

The sound of the rotor blades echoed from the mountain as the helicopter soared above the trees towards the burning farm. I estimated that I was a mile away from the scene and I elected to follow the wall to the right simply because it took me further away. Three hundred yards on, there was a gate and thankfully it was open. I guided the quad through it and opened up the throttle. As I picked up speed, I glanced behind me. Two sets of blue flashing lights were moving quickly along the coast road from the direction of Nant-y-Col. They'd responded quickly, so I assumed that they'd been part of a roadblock on the main road who had then been dispatched to investigate the fire. The helicopter searchlight illuminated the farmyard and I could see that the fire had spread to one of the barns. I couldn't tell which one from that distance, but I hoped it was the one which contained the bodies of Bryn and his father. That would be two bodies that couldn't be attributed to me if the barn burned down.

The ground began to slope away, and I let the gradient take the quad, praying that there were no ditches dissecting the fields. As my speed increased, so did my confidence. It was only a matter of time before I stumbled across another farm track and as long as I took the downhill direction, I would eventually reach the coast road. As I was planning what I would do when I reached Barmouth, headlights appeared three hundred yards to my left. I could hear a throaty diesel engine and from the direction of the beams, the vehicle was set on a collision course with the quad. Even though it was dark, I knew the vehicle had entered the field via a gate further up the slope, which meant that I was heading in the wrong direction. I was steering towards the corner of a massive square, blindly following the gradient into a dead end. The vehicle adjusted direction, aiming straight towards me; the headlights blinded me.

There was little point in driving blindly anymore. I switched on the lights and steered the quad at an angle from the oncoming vehicle. Illuminated in the beams I could see that it was a short wheelbase Land Rover, which meant that it wasn't the police. The driver of the vehicle altered course again, determined to meet the quad head on. Whoever it was, they weren't coming to tell me to get off their land. With the field between us illuminated, I opened up the throttle and steered directly into the path of the speeding Land Rover. I thought about raising the shotgun and blasting the windscreen through but as I'm not Bruce Willis and it wasn't a movie; I didn't think that I could shoot and stay on the quad simultaneously. As the vehicle neared to within a hundred yards of me, I could see a blackened face beneath a flat cap. A bulky figure was hunched over the steering wheel, his teeth bared in a fixed grimace. He looked determined not to swerve out of the imminent crash. Had I been in the two-ton vehicle, I probably would have done the same thing, however I wasn't, so my choices were limited. Keep going and hope that he bottled it or change direction at the last minute and go around him.

I heard the transmission grinding as the driver dropped a gear to increase his speed. In response, I slowed the quad and tried to gauge the right moment to swerve. As I've said before, this was no film script and I was no expert on a quad bike. I leaned to the right, opened the throttle, and swerved hard. The front of the bike reared like a rodeo stallion and I was thrown into the air like a marble from a catapult. I heard wrenching metal and there was a shower of sparks but the cataclysmic collision I was expecting, didn't happen. I landed like a sack of potatoes fifteen yards away. I was winded but grateful not to have broken my neck. I blinked and the stars became clear and bright, tiny diamond pinheads on a black satin board. The sound of the Land Rover skidding on the grass forced me to move. I saw the Land Rover's reversing lights come on heard the gearbox crunch. I looked across the field to see what state the quad was in. It was upright, facing up the slope but missing one mudguard and headlight. I sprinted the short distance to the quad and then quickly checked that the Mossberg was still there.

Young Bryn would probably have ridden the quad and run the Land Rover ragged, out pacing and outmanoeuvring the heavy vehicle but I could barely stay on it at speed. I took the shotgun from the seat and walked ten yards away from the quad. When this was done, I would need wheels, so the motorised jousting would have to stop. The Land Rover turned and skidded to a halt; the headlights bathed me in light. I couldn't see the driver, but I knew that he was weighing up his options. What I didn't want right then was him to come up with a good plan. If he had realised that I'd walked away from the quad because I needed it, then he would have put me on the back foot by ramming it out of action. I had to put him under pressure before he made a decision.

I shouldered the weapon, ran towards the vehicle and squeezed the trigger. The blast shattered the left-hand headlight. He crunched the gears as I fired again, and the remaining headlight exploded. My eyes were struggling with the sudden darkness, but the Mossberg was aimed at the Land Rover. I fired blindly and heard the windscreen splinter into a thousand pieces. The engine roared and I ran to the left so that I could get a shot at the driver, but he had put the vehicle into reverse and the transmission whined as the vehicle lurched backwards at speed. I slammed cartridges into the gun and fired off three shots, blowing the front tyre to ribbons. The Land Rover went into a severe swerve and then the rear end disappeared as if swallowed up by the ground. The front of the vehicle lifted, wheels spinning in mid-air, the underneath of the Land Rover exposed. Exhaust fumes and steam spewed into the air and the engine screamed one last time before it spluttered and died. I heard a cry of pain and anguish as it dropped into a deep irrigation ditch. This was my opportunity to get away.

I glanced towards the fire in the distance, the slope of the earth hiding most of it, but I could see that the helicopter was positioned above the farm. They hadn't heard the gunshots or if they had, the echoes from the mountain had confused them as to which direction they'd come from. I jogged back to the quad, fastened the Mossberg and steered the bike up the slope in search of the gate that the Land Rover had entered through. The quad seemed unscathed mechanically and one headlight was better than none. The altercation with the Land Rover had done me a favour. I would have ridden straight into the ditch that it had fallen into. Looking back, I can only guess at who the driver was, and my instincts tell me he was part of the shooting party who went to the farm to kill me. I never heard any mention of him when the deaths at the farmhouse hit the news. It's not like he could report the incident to the police without having to answer some very tricky questions himself.

As I trundled across the fields and down pothole riddled tracks, I thought about the news coverage that would be broadcast the next day; an armed siege at the campsite thwarted by my escape and then the ensuing fire and deaths of a number of local men. Could people really believe that the people killed were just unfortunate victims, who were in the wrong place at the wrong time? Surely the police would find their weapons and realise that they were hunting me and that I'd acted in self-defence. I decided there and then that before I headed for my showdown with Fabienne Wilder, I would share my version of events with the media. I'd turned the tide of public opinion once and I needed to do it again, even if it was only to cause the police investigation to intensify its efforts against the Order of Nine Angels. There was no doubt in my mind that if I didn't do it now, I wouldn't get another chance. I didn't believe that I would survive my showdown with the Niners.

CHAPTER 28

I reached Barmouth two hours later. The farm tracks led to a back road which weaved down the headlands and eventually merged with the coast road. Blue flashing lights were zipping up and down the main road, so I entered a housing estate which looked rundown and sprawled for a mile before it mingled with the older more expensive dwellings. I wiped the quad down and left it on the edge of some playing fields with the keys in it. Bryn didn't need it any longer and I figured that a couple of proud ASBO owners would be delighted when they found it. They would strip it, repaint it and terrorise their neighbours on it for weeks before the police connected it to the campsite; if they ever connected it at all. I couldn't risk walking the streets with a shotgun under my arm, so I took a gamble. Taking cover in a clump of trees, which bordered the playing fields, I took out a crumpled business card from my back pocket and dialled the number. I was about to test the offer of help, which had been offered the previous day.

'Hello.' The line clicked and buzzed as if there was interference.

'Joseph,' I said.

'Yes,' he sounded sleepy. 'Who is this? Have you got any idea what time it is?'

'No, not really,' I answered honestly. 'This is Conrad and I need help.'

'Fucking hell.' his voice suddenly sounded wide awake. 'Where are you, how can I help?' I heard him fumbling around for something and then the sound of a lighter wheel against a flint. The sound of a cigarette being lit sent the nicotine receptors in my brain alight like a thousand tiny blowtorches burning in my brain.

'Well I could do with one of those cigarettes for a start,' I mused. It had been hours since my last smoke. My cigarettes were in my Landy. 'Has there been anything on the news about the campsite at Nant-y-Col?'

'Are you joking?' I heard him take a deep suck on the smoke. '*Sky News* was showing nothing else but a reel about how the police allowed an armed fugitive to escape through the back of his tent. My tent as well; I sold you that; my tents are famous, eh?'

'You need to design and sell 'escape tents' with a zip at both ends.' I laughed sourly, 'there's a gap in the market there. Every fugitive should have one.'

'Funny,' he inhaled again. He sounded almost excited. 'Seriously though, how can I help you?'

'Well I need a lift for a start, a cigarette, a beer and an Internet connection.'

'I think I can manage all that,' he said seriously. 'Anything else?'

'Oh yes,' I added, 'I need a boat that will stay afloat long enough to sail me to Anglesey.'

'Fucking hell,' he whistled.

'Oh, and someone who can sail.'

'One thing at a time,' he said calmly. 'Tell me where you are, and I'll come and get you.'

***

Half an hour later, I heard a diesel engine approaching and then headlights swept across the playing fields. Joseph flashed the beam twice as we had agreed. I stepped out of the trees and jogged fifty yards across the grass to his dark blue Jaguar. There was a moment of nervous anxiety as I opened the door. I was putting my liberty and possibly my life into the hands of a stranger, but my situation was so dire that I had little or no choice. I couldn't get out of Barmouth by road or rail and I didn't have enough time to lie low for weeks until the roadblocks disappeared. I put the Mossberg into my left hand and slid into the front seat. He reached over with his right hand and I accepted the gesture gladly.

'You've stirred up a hornets' nest,' he said. 'There are police racing up and down the coast road. The news is warning people to stay indoors as there's an armed fugitive in the area.'

'There is,' I shrugged and tried hard to return his smile but failed miserably. 'Can I steal one of your cigarettes please?' I needed to get my priorities right. He chuckled and passed me a Sterling from a new packet. I lit it and inhaled deeply.

'Keep them. They're for you, menthol, right?'

'Right.' I looked at him sternly. 'How do you know that?'

'There's been quite a few profiles about you on the news, you know, interviews with people who claim to know you and the little titbits about you lead to 'be on the lookout for a shaven headed male, who smokes menthol cigarettes' blah blah. Some of them are showing an interview with your ex, you know, Constance Bonner's mother. She's claiming that you're a hero for rescuing her daughter and pleading you to give yourself up.'

'Funny how the people you haven't seen for years claim to know you the best. I see she hasn't learned to stay out of the limelight,' I relaxed a little. 'Thanks for the cigarettes. I was gasping. You're a star. We'd better get going. It looks a bit odd sitting here at this time of night.'

'I'm making sure that I haven't been followed first,' he looked in the rear-view mirror. I looked over my shoulder nervously. The roads around us were dead. He scanned the playing fields once more before starting the engine. 'I live up the hill,' he explained as he drove away from the kerb. I found his cautionary behaviour comforting and yet disturbing in equal amounts. He wasn't your average guy. 'You can rest up tonight and then we'll sort out what you need tomorrow.'

'Thanks for your help.' I sunk down into the leather seat and pulled on the smoke. The cigarette felt like a little piece of heaven in my hand and I savoured the soothing effect. The Jaguar purred as we drove through the council estate before taking a left and heading towards the headlands above the river. In the space of a few hundred yards, the buildings had changed from prefabricated terraces to four-storey Victorian detached.

'No worries,' he said seriously. 'Most people are right behind you. Did you know there was a half hour news special on you yesterday?'

'No,' I felt my stomach tighten. My ability to move freely across the country was dissipating day by day. 'Did they make me out to be a lunatic?'

'Far from it,' he shook his head. 'They painted you as a victim, if anything, they were scathing of the police investigation into the cults and they made a big deal about you rescuing your daughter.'

'They don't know it was me at the mill for sure, do they?'

'They have your voice on the recording of the 999 call,' he looked at me. 'It's faint and in the background but some of your friends identified it as you.'

'Friends, eh?' I laughed. 'Who needs friends like that?'

'Well it must be nice to know you have some,' he joked, 'the programme was scathing about these cults though.'

'Cults as in plural cults?' I asked, confused.

'Yes,' he nodded. 'Seems that your Order of Nine Angels has a number of affiliate groups, The Church of Satan and The Temple of Set being the most obvious names that I can remember and then they were showing footage of some of the right-wing extremist groups, who sympathise with their ethos. The newspapers are dragging up all sorts of connections going back decades. There's been some pretty high-profile arrests made and half a dozen untimely resignations. It's big news at the moment.'

'Good, but the Press is diluting the story by bringing the other groups into it. The Niners hold all the other groups in contempt,' I explained. I was frustrated that the Press had still not got a handle on just how bad the Order of Nine Angels were in comparison to the other self-proclaimed Satan worshippers. 'The other groups are like the boy scouts in comparison to the Niners. The Press doesn't realise just how insidious they are.'

'What's the difference?'

'Culling and breeding for abuse.'

'Culling,' he repeated. 'As in seal culling?'

'Exactly,' I drew deeply on the smoke again. 'They actively encourage the slaughter of those who they see as weak, or people they deem to be a threat to them. They choose their sacrifices from the sea of human dross that floats around out there. Drifters and the homeless, kids from the care systems, people who won't be missed. Of course, killing people who threaten to expose them is just a necessity.'

'People who threaten them.' He smiled. 'Like you?'

'Especially me.' I laughed. I couldn't remember the last time I'd felt relaxed enough to laugh.

'Well, whatever these Satanic groups are up to, they're in the spotlight and running for the shadows. Worshipping Satan is not PC at the moment.'

'Good.' I finished my cigarette and exhaled as I spoke. 'It's got fuck all to do with worshipping Satan for most of them. It's all about sex and abuse. Only the hardcore really believe that Satan is their God.'

'That's what they're saying on the news now. Your message is getting there,' he glanced at me. There was thirty seconds of uncomfortable silence. 'What happened at Nant-y-Col?'

'To cut a long story short, the campsite owner bubbled me. I fell asleep and woke up surrounded. I legged it through the forest.' I lit a second Sterling, 'The owner's son, a young lad called, Bryn helped me escape. I was hiding from the police in a farmhouse which belonged to their family and it turned out to belong to a Niner.'

'Was that a coincidence?' he grimaced. 'Did the son set you up?'

'Fuck knows,' I said. 'If he did, then he paid a hefty price. They slit his throat and crucified him to the barn wall. His old man was one of them.'

'What?' Joseph shook his head in disbelief. 'He slaughtered his own son?'

'I don't think so,' I thought back. 'He was burnt badly in the fire, but he thought that I'd killed Bryn. I think one of the others knew he'd helped me escape and they killed him as a warning to anyone else who thinks about helping me.'

'Are you trying to put me off?' Joseph wasn't perturbed by the implication. 'I'll take my chances.' It wasn't said boastfully, but I got the feeling that he probably fancied his chances in most situations. 'I'm intrigued about the farm, carry on.'

'They came for me with shotguns. I set fire to the place and left a tin of petrol on the stove to cover my escape and they were caught in the explosion. The flames alerted the police helicopter and here I am.'

'Very clever.' He tilted his head. 'I've read your bio, but have you been in the military?'

'No.' I shook my head and smiled at the thought. 'Just shit I've picked up researching books.'

'Well it obviously works,' he nodded. 'Were there any more dead?'

'Yes.'

'How many?'

'I don't know. Maybe four.'

'Oops.'

'Oops, indeed.'

I looked out of the window and caught sight of a drawn face with dark circles under the eyes. He looked tired, exhausted even. Although I was aware that it was my reflection, I was fascinated by how haunted the face looked. The gentle movement of the vehicle and the quiet purr of the engine combined and acted as a powerful tranquiliser. I was asleep within seconds. I felt safe for the first time in as long as I could remember, and my mind surrendered to slumber. I couldn't have slept for more than ten minutes but my dreams were the most pleasant that I'd had for months. I was surrounded by familiar faces, all of them smiling and reassuring me that they didn't judge me for what I'd done. My dear departed father appeared just before I awoke; his blue eyes as vivid as if he was there. He smiled and was about to speak. I knew it was a warning. A voice dragged me back to a dark reality. I sat up and couldn't move properly. I gripped the gun and looked around with panicked bleary eyes.

'It's okay, Conrad.' Joseph placed a calming hand on my arm. 'Relax we're at my house.'

I realised that the reason that I couldn't move was my seat belt. I sat back and took a deep breath. 'Sorry.' I sighed. 'I'm tired and jumpy.'

'Well, you're safe for now.' He opened his door and the interior light came on. I could hear a winch motor and saw a garage door closing behind me in the wing mirror. As the door closed, the lights came on automatically. A bank of six fluorescent tubes flickered into life illuminating the interior of the double garage with the power of a small sun. I blinked and looked around. It was painted white and was pristine and spotlessly clean. The walls were lined with pegboards and shelves, which were filled with enough DIY hardware to stock a B&Q. Everything was aligned neatly and symmetrically in rows and columns. It looked like there was a small saloon car beneath a tarpaulin in the second side of the garage, maybe a restoration project or something similar, although I couldn't see any wheels. A Jeep was parked in front of it. Thick metal stanchions supported the house above the cavernous garage. 'Come on let's get you inside.'

I opened the door and reluctantly climbed out of the vehicle. I could have curled up and slept for a month. I carried my bag and the Mossberg as if they were the crown jewels. Joseph offered to carry the bag but that would have been too traumatic to handle. The garage smelled of timber and creosote. It was a pleasant smell. I envied the order and normality of Joseph's garage. He was obviously a conscientious DIY fan. Not someone who dabbled to save paying a tradesman but someone who took on a project for the sense of accomplishment and pride. Joseph punched a six-figure code into a digital keyboard which was fixed to the wall and the door into the house clicked open.

'I'm always losing my keys, so this was a no-brainer.' He guessed what I was thinking from the expression on my face. 'I bought this cheap on eBay.'

'I'm always losing my keys and forgetting my pin code so it would be of no benefit to me. I'd be screwed either way.'

'Follow the stairs up to the top,' he switched on a light, which illuminated a carpeted stairwell. There were ten steps and then a small landing as the stairs turned 180 degrees and then there were another ten to the top. I noticed a door on the landing, which seemed to lead to a hallway with several rooms leading off it. When I reached the top of the stairs, I was greeted by a huge split-level living area with a vaulted ceiling and a wooden floor; three low leather couches and a smoked glass coffee table the only furniture. A plasma television was bolted to the wall where it could be viewed from any angle. Panoramic windows made up two walls, offering a view over the entire resort, which was three miles below us. The river was to the left and the sand dunes and beaches to the right. The remaining walls were made from rectangular slate bricks and at the far end of the room was an open kitchen which looked to be made entirely from granite and chrome. 'I renovated the place myself,' Joseph said proudly from behind me. 'It was a bungalow, but we blasted into the cliff to add height and depth.'

'It's amazing,' I said impressed. 'Were you a builder?'

'Sort of,' he said, laughing. 'My father was a property developer and we worked together for a while when I left school but then I chose a different career. He taught me the basics and I learned the rest along the way. It's not rocket science.'

'Beautiful location, Joseph,' I said impressed. I stood by the windows and saw the wooden decking beyond. The house was built into a steep incline, so the wide deck was supported from beneath by metal stilts forming an 'L' shaped balcony at the front of the house. I guessed that the bedrooms were beneath us accessed from the doorway on the landing. 'What a view. At least I'll be able to see the police coming.'

'I like it.' He opened one of the sliding windows as he spoke. We stepped out onto the expansive deck and I inhaled the sea air deeply. Sirens spoiled the silence and the rumble of a helicopter echoed off the mountains behind us. 'You can see why I don't want the ex-wife to get her claws on it.'

'Definitely.'

'Do you want that beer yet?'

'Yes, please.'

'I'll get them and then you can tell me what you need.'

I took in the view again. The half-moon was reflecting off the ripples close to the shore, the wide sandy beach taking the momentum from the swell further out in the bay. Despite the late hour, the streetlights and neon signs in the town beckoned the onlooker to enjoy the bars, funfair rides, arcades and gift shops. They'd closed hours earlier, but the lights burned through the night. I imagined the empty streets, fish and chip wrappers swirling in the sea breeze while the resort slept. Yesterday it was just another declining seaside resort. Now it was my Dunkirk. A peninsula sealed off by the police and my only remaining exit was the inky black sea, which stretched to the horizon where it met the star-studded infinity of the sky. I inhaled again, savouring the fresh air and then followed Joseph inside.

'Can I put the news on?' I asked. 'I'm curious about what they're saying.'

'Take a seat,' he said opening a fridge which was the size of a wardrobe. 'I'll stick *Sky News* on for you.'

The plasma came on and the crystal-clear picture impressed me. The colours were as vivid as I'd seen on any screen. Joseph passed me a beer and made me a plate of chicken sandwiches while I was engrossed in the news. I ate them hungrily and we sat in silence mesmerised by the images. I watched twenty minutes of news footage before it began to repeat itself. The reporters were bandying about the word 'vigilante' far more than I expected. It's a word defence lawyers use for killers to justify murder. I was labelled a victim twice and they indicated that I was fleeing for my life rather than hunting for random victims to shoot. Victims of abuse from all over the world were coming forward claiming to have been forced to have sex during rituals of varying descriptions and the list of missing persons connected to the nexions was growing.

'It sounds like the message is getting through,' I shrugged when I'd heard enough. 'I wanted to upload a message giving my side of events, but maybe I don't need to.'

'I think that you should,' Joseph sipped his beer. 'Tell me how it all began and what you're planning to do next and we'll take it from there.'

One hour, four bottles of beer, and ten menthols later, I'd told Joseph the whole sorry tale. His voice was impassive when he asked questions and his eyes showed no judgement or disgust when I recounted the killings. 'Jesus, Conrad,' he said when I was done. 'You need to record everything that you've just told me. I'll keep it on a memory stick and when you get away from here, I'll upload it to every news station that wants to see it.'

'Okay,' I thought it was a good idea, 'but I need you to upload it between me leaving and Friday night.'

'Why Friday?' he asked confused. 'What's the rush?'

'Friday is Lammas Day on the Satanic calendar,' I explained. 'This year, it also coincides with the full moon. The Niners are going to use the ley lines and standing stones on Anglesey to tap into a mystical energy source and I'm the guest of honour.'

'Sounds like bollocks to me.'

'A year ago, I would have said the same thing, but that's where they will be.'

'How do you know this?' Joseph frowned.

'She called me,' I smiled. 'I took mobiles from the dead Niners and she guessed that I had them, so she rang me and invited me to their little shindig.'

'Where?'

'I don't know exactly.' I sighed. 'She told me to go to Trefignath, which is a site of ancient standing stones on Holy Island. It's special because it's on the intersection of three ley lines. Experts call it a ley gate, but I don't think that she'll be there. I think Trefignath is a decoy, a trap to capture me and then they'll take me to wherever the real ceremony is taking place.'

'Ceremony?'

'There's a Satanic calendar which specifies what they do on certain dates, orgies, rape, sacrifice of a female, male or child, depending on the date,' I explained and watched his expression darken.

'How the fuck do they get away with it?' He was incredulous. 'I mean where do they get their victims from?'

'Some of them are willing victims of the abuse,' I shrugged, 'some are less willing obviously. As for the children, they breed them.'

'Breed them?' he frowned. 'You're going to have to explain that one to me. Sounds like pig farm.'

'It's the only way they can use children in their rituals without attracting attention,' I said trying not to sound patronising. 'Missing children are big news. A child disappears and the search goes viral in days. They can't risk that kind of exposure, so they breed within their tribes. They're organised into nexions or what they call sinister tribes, which consist of adults, husbands and wives, boyfriends and girlfriends who have kids, right?'

'What and they use their own kids?'

'Bingo.' I looked at the expression on his face. He looked shocked. 'Let's say they find a weak female, a homeless girl who has been abused all through her childhood, someone who doesn't know any different.'

'Okay, I'm following.'

'They befriend her, give her a nice place to live, feed her, spoil her with nice clothes, introduce her to their little gatherings and then snap the trap closed,' I slapped the settee with my hand making Joseph jump. He eyed me warily. There was something about Joseph. He had an aura of strength and calm. He was dangerous but meant no harm to me. I could sense it. 'She's hooked and they impregnate her. No one knows about her; let alone any children she may have. Multiply this process by dozens of lost females across the country and there they have their own battery farms breeding children who will never be missed, because they never existed. If they're born into the tribe, then they don't know any difference but abuse.'

'It sounds impossible to comprehend.'

'It's a fact,' I challenged him. 'Have you heard of Aleister Crowley?'

'His name has been mentioned on the news a few times.'

'He was a nutcase, but he's revered by the Niners because he openly admitted to holding orgies where men and women and children were raped,' I looked at the television screen as I spoke almost wishing it would show something that would back me up. 'He admitted to sacrificing hundreds of children to Satan.'

'Hundreds?' Joseph whistled. 'They're sick in the head. This is madness.'

'The world is mad,' I chuckled. 'Humankind makes it mad. You call them sick, yet they see civilisation as mundane and a waste of their short lives. They think we are mad for living a life within boundaries set by leaders we neither like nor trust. 'Do as thy wilt' is their philosophy. Do what you want, whenever you want to, and fuck what anyone else thinks. If anyone tries to stop you, kill them.'

'And that's what they have in mind for you,' he raised his eyebrows as he spoke.

'Without a doubt.'

'You know it's a trap, but you're still going there?'

'What else can I do?' I laughed sadly. 'To kill Fabienne Wilder, I have to go to her.'

'Giving yourself to them is pointless after everything that you've been through,' he emptied his beer. 'Are you going to die like a rat in a trap and let them win?'

'Well I'm intending to live long enough to blow Fabienne Wilder back to hell.'

'What about the police?' he looked serious. 'If you know where she is, let the police arrest her.'

'It would never be over, Joseph.' I sighed wearily. 'Look how easily she escaped last time. As long as she's alive, they'll be after me and they'll get me in the end.'

'Okay,' he said, smiling. 'She has to die but we need to find a way of doing it that doesn't involve you dying too.'

'I'm all over that if you have any ideas.' I laughed again. His simple acceptance of the fact that I was going to kill Fabienne Wilder regardless, seemed extraordinary. I couldn't work out what made Joseph tick. He was different.

'There's one thing that I don't get though.' He sat forward and looked me in the eyes. 'Why you, Conrad?'

'Because I wrote a book which implicated them in several murders,' I replied. 'The exposure it caused pissed her off no end.'

'And you think that all this is about the book?' He shook his head as if the concept didn't sit right with him.

'Well it started there and then they tried to burn my house down.'

'And you shot the copper and went on the run?'

'Pretty much.'

'But they didn't leave it there?'

'Neither did I.'

'Why?'

'Because I can't leave things alone and everything that I touch turns to shit.'

'What do you mean?'

'Jobs, relationships, businesses and even my writing,' I replied, being brutally self-scathing. 'I become obsessed with things to the detriment of those around me. I have a talent for fucking things up.'

'Sounds like you're beating yourself up.'

'Not really.' I smiled. 'It's true.'

'I still don't get it.' He frowned. The muscles in his jaw twitched. His neck was thick and powerful. He looked like he could be a handful if crossed. 'I don't see why they didn't just walk away and leave things to settle down.'

'I'll ask Fabienne when I meet her,' I said sarcastically. 'She seems to be calling all the shots, so she is the only one who can answer that question.'

'So, do you really believe that this woman is something other than human?'

'Right here and now, no, but when I was near her, there was something about her that I can't explain. Maybe it's all just in my head.'

'But you said you felt a connection with her immediately.'

'I did,' I thought back. It all seemed so hazy now, like a dream. 'She has got something up here.' I tapped the side of my head trying to explain the telepathic connection, which I'd felt with her. 'I can't explain it rationally, but she knew things that she shouldn't. Things that I'd seen in my head.'

'Did anyone else feel her 'power'?' Joseph tapped his head cynically. 'You know, people involved in the initial interviews?'

'Nobody mentioned it if they did.'

'So, she singled you out.'

'Maybe, or maybe I was just weak and susceptible to her thoughts.' I remembered back to the first time I'd seen her in the secure unit of the mental hospital. 'She said it was because I was a writer, because of my imagination. My imagination made it possible for her to connect.'

'I don't buy that.' He frowned. 'It sounds to me like she staged the whole thing to get to you.'

'It did feel as if she set me up from the start,' I agreed. 'I've thought about that but then it just makes me feel paranoid. You know, when you're on your arse and you wonder, why me?'

'Maybe she did set you up.'

'Why though?' I asked myself out loud. 'I just think that there has to be more to it than that stupid book.'

'Why?'

'Because as you said earlier, the focus would have moved from them eventually,' I shared my theory, which had been developed during many hours of lonely contemplation. 'She could have stayed in the shadows and sooner or later, she would have been forgotten.'

'You said she disappeared from the hospital and then turned up at that farm with the funny name?'

'Brunt Bogart,' I reminded him. 'They told me at the hospital that she'd committed suicide and then the next time I saw her, she was being bundled from the back of a car. I thought she was dead. A doctor at the hospital told me, so why would I think otherwise?'

Joseph stared at his beer bottle and peeled off the label, deep in thought. I hadn't noticed before, but his forearms were wiry and strong. The tendons looked like steel cables beneath the skin. 'She suckered you at that farm,' he drained his beer and went for two more.

'Do you think so?'

'Definitely,' he plonked a fresh beer next to me. 'She knew that you'd go and try to rescue her. Why else would she let her followers put her in the boot of a car?'

'Because she was wanted by the police?'

'She could have put a flat cap and sunglasses on,' he joked. 'It worked for you.'

'Yes, for about an hour.' I laughed and it felt good. Talking about the entire crazy story with an outsider gave it some perspective. Joseph was completely objective; thus, he saw things with a clarity that I didn't have. 'But if she wanted me to go into that farm, then she must have had an idea what would happen.'

'Maybe she didn't care if any of them got hurt.'

'What do you mean?'

'Let's assume that her number one objective was testing your resolve,' he shrugged, 'to see if you would kill to protect her.'

'To see if I would kill them?'

'Maybe.'

'She asked me to let go and join them,' I pondered her words. 'She was like a wild animal, Joseph. I had scratches and bites that didn't heal for weeks.'

'I had a girlfriend like that once,' he chuckled.

'Not like this one, trust me.'

'Maybe she wanted to see how far you would go before she tried to recruit you?'

'Who knows?' I shook my head. I'd been over it all in my head so many times that none of it made sense anymore. 'If all this is right, then the entire thing was planned.'

'You said she had a child soon after and that she says it's yours.'

'Yes.'

'You did have unprotected sex with her.'

'In a fashion,' I squirmed uncomfortably.

'You either did, or you didn't.'

'Okay we did,' I said resigning to the obvious truth.

'And was the timing of the birth, about right?'

'Yes, I think so.'

'You said that after you had sex, she tried to kill you.'

'Yes, Evie Jones saved me.' The mention of my dog's name made me cry inside. I missed her terribly. I missed my old life terribly. My recent past had been a melee of blood and fear. My future would be more of the same. I wished that I could see Evie one more time.

'So, she had what she wanted from you and then you were just another sacrifice, but the key is she got what she wanted.'

'Sex?'

'Sperm.' He laughed. 'She wanted to be impregnated.'

'That still doesn't explain why she targeted me.'

'Because she chose you,' he pointed his finger as he explained his idea. 'You had a connection and you killed people who tried to kill you and you killed to protect her,' Joseph offered an alternative theory. 'You passed her test.'

'She has thousands of followers,' I disagreed. 'Anyone would have done the same.'

'Bullshit.' Joseph laughed. 'Are you taking the piss?'

'No.' I was taken aback.

'You shot anyone who stood in your way and killed Niners without giving it a second thought,' he changed his tone. 'How many of these so-called followers are truly capable of blowing someone away without any thought of the consequences?'

'Not many, I suppose.'

'When your house burned down and you shot that rogue copper, most people would have crumbled and turned themselves in. You lived on the run for how long?'

'Over two years.'

'That's what makes you so special.'

'What?'

'She wanted a child,' he pointed again, 'your child.'

'She could have picked any of her followers,' I disagreed. 'It would have been much easier.'

'No, think about it for a minute,' he raised his eyebrows. There was something very rational about his manner. Even when he disagreed it felt like he actually agreed. 'She wanted a child with someone who was on the same wavelength as her, someone who could kill at the drop of a hat.'

The concept he described was as if someone had kicked me in the guts. I knew what I'd become, but could she have seen that in me? Could she tell that I had the capacity to kill without remorse or regret?' 'If you're right,' I closed my eyes. 'Then this is all about the child.'

'Exactly,' Joseph agreed as if that was his point all along.

'She once said to me that the baby would be 'A Child for the Devil' but I didn't really put much thought behind what she'd meant.'

'You mentioned that Friday is something special to them, right?' Joseph stood up and grabbed a slim silver laptop from the kitchen counter. 'If we can work out what this ceremony is all about, then maybe we can come up with some answers.' He opened it up and googled Lammas Day. A page of sites about the first day of autumn appeared. Most of them linked the date to a celebration of harvest, nothing to do with Satan. 'This all looks innocent enough.'

'Put the year in too,' I said. 'I read somewhere that some of their sacred days don't happen every year. Put 2019 in.' Joseph typed it in and this time the search revealed much darker sites. 'Click on that.' I pointed to a posting about 'The Feast of the Beast'. It opened and we read it before looking at each other in amazement.

'At the Feast of the Beast on the twelfth day of the eighth month in the year 2019 a virgin child born of two of the blackest hearts, one mortal and one shapeshifter, will be presented to Satan himself as a bride. The child must be of mixed blood and colour. The sire of the child will be sacrificed on Lammas Day, twelve days before, in conjunction with the full moon near to the sea. When the dark one appears among the mortal and immortal, he will choose to take the child for his own, or he will share her and feed on her during the ensuing feast. The ceremony must take place within the walls of a sinister dwelling on European soil.'

'Fucking hell,' Joseph said wide eyed. 'Do these freaks really believe all this shit?'

'Oh yes,' I nodded. 'They believe every word of it.'

'So, you're the sacrifice at the full moon,' he pointed to the text. 'The child is for the Feast of the Beast.'

'Born to two of the blackest hearts,' I said to myself.

'What?'

'She keeps on telling me that my heart is blacker than any of her followers.' I sighed exhausted by it all. 'I didn't know the meaning behind what she was saying until now. She chose me to father the child because I'm as evil as she is?'

'She's a fucking lunatic.'

'Is she?' I drained my beer. 'She's right though.'

'What do you mean?'

'She keeps on telling me that I'm a killer, an evil, stone-cold killer and you know what?' I shrugged. 'She's right.'

'You've killed for a reason.'

'Yes, my reasons and I haven't blinked once, any time that I've pulled the trigger or watched them burn or hang. I haven't given their families a single thought before, during or after killing them.'

'Neither would I but it doesn't make me evil,' he argued. 'It makes me human. Scum like that don't deserve families. Imagine finding out that your husband or dad was dressing up as a goat and abusing children. Fuck them.'

'Whatever we think,' I shook my head. 'They have their virgin child born of two of the blackest hearts, one mortal and one shapeshifter. There it is in black and white. That's what they believe, so to them, it is true.'

'Fuck what they think,' Joseph searched some more. 'This is giving us clues as to where they will be.'

'What do you mean?'

'Look at the spelling here,' he pointed to the word 'color'. 'American English or old English and the baby must be mixed blood, so they mean race. She's black, right?'

'Right.'

'A mixed-race child,' he stared at the screen. 'What the fuck is a shapeshifter?'

'Therianthropy.' I shrugged. 'The myth is as old as the seas. It's the power to change shape, from human to animal like a man to werewolf or a vampire from humanoid into bat.'

'So, it's mumbo-jumbo.' Joseph dismissed it.

'I'm not so sure,' I shrugged remembering her at the farm. 'At Brunt Boggart when I was hallucinating, her face changed. Her jaw distended and her strength was incredible, almost superhuman. Her face became animal like.'

'Did she drug you?' he dismissed it again.

'I don't know if what I saw was real, but I do know that I saw it.'

'You know that you think you saw it.'

'Whatever.' I sighed.

Joseph wasn't willing to debate the subject and I couldn't be bothered trying to explain something that most people would consider as madness. The entire episode was too far-fetched to expect rational minds to contemplate it. 'You think that these ley lines are the reason they're going to Anglesey?'

'I'm guessing, but yes I do.'

'We need to get an Ordnance Survey map of Anglesey,' he held his chin between his forefinger and thumb. 'Using a compass, we can plot all of your ley lines on it and see which standing stones sites and buildings are on those coordinates. You know the island well, don't you?'

'Yes.' Something else was on my mind as he spoke. It occurred to me all of a sudden. I thought back to our first encounter at the camping shop when he saluted me as I drove away. His behaviour and mannerisms were consistent with others I'd met through my writing and research.

'You need to think hard about any old buildings, which could be considered 'sinister', whatever that means.'

'Everything on Anglesey is old,' I chuckled as I searched my memory banks for ideas. 'The text says that it has to be done 'within the walls', which rules out all the sites where the standing stones are, doesn't it? It won't be outside.'

'Yes,' he agreed. 'Do you still have their mobiles?'

'Yes.' I reached for my bag. 'I've got seven of them.'

'You have been busy,' he said sarcastically but there was something in his eyes. I think it was respect. 'We need to go through every phone and write all the numbers down and then we cross-reference them. Any number that's on two or more phones we keep. Any number that's on four or more, we prioritise and if any are on all seven, we're going to ping the numbers and see exactly where they're at.'

'Why didn't I think of that?' I asked shocked at my oversight.

'You have too been busy shooting them and avoiding the police.' He smiled cheekily. 'You would have thought of it in time.'

'Of course, I would,' I said. 'It was my very next plan.'

'I thought your next plan involved walking blindly into a trap with your fingers crossed that you can get out of it?'

'It's more like, kill everyone and then go home. Except I can't go home.'

'It's flawed at best.'

'That was plan A,' I said. 'Plan B is better.'

'Plan B is always better, trust me on that—' he nodded knowingly, which added to my growing realisation '—we'll check the OS map for possible EHQ. There can only be a handful of possible buildings that qualify and then we'll cross-reference them with the mobile phone locations.'

'Were you in the military?'

'What makes you ask that?' he said wryly.

'OS maps, EHQ,' I said. 'Enemy Headquarters, right?' I guessed, 'add the compasses and the way you think strategically and I'm guessing you're a scout leader or military.'

'I was 1st Assault Group, Royal Marines,' he saluted again. 'Served in Bosnia, Kosovo and Sierra Leone. Broke my dad's heart when I left the family business, but he was proud when I earned my Green Beret.'

'I bet he was,' I mumbled, a little in awe of his career. 'Makes my story sound like a walk in the park, eh?'

He looked me in the eyes and shook his head. 'Not at all but now you know why I don't judge you for killing the men that you've killed,' he said honestly. 'You're not a lunatic or a freak. I pulled the trigger without questioning who I was killing. I've laid charges, which killed dozens and I've never given it a second thought. I killed because I had to and so did you.'

'Do you think my flat cap is up there with your Green Beret?'

'Not a fucking chance.'

'If I get caught will you act as a character witness in court?'

'Maybe you are a lunatic after all.' He laughed.

'There's no doubt about it,' I countered. 'Where can we find an OS map?'

'I've got one in the garage.'

'I knew you were going to say that.'

'You need to go and get some sleep.' He put the laptop down on the table. 'We need to be fresh and alert when we begin. You look like shit and I need you to be sharp.'

'Okay,' I replied without any argument. 'I guess a few hours won't hurt.'

'Down the hallway off the landing—' he pointed to the stairs '—take the second room on your right. The bed's made up and there's shower gel and towels in the bathroom.'

'I need a shower badly.' I stood up and my legs felt like jelly. Running up the mountain away from the police had been a mammoth effort and my muscles and joints were screaming with exhaustion. Only the will to survive and adrenalin had kept me going. Now they'd worn off and I needed to rest.

'You do,' he nodded sympathetically. He nodded to the shotgun. 'Leave the Mossberg with me.'

I felt a bolt of fear shooting through me. 'I don't leave it anywhere,' I said defensively. 'Sorry but it stays with me.'

'That weapon needs to be stripped and oiled if you want it to keep working,' he said stoically. 'Do you know how to do it?'

I shook my head. I knew it made sense, but I'd been on the run for so long that trusting someone was unnatural.

'If we're going to do this together, then you need to trust me,' Joseph said reaching for the gun. With the twist of his wrist and the click of a catch the Mossberg was in two pieces and rendered into useless scrap metal. 'I'll service her and leave her next to your bed when I'm done. If I'm coming with you then I need to know that your weapon isn't going to seize up when we're knee deep in blood and shit, understand?'

I thought about the implications of what he was suggesting. It meant that I wasn't alone anymore. I had more chance of ridding the world of Fabienne Wilder if I had help, especially the help of a man who had made a career out of killing. 'Okay,' I agreed. 'I'm grateful for your help and somewhere to sleep but I don't think you realise what you're offering to do.'

'I know exactly what I'm doing,' he smiled. 'I'm stopping you from killing yourself for nothing. On your own, you have no chance. Together we have a good chance. If we can find them, then we go to them before they even realise that you're not going to turn up at their trap. We hit them unexpectedly, kill this bitch and anyone else who fancies dying with her and then we get away before they're even cold. We can be back here before the police get a sniff of it. What they find won't be attributed to you or me.'

'You're assuming that Fabienne Wilder is just an evil woman,' I turned towards the stairs before turning back to look Joseph in the eyes. 'What if she is what she says she is?'

'Then we'll have to hope that God is on our side,' he shrugged and began stripping the shotgun. There was a flicker of something in his eyes, but it wasn't fear. I felt lifted and optimistic for the first time in an age. Hope. I had hope.

'God? I don't think he's watching.' I smiled tiredly and walked down the stairs. 'And if he is, then he's having a fucking laugh on my behalf,' I muttered to myself. I hoped that Joseph was right. Hope is a powerful emotion and I could feel it spreading through my soul.

CHAPTER 29

When I woke, it took me long seconds to remember where I was. The bedroom was half lit by the morning sun, which filtered between the dark curtains and the wall. The Mossberg was leaning against the bedside table next to the bed. The metal gleamed and the stock was polished. I touched the barrels with my fingertips. My old friend was in the shape of her life and ready to do what she did best, blowing the shit out of Niners. The smell of bacon cooking drifted into the room from upstairs. I'm not sure if it was the smell of bacon or the excitement of renewing my search for Fabienne Wilder which motivated me the most, but I leaped out of the bed and headed into the bathroom.

Powerful jets of hot water washed away all the sleepy fog from my mind. The ache in my muscles seemed to run away down the plughole, along with the dried blood and grime from my skin. The lemony soap bubbles invigorated me as they cleaned the filth from my body. I marvelled at the colour of the water as it flowed into the tray. It was hard to comprehend how much muck could come from one human being. I must have smelled like a dead donkey in a manure pile. The urge to shave the bristles from my head and face was almost unbearable. I'd needed to keep as much of my face covered as possible but that day, I didn't care. Using a disposable razor, I took the hair from my head and face. It felt amazing. I reluctantly stepped out of the shower and brushed my teeth at the sink.

When I walked back into the bedroom, I noticed that my clothes were gone, replaced with a clean pair of olive-green combats, fresh underwear and a black T-shirt. My boots had a pair of new socks stuffed into the tops. Joseph was obviously organised to the point of being obsessive, but I wasn't going to complain. Looking and smelling like a member of the human race, I loaded the Mossberg and carried it upstairs following the intensifying smell of bacon.

'What's that for?' Joseph nodded to the shotgun. 'In case anyone steals your breakfast?'

'Force of habit,' I said sitting on a tall stool at a granite topped breakfast bar. He plonked a pint mug of coffee and a packet of menthols in front of me. 'Thanks, kick-starters,' I said lighting one up and slurping the hot brew. I looked over at a pile of books, which were stacked up on the coffee table in the living room. Beneath them Joseph had spread out a map. There was a ruler and a compass next to some coloured pencils. 'Looks like you've been busy. Thanks for the clothes, by the way.'

'No problem.' He slid a bacon sandwich across the worktop. 'Once I got started, I couldn't stop. There're acres of stuff on the Internet about your ley lines. Most of it is bullshit but there is some interesting stuff too.'

'I warned you about getting involved,' I said with a mouthful of butty. I washed it down with coffee and then took a drag on the menthol. Joseph shook his head as he watched me trying to shovel three things down my throat simultaneously. 'Sorry but I've learned to eat in a hurry lately. I never know when it's going to be my last meal.'

'Carry on.' He smiled. 'I've been there myself, remember.'

'Yes, sorry. I know you have.' I swallowed before carrying on. 'I did a lot of research on ley lines especially the ones on Anglesey. Some experts say they are burial mounds, others a place of sacrifice, while others believe they're a source of energy, which can be channelled. Others say they're signposts for alien visitors. The information that I found pointed to the fact that there might be something in it.'

'Seriously?' He raised his eyebrows.

'Seriously.' I stuffed the remainder of the sandwich into my mouth. Chewing furiously, I walked over to the map. I studied the work that Joseph had done the previous night. 'Ah, now then, you have made the exact same mistake that I did when I researched them. It took me weeks to see the mistake I'd made.'

'I've marked the lines exactly as they're plotted in all the information I found on the net.' He pointed to the books. 'I checked them in these reference books too. They're walking guides but they mention the standing stones on the island. I've plotted the lines precisely.' He looked offended. 'There are no mistakes.'

'Okay, it's not a mistake with the plotting on the island as such, it's an oversight.'

'An oversight?'

'Yes.'

'There are no oversights.'

'There is one big one.'

'Where?'

'You have taken the ley lines and plotted them along the latitudes which follow the standing stones, right?'

'Yes.'

'And then you've plotted the lines east all the way across Snowdonia to the edge of the map, right?'

'What's your point?'

'I did the same thing.'

'So, what?'

'I didn't finish the job and continue to plot the lines west in the other direction.'

'That's the Irish Sea.'

'I know it is,' I smiled smugly. 'Thanks for the geography lesson.'

'I still don't get your point.'

'Watch this.' I took his ruler and continued one of the ley lines across the blue area of the map. Joseph frowned. 'Bear with me.' I grinned and did likewise with a second ley line, then a third and then a fourth and fifth. Joseph's eyes widened.

'Fucking hell,' he looked from the map to me and back again. 'They all intersect in the sea near these islands. The Skerries?'

'The north coast of Anglesey lies on the main shipping route to Liverpool, which I'm sure you know was one of the biggest ports on the planet and at onc time, during the nineteenth century, thousands of ships passed the island on the way to Liverpool. The Skerries has had a lighthouse for as far back as shipping records go,' I explained and pointed to the islands. 'Despite the lighthouse warning shipping, records show that in this area one mile to the west of the Skerries and a mile to the east of Lynas, where the ley lines intersect, over three hundred shipwrecks have been recorded and there are probably many, many more, which disappeared, but actually sank here.'

'More?' he asked incredulously. He was still digesting the news. 'How would you know that there were more?'

'From the number of ships which left their ports and never arrived in Liverpool, but they were spotted rounding North Stack by the lighthouse keepers on South Stack. They kept logs of all passing vessels.'

'So, they sank somewhere in this area?'

'Yep,' I sat back and nodded. 'It surprised me too. I published some of it on my blog, but the theory was dismissed as nonsense.'

'Coincidence?'

'I don't do coincidence and you can't refute the number of ships lost there.'

'So, the area is jinxed because it's at the intersection of ley lines?' He scoffed.

'Which came first,' I asked, 'the chicken or the egg?'

'What?'

'Whoever built those standing stones built them in a linear pattern which intersects at this point, right?'

'Right.'

'Maybe they were built as a warning that that area of the sea was incredibly dangerous,' I shrugged as I offered an explanation. 'Imagine if the early sailors and fishermen were dying regularly in that area, so they pointed it out.'

'What is the other option?'

'That the area is a ley gate.' I laughed at the thought. 'It's the centre of some kind of mystical cosmic power and our ancestors on Anglesey knew how to map its flow and tap into it. The key to understanding their theories is the word 'gate',' I tried to make it as clear as I could, although it was as clear as mud to me too.

'Gate?' He frowned.

'Ley gate,' I sat back, 'it implies that where ley lines intersect, there's a gate, a portal, through which things that don't belong here can pass. Evil things.'

'Like demons and dragons?' he chuckled.

'Who knows?'

'And this evil which comes through the gate makes ships sink?' Joseph looked at me as if I was mad.

'Look, ships have sunk there in the hundreds yet there has always been a lighthouse to warn them of the rocks. Why have so many ships sunk there and why did our ancestors think to plot their standing stones to intersect at that point?'

'You tell me.'

'Think about it,' I explained, 'thousands of years ago somebody moved massive slabs of stone, which feasibly couldn't be moved and they aligned them to point to one of the most dangerous areas in the sea. They are the facts, so you give me a reasonable explanation and I'll take it.'

'I haven't got an explanation.'

'Neither have I but lots of people seem to agree with the energy theory.'

'Do you think that there is something in it?'

'Who knows? Mediums pick up on the energy of the dead, right?'

'I suppose so.'

'Well, how many people have died in that part of the sea?'

'Hundreds.'

'More like thousands.'

'And the point is?'

'All those 'souls' died in a traumatic way, drowned at sea before their time.' I looked at Joseph to see if he was open to the concept. 'Could there be a mass of bad or tortured energy concentrated in that area because of all the death?'

'It's a bit of a stretch for me,' Joseph shook his head. 'Do you believe that?'

'I don't know,' I shrugged again, 'but what I do know is that Fabienne Wilder and her sicko friends think that there is.'

'Okay, let's say she does believe that there is an 'energy' there,' Joseph sat down as he spoke. 'What is she planning to do with it?'

'Feed on it to make her stronger, maybe or use it to open a door from one dimension to another.'

'Oh, for fuck's sake.' Joseph couldn't get his head around it. He put his head in his hands and laughed. 'Come on, Conrad.'

'She was like a woman possessed at that farm,' I shrugged, 'I've never fought anyone physically stronger. She threw me around like I was a rag doll. I shot her in the face with that Mossberg and she managed to leave there and survive?'

'I think you were drugged.'

'How?' I asked, 'with what?'

'I'm not having this 'doors to another dimensions shit' okay.'

'I don't blame you but believe me when I tell you that there were others at that farm,' I frowned as I searched for words. 'The room was empty one minute, but when she attacked there were other things in the room. Evil, grotesque things. I could sense them, hear them, and smell them. The room was heaving with… something.'

'It was hysteria,' he insisted. 'Or hypnotism.'

'Have you ever seen the film *The Exorcist*?' I sat back as I spoke. It's hard trying to convey an idea to a sceptical person when you're not convinced by it yourself. Joseph nodded that he had but sighed as if he didn't want to hear what I had to say. 'A demon or devil comes through from another dimension and possesses the girl.'

'I don't see the relevance.'

'What if there is another dimension, which we can't comprehend?'

'I don't believe that there is.'

'Okay then, where does space end?'

'What?'

'Where does space end?' I sat forward again. 'Does a fish comprehend that the surface of the sea is not the end of the universe?'

'What are you on about?'

'Answer my fucking question.' I snapped frustrated. 'If you can't even try to understand what we're dealing with, then we're fucked before we begin.'

'Okay—' he took a deep breath '—I don't know what a fish thinks.'

'Don't take the piss.' I smiled trying to calm things down. 'The surface of the water is as far as a fish can go, yes?'

'Yes.'

'Birds cannot leave the atmosphere.'

'Okay.'

'But certain birds can go underwater for a while at least, but they have to return to the air, eventually.'

'Yes.' He shook his head baffled.

'They physically cross from air to water to feed but they cannot stay there.'

'I'm lost.'

'we've explored space, yet we cannot explain what is beyond it,' I tried my best to explain my view of things. 'Where does it end and what is beyond it?'

'We don't know.'

'Why don't we know?'

'We just don't.'

'No,' I insisted, 'we don't understand. We don't understand because our minds work in three dimensions. Everything has a beginning and an end, full stop. That's why we can't explain space.'

'I can see what you're trying to say, sort of,' he reluctantly nodded agreement.

'Everything has to be three dimensional for us to comprehend because that's how our brains are wired up but we know there must be an end to space and a beginning of something else because otherwise it doesn't make any sense. We cannot comprehend infinity.'

'I follow so far.'

'What if there are parallel dimensions, which exist right here with us, but they cannot co-exist in the same place at the same time?' He put his head in his hands as I spoke. 'But there are certain places where energy and power allow one to cross over into the other like a bird diving for fish.'

'You're really stretching my imagination now.'

'Have you ever filled a balloon with water and put a pin through the bottom without bursting it?'

Joseph laughed and nodded. 'Yes, I have so what?'

'There are only a few places on the surface of a water-filled balloon where a metal pin can penetrate the membrane into the water without causing it to explode. And more to the point, it's a state which is unsustainable. It can only be maintained for a snapshot of time. When you remove the pin, something catastrophic happens to the balloon.'

'Sadly, I'm beginning to follow your point,' he grimaced.

'The pin crosses through a membrane into another dimension but remains in both simultaneously. Pick the wrong spot and the balloon will explode. A child couldn't do it but we can because we know how to. Now what if Fabienne Wilder, or more to the point, whatever possesses her knows how to penetrate the balloon into our world?'

'What if it does?'

'Then something from another dimension.' I held up my finger, 'an evil dimension penetrates the membrane into Fabienne Wilder. She is the water-filled balloon and eventually when the balloon bursts and it always will, the entity finds another water-filled balloon to penetrate. She is nothing more than a vessel which it uses for a period of time before her body deteriorates and it has to move on.'

'And the ley lines?' he frowned.

'They're like seams, strong points. The intersections are where we'd pierce the balloon with the pin.'

'So, to carry out this ceremony, they need to be near the bottom of the balloon, or near the intersections to cross over?' Joseph stood up and walked to the patio window. His hands were clasped together behind his back. He stood rigid like an officer inspecting his troops before battle. 'Let's say that I can't accept that theory although I understand it. However, I'll bear in mind that you do.'

'Okay, that's fine by me.'

'You believe that the ceremony you interrupted at that farm gave her an unusual level of physical strength and allowed evil to seep through from wherever it lives into her making her stronger?'

'Yes, I do.'

'So, if what we've discovered is correct,' Joseph turned to face me before continuing, 'The ceremony involving you is just a prelim to the 'Feast of the Beast', which is going to be held at an intersection of ley lines on one of the most sacred days in the Satanic calendar?'

'Yes.'

'Why though?'

'Maybe at certain parts of the year, sun, moon and stars are all in the right place at the right time to facilitate this exchange.' I shrugged.

'Exchange?'

'Yes,' I explained. 'Push a needle into a balloon, if some of the water seeps from the balloon then the atmosphere squashes the balloon. Let all the water out and the balloon becomes flat. Physics won't allow it to remain inflated. If they leave their dimension, then someone must replace their entity to maintain the equilibrium. They take one from here, me for instance, and one of them can cross momentarily. Everything in nature has a balance.'

'Which means that if you're correct, her 'power' and the amount of evil which could potentially be siphoned through, would be magnified in comparison to the ceremony you witnessed. She'll become much stronger physically?'

'Yes.'

'If we get up close to them, then we'll be outnumbered, probably out gunned and potentially we could be overcome by a force, which in your experience was undeniably powerful.'

'Yes.'

'Which tells me that we have to do whatever we can to kill her from as far away from her as possible,' he said calmly. 'If you are right, then we cannot risk getting too close to her or her people. We need to take her out from a distance.'

'I'm listening.'

'We identify where they'll meet. We wait for them to arrive and then we blow them up.'

'You're forgetting two things.'

'What?'

'The ceremony is all about sacrificing me.'

'I don't get it.'

'The father of her child, blah, blah, blah,' I rambled. 'If I don't turn up, then will they meet at all?'

'That's one thing.'

'What?'

'You said there were two things?'

'The baby,' I added. 'What about the baby?'

CHAPTER 30

'We can't wait until Friday.' Joseph looked at the map. 'Have you had any thoughts about where the ceremony will be?' he asked studying the map again. 'If we can work out where it will be, we may be able to work out where she will be beforehand.'

'Let me look at the ley lines on the map and think about it. If I remember rightly from my research, there won't be many alternatives.' I leaned forward and studied the map. I searched for intersections. The single lines ran though very few buildings, but they merged near the shore and one area stood out immediately. 'Did you go through the numbers on the mobile phones?'

'I did,' Joseph said reaching for a notepad.

'Can we ping them like you said?'

'I think so.'

'How does it work?'

'Mobile phone companies can locate a phone's remote location through 'pinging', which basically means that a phone company can pinpoint your phone's location by locating the phone tower closest to where your cellular device most recently sent and received a signal.'

'How accurate is it?'

'Not very. It gives you an area so in a city, it's useless but in a rural area like the island, we may have a chance of pinpointing a building.'

'Can we do it though?'

'The police and rescue workers use it in locating criminal suspects, people who need urgent medical attention and missing persons, but it's illegal for a civilian to ping a phone they don't own.'

'So how can we do it then?'

'It can be authorised by the military. I've narrowed the numbers down to two,' Joseph pointed to a list of scribbling on the pad. 'These two numbers are on five of the phones. This one is on them all.'

'That has to be the one we need to ping then,' I asked excitedly. 'How do we do it?'

'We need to find out whose number it is, what network it's on.'

'Then we can pretend to be the police and tell the provider that we're searching for a suspect in a major crime who has stolen the phone in the process,' I shrugged. 'I can't see how they can verify if we're the police. I could tell them you're a detective and I'm your senior officer. They might ring me for verification?'

'Worth a shot in one of your books.' He laughed. 'That's up there with your hat and sunglasses disguise.'

'smart-arse.' I laughed, 'what are you going to do then?'

'Like I said, the military can authorise it.'

'You still got contacts?'

'Yes, it's the best way.'

'It has to be.' I smiled. 'Saves me from fucking it up, anyway.'

'Exactly.'

'I'll just look at the map, shall I?'

'Okay, you find me a building where you think they may be,' Joseph reached for his laptop. 'I'll find out which network it's on and who it belongs to.'

'I've got a feeling you've done this before,' I asked looking at the map.

'Find a mobile phone number and you find the owner,' Joseph winked. His face darkened and I could only guess that a bad memory caused it.

'I found a few of them using the same theory,' I agreed, 'but I didn't know how to ping their phones. I just sent them a text message.'

'Whatever works,' Joseph shook his head at my lack of finesse. 'I'm amazed you got as far as you did, no offence.'

'None taken. Who were you looking for the last time you did it?' I asked. Joseph looked up sharply, his jaw twitched, and his eyes narrowed. His eyes went back to the laptop screen quickly without a reply. 'Sorry, just curious.'

'It's not a problem.' He tapped away on the laptop. 'You must have had some hairy moments sending text messages and then waiting for someone to turn up.'

'Oh yes,' I grimaced. 'One of them turned up in the forest with his wife.'

'At Miner's Bridge?'

'Yes.'

'They dragged the bloke out of the river north of Corwen,' Joseph recalled the news. 'He had a human skull, a jar of pig's blood and a ceremonial dagger of some description in his bag. You didn't know the wife was in on it?'

'Not until she turned up with him.'

'I saw her on the television being taken away by the police,' Joseph looked up. 'She was pleading innocence, but they found similar weird shit in her bag too.'

'She was one of them,' I assured him. 'No doubt about it.'

'You didn't shoot them though?'

'I would have but the Mossberg was in my Landy,' I confessed.

'What?' Joseph was shocked.

'I went to buy supplies and got rumbled. I was cut off from the Landy and had to wing it.'

'Tell me again,' he frowned. 'How did you get this far?'

'God knows.'

'Mark Friedman,' Joseph threw in a random name.

'Who is that?'

'He was the last guy I found by pinging his mobile,' Joseph looked thoughtful, 'a guy from my unit lost an arm in Bosnia. Six months after his discharge, he got in touch begging for our help to find this guy, Mark Friedman. He was his daughter Susan's ex-boyfriend. She'd been raped in her own bed and left for dead. He'd been knocking her around for months before she finished it. We found him and dispatched him cleanly. The police didn't have a clue who had killed him. Everyone thought the bastard got what he deserved until the police arrested a known sex offender a month later. He confessed to raping three others, including Susan. Not my finest moment.'

'Swings and roundabouts.'

'What?'

'Unlucky.'

'What do you mean?' Joseph looked amazed.

'You know, what goes around, comes around. The ex-boyfriend was unlucky but if he hadn't been a twat and beat her up in the first place, then no one would have suspected him in the first place. Unlucky.'

'Never thought of it like that before.'

'You're either lucky or not but you have to make your own luck sometimes too,' I nodded. 'I've had to.'

'I hope your luck runs long enough for us to get this done and get back.'

'Me too.'

Joseph clicked another button of the laptop and then put it down on the coffee table. 'I've e-mailed the number to my old mate.' he stood and went to the patio. Lighting a cigarette, he opened the door and stepped out onto the patio. 'We should have a position within the hour.'

CHAPTER 31

I looked at the OS map, but I wasn't really looking at it; I was miles away watching images of my youth on the big screen in my mind. Three of the ley lines intersected at the point where Holy Island climbs from the sea to become Holyhead Mountain. At the base of the mountain is an abandoned quarry which supplied the rocks to build the breakwater. The breakwater stretches a mile and a half into the sea and is wide enough to drive two articulated lorries side by side. In the 1800s a grand hotel called Soldiers Point was built overlooking the breakwater. Soldiers Point was now a derelict hotel, castle-like in its appearance and it was the building which haunted my dreams. It couldn't be a coincidence, something in my mind had been telling me not to go there, no matter what happened. Once a Victorian edifice used by only the rich seafaring merchants and wealthy visitors to the port, it was now a crumbling shell. It had been plagued by misfortune, tragedy, suicide and even murder. Maybe the perilous region of the sea highlighted by the ley lines had tendrils of bad energy which encompassed that part of the island too. It could certainly be considered 'sinister'.

The ruins would make the ideal place to hold a Satanic ceremony in a movie but as ever, I was not in a movie and the last time I'd explored the remains, I was amazed by how fragile the entire structure had become. A few determined Niners could penetrate the shabby mesh fences which formed a flimsy perimeter around the hotel, but if they were in numbers, then I doubted the rotting floors would support them. The hotel had plagued my sleeping hours for months and now I knew why. It would have something to do with the climax of my journey, of that I was certain.

It was the building next to it which drew my attention and made the skin on the back of my neck crawl. 'I think I've had an epiphany,' I said reaching for a menthol. 'I don't know why it hasn't dawned on me before.'

Joseph was in the kitchen making more coffee. Anyone who liked coffee and cigarettes as much as I did had to be okay. He put his cig between his lips so that he could carry both mugs. The smoke drifted into his eyes making him squint. 'I think I met her in a pub in Plymouth once.'

'Who?'

'Epiphany,' he plonked the cups down avoiding the map and ever-growing bits of notepaper. 'I was joking.'

'I know.'

'What have you found?'

'More coincidences.'

'You don't do coincidences.'

'I don't.'

'What is it then? Spit it out.'

'When I was a boy I lived here, number 9 Porth-y-felin,' I pointed to it on the map. 'It's right near the sea and my bedroom was at the back of the house overlooking here.'

'The marina, the breakwater, the mountain,' Joseph studied the area. 'Must have been some view.'

'It was but look,' I followed one of the ley lines with my finger.

'It does run very close to your old street.'

'Here,' I said pointing to the old hotel and the building next to it. 'Soldier's Point is a possibility, although I think it's way too dangerous for more than a handful of people. It's a death trap but the building next door would be perfect.'

'What is it?'

'Porth-y-felin House,' I answered. 'Coincidence or not, that's what it's called.'

'Same name as the street you lived in.'

'And I lived at number nine, Niners, Order of Nine Angels, maybe this has always been on the cards?'

'You're stretching again,' Joseph shook his head. 'Get your feet back on the ground and think straight. Drink your coffee and tell me what you know about the place.'

'It's a huge building, the size of a big hotel. It was built by the foreman who built the breakwater. He must have been minted, it's massive. The main gate is off this track here. The grounds run right down to the marina here.'

'What's this?'

'It's a jetty,' I replied looking at the map.

'How come?'

'It was commandeered by the RAF and used to operate a marine rescue unit called the Marine Craft Unit,' I explained. 'I was friendly with some of the lads from there and they had a bar in the cellar called the Bilges. I used to go there all the time.'

'What was the jetty used for?'

'That's where they moored their launches.'

'What is it now?'

'Abandoned,' I gulped my brew, 'it was closed in 1986, been empty and boarded up ever since.'

'When did you last see this building?'

'A year ago.'

'Was the jetty intact?'

'Yes,' I thought back. 'I was staying here in my brother's place.' I pointed to a new apartment block, which had been built overlooking the marina. An armada of white yachts of varying size appeared in my mind; the sound of rigging clanking against their metal masts rang in my mind. The noises carried at night keeping me awake and driving me to distraction. 'I could see the jetty from his balcony. It looked pretty solid to me.'

'What about the ladders?'

'Yes, they're still there.'

'You're sure?'

'Yes,' I nodded. 'I remember watching a couple of old blokes emptying their crab pots when the tide went out. They used the ladders to climb up the jetty and then walked down this path here into this cove here.' I pointed to the area on the map. 'Do you know someone with a boat?' I asked, guessing as to why he was interested in the jetty.'

'Yes.' He smiled. 'Me. I've got a 16ft rigid in the garage.'

'Under the covers?'

'Yes.'

'Will it get us to Anglesey?'

'It would get us to France if the weather permitted.' Joseph pointed to a picture on the wall. He was standing with a group of men all dressed in orange waterproofs. The rigid was behind them. There were more boats in the background. 'We taxi boat owners out to their yachts in the summer. Along with the shop and my pension I do all right.'

'Where will we sail from?' I looked out of the patio windows. 'There are police all over the town.'

Joseph stood and walked to the window. 'The ramp I launch from is beyond the fairground to the left of the station there. Can you see the rollercoaster?'

'I see it.'

'I'll put you in the rib under the boards before we go,' Joseph shrugged. 'No one will stop me on the way to the ramp. Once we're out of the bay, you can get up.'

'Okay,' I liked the idea. It sounded too simple, but it beat trying to get to Anglesey by road. 'Then what?'

'We blow the fuckers to hell.'

'What are we going to blow them up with?'

'You made pipe bombs before, didn't you? Before you went to the farm.'

'I did,' I replied proudly. 'Fireworks and lead pipe. They worked a treat.'

'We're going to do the same but no fireworks.'

'No fireworks?'

'No.'

'What are we going to use?'

'Tovex.'

'Fucking hell,' I remember being very surprised.

'You know what it is?'

'I've used it a few times,' I smiled, 'in a book though. It's the terrorists' explosive of choice nowadays. That stuff is the reason why we can't take liquids through an airport.'

'Well then, you know how explosive it is then.'

'I know what I've read.'

'We're going to use the same principle as you used for your pipe bombs, except we'll be using Tovex in plastic bottles,' he demonstrated with his hands. 'It becomes unstable next to metal. I've got enough Tovex to make three or four bombs which will level that building and the hotel. If that doesn't take them all out, then we're fucked, anyway.'

'Where the hell did you get Tovex from?'

'The builders used it to blast the rock from the back of the house when we started building.' He laughed dryly. 'I ordered a bit too much just in case. You never know when you'll need it.'

'We had better get busy then.' Suddenly I wasn't happy at all. 'A boat, explosives, I feel like I've bumped into *Rambo*. This is all too good to be true.'

'Like you said,' Joseph frowned, 'you got lucky.'

'Funny but I don't even know your surname yet you're willing to put your liberty and life on the line for a stranger.'

'Walcott.' He walked away towards the kitchen as he spoke. He picked up a piece of crumpled white card and brought it back, thrusting it into my hands. 'I took this out of your trousers when I washed them. My surname is Walcott. It's on the business card which I gave to you and you're a cheeky bastard.'

'Cheeky bastard is better than dead bastard.' I blushed.

'One can lead very quickly to the other,' he picked up the laptop and walked back to me. He handed me the computer and then went over to the kitchen cupboards. He pulled out a blue photo album and dropped it onto the worktop. 'Here are my photos and you can check out my record on there. Ask me anything.'

'What year was your unit sent to Bosnia?' I couldn't work out if he was a warrior who couldn't hang up his sword or if he was a plant. My gut feeling told me that he was a warrior, but I decided that I had to be sure.

'1995,' a thin-lipped smile parted his lips. '97 to 98, Commandos went to the Congo and then in 2000 I was part of Operation Agricola in Kosovo.'

Although I felt awkward, I put the laptop down on the coffee table and stepped over to the kitchen. I flicked through the first three pages of the album which were made up of Joseph's training and passing out parade. The face was fresher and much less lived in, but it was Joseph. They were genuine, not photoshopped. 'Look at the state of that moustache,' I joked.

'They were fashionable then,' he countered.

'You look like an extra in a 'YMCA' video.'

'Fuck you.'

'See.' I raised my eyebrows. 'Definitely Village People material.'

'Are we going to do this or not?' he stopped laughing. 'I'm coming along because I happen to think this is worth fighting for. One less paedophile and I'll be happy but if we can frazzle a bus load of them together, then I wouldn't miss it for the world.'

'Yes,' I held out my hand as I spoke. Joseph shook it, 'what's first?' I relaxed, happy that Joseph was trustworthy.

'Okay.' Joseph clapped his hands together. 'We think that we know where she is. As soon as we get the ping on the mobile to confirm your theory about the venue, then we'll sail. We need to get ready to move. We'll sail as soon as it's dark and hit them first thing in the morning before the sun comes up.'

CHAPTER 32

The next two hours were exhausting. Joseph's garage was a hub of activity which would be befitting of a terrorist cell. Handling the most explosive gel on the market makes you twitch like a mouse's nose at a cheese festival. The explosive is packed into sausage shaped plastic tubes which are stapled at the seams. I poured it into three plastic bottles, leaving a two-inch gap at the top. Joseph placed three boxes on the workbench next to me. I opened them and polished metal glinted in the lights.

'Four-inch nails, three-inch wood screws and a box of galvanised panel pins, all nice and sharp.' When he plonked three rolls of duct tape next to them, I knew what I had to do. 'Use the entire roll of tape on each one,' he explained. 'It's not rocket science, but it's important that you put a layer on at a time, the tighter the tape, the more concentrated the explosion.'

'Do you want me to use a full box of nails on each?'

'Yes,' Joseph opened a storage drawer as he spoke. He took the lid from a tin of clear plastic glue. 'This stuff dries very quickly. Tape, glue, shrapnel, tape, glue, shrapnel, and so on and pack as much metal between the layers as you can.'

'Sounds simple enough,' I said with sweat running down my back. 'What makes it go bang?'

'Liquid metal.' He took a bottle from another storage unit. Its label said everything that I needed to know, 'Liquid Metal'. 'The gel is harmless until it's sensitised. Liquid metal mingles with it and it becomes sensitive. When that happens, we need to make sure we are a long way away. Are you happy?'

'I'll be a lot happier if you take that bottle away from this bottle,' I said pointing to the liquid metal.

'It's two metres away and the lid is on.'

'I'm still not happy.'

'It also needs a detonator, you dummy,' he reached onto a shelf and grabbed three of the Niner's phones. 'It seems fitting to use their own phones to blow them to hell and back.'

'I've seen a few videos of how to do this,' I said trying to remember how it worked. 'I have to strip the phone down, find the vibrator and drill a hole in the casing, right?'

'Spot on so far,' he said impressed. 'Then what?'

'I use a low amp wire to connect the vibrator to a couple of batteries and then run a wire from the batteries into the explosive mixture. When I call the phone, the vibrator spins making the connection. The battery makes the fuse wire live, it sparks, boom.'

'You learned that on the Internet?'

'Yep.'

'That was a two-day session on an improvised explosives course for me.'

'The theory is fine, but you know how to put it all together practically,' I moaned. 'I think you should make them.'

'Stop whingeing, you'll be fine, and we'll test them first.' Joseph laughed. 'I'll get the rigid ready and make sure all our ammo is stored in dry-boxes because we'll get wet on the way. I'll need to get some fuel from the local garage and some packaged food, bottled water, synthetic engine oil, and she'll be ready to go.'

'Have you heard from your contact yet?' I wanted confirmation that the mobile was in the right area.

'I'll check the email now before I go.'

'Okay,' I returned to becoming a nail bomber. I had an unusual feeling inside me as I manufactured three powerful explosive devices. Memories of the devastating injuries which I'd witnessed first-hand following the IRA bombing of Bridge St, Warrington in '93 replayed in my mind. They never faded like other memories. The images of the victims were embedded in my memory banks in wonderful high definition. If all my memories were as sharp, I'd be happy. I heard Joseph coming back down the stairs. 'We're only going to use these where the Niners are,' it wasn't a question. It was a statement of intent. 'If there's any chance of passers-by being injured, we abort using them.'

'We can only make an educated judgement,' he stared at me. 'We won't arm them if there's any doubt, but once they're primed, they cannot be stopped from exploding. It's a chemical reaction which cannot be reversed.'

'I guess that we'll have to be sure then.' I smiled weakly. My hands were trembling as I spread a thick layer of glue to one of the bottles. I tipped the box of nails onto the bench and then rolled the bottle over them like a rolling pin over dough. The glue picked up the metal in a thick even layer.

'Good idea.' Joseph looked surprised. 'I think you missed your calling. Did you pick that technique up researching a book?'

'No.' I grinned. 'Watching *Celebrity Master Chef*.'

'That figures.' He laughed. 'Nothing on the mobile ping yet.'

'Maybe it's not switched on.'

'That won't matter.' Joseph shrugged. 'It gives you the position of the last place it was used, which may not be where it is now, doesn't matter if it's on or off.'

'He might be busy.'

'Maybe, but there's no rush, we'll know before we leave, anyway. Try not to kill yourself or blow my house up,' he pressed the remote and the garage door kicked into life. He opened the driver's door and climbed into the Jaguar. 'I'll be an hour, tops.'

'Be careful out there and stay out of trouble,' I waved. Two four-inch nails were welded to my fingers with glue. They looked like demonic claws. It crossed my mind to make a full set for both hands. I scratched an itch on my nose with one of them and then formed a claw and pulled a scary face. Tears rolled down my face as I laughed out loud. It was a proper belly laugh; you know, the type where you can hardly breathe. It really wasn't that funny but maybe it was just a pressure release. My bizarre world had taken another twist.

As the garage door closed, the sea air mingled with exhaust fumes. My view of the town and the sea narrowed to a slit and then disappeared completely as it clicked shut. I was alone again. When I'd finished wrapping my bombs in tape and shrapnel, they weighed about three kilos each. Making the first detonator took me half an hour. I switched on the phone and dialled the number. A second later, the fuse wire sparked. To say that I was ecstatic would be an exaggeration, but I was very pleased with myself. The other detonators took ten minutes each and I had a huge sense of accomplishment when I was done.

I took a cloth from the bench and tried to peel the thick layers of glue from my fingers. The rib was exposed now, the covers removed. There were three green boxes lined up on the floor beneath the solid orange hull. Joseph had been filling the thick resin storage boxes before he left. I looked inside and smiled. One of them was crammed with shotgun cartridges, in the other were 9mm shells and four spare clips all fully loaded. The clips looked like they belonged to a Glock-17 although I couldn't be sure. I knew that the Marines were once equipped with a 13-round Browning, but the Glock was lighter with a shorter barrel and because of the obvious advantage of a 17-round magazine, most commandos opted for the Glock. I wondered where the Glock was. The third box was empty, so I assumed it was destined to carry the bombs.

The Jeep was already hooked up to the boat trailer and I opened the rear door and looked into the back. There were two camouflage jerrycans. I tapped them with my knuckles to see if they were full. They were. I opened one and sniffed the fuel inside. It was unleaded of some description. The Jeep had a diesel engine, so I knew the jerrycan were for the rigid's engine. That begged the question as to why Joseph needed more fuel. When we studied the maps, he had told me that it was approximately sixty-two sea miles, past Bardsey Island and the Lleyn Peninsula, over Caernarfon Bar and into the Straits. There we had to decide whether to risk the twenty-six sea miles of rough seas off South Stack or risk sailing through the treacherous Straits to take thirty-five sea miles on the sheltered route past Puffin Island. Both choices sounded dodgy to a landlubber like me. He said that with the wind behind us and right tides we could make it there and back on a full tank but if we had to sail into the wind against the tides, we'd triple our fuel consumption. I had to assume that he was erring on the side of caution by taking more fuel. Our preparations were nearly ready. Happy that I'd done all that I could do, I went upstairs to the living room to wait for Joseph to return.

CHAPTER 33

I found my way around the dozens of polished kitchen cupboards and made myself a brew. Everything had a place. The tins were stacked neatly in lines two high resembling supermarket shelves rather than a single man's home. I found the cutlery drawer after opening five others and wasn't surprised to see the knives and forks lined up symmetrically. The tin opener had its own slot next to the teaspoons which were stacked on top of each other facing in the same direction. Everything in the house indicated that Joseph had an ordered mind. I felt like putting a few forks into the knife section and turning some of the spoons around the wrong way. If I'd known him better, I probably would have done and put some of the beans into the tinned pea line just to top it off. It would drive him bananas. Now wasn't the right time to play practical jokes on the only ally I had. Maybe there was some of the old me left after all.

I opened a tin of tuna and tipped the brine into the sink. The stainless steel looked flawless. I drowned the pink meat in malt vinegar and ate it from the tin with a teaspoon. I remember being enthused with anticipation. I actually felt like I was on a level playing field at last instead of being one man hunted by many. Not only were my adversaries legion, they were disguised, camouflaged to look like ordinary people. Now I had the advantage of a well-trained killer on my side and I knew where they would be. At least I had a good idea where they would be. I took my lunch and flopped in front of the plasma, turning the news channel on.

Images of the fire from the night before were interspersed with shots of Nant-y-Col campsite the farmhouse and the barns were nothing more than smouldering black rectangles against the green of the land. The silo stood defiantly untouched by the inferno. Yellow crime scene tape flapped in the sea breeze. Then came an old photograph of me, followed by a series of artists' impressions of how I may look now. Most of them looked like a four-year-old had drawn Mr Potato Head with glasses on and a variety of hats and facial hair. They may as well have been looking for Uncle Fester in a trilby and shades. Although the search was centred literally just miles down the road, I felt safe where I was. Hiding under their noses was as good as being a hundred miles away. They would think that I was miles away and I relaxed and waited patiently.

Joseph's laptop was on the table in front of me. I thought about checking his email to see if there was any news on the ping, but I didn't like to betray a trust. I pressed return on the keyboard and the screen displayed his email homepage. He hadn't logged out, so I didn't think it counted as a betrayal if I just peeked at his new mail. It was empty. Nothing new had come through. In the in-box, there was one message. I opened it and read one line.

Number is out of service. No trace.

That was all it said. I was a little disappointed but not desperately. My thinking was that Fabienne had told me to go to the stones because she wasn't far away from there. The fact that the ley lines intersected there had convinced me. I was playing my best guess and what did I have to lose, anyway? If she was there, game on. If she wasn't, I would live to find her another day. It was all just educated guess work, common sense and as I thought about things again, something occurred to me. Joseph told me that there had been no reply about the phone. I read the email again. Joseph had read it before he left. He told me himself that the ping gave you the location of the mast closest to the mobile when it was last used. If that was the case, then you would still get a location, it just wouldn't be current. Either I was misunderstanding the process, or someone was lying about the results. Either way, Joseph had lied about receiving it.

I couldn't think of a way of replying to the email without blowing my whereabouts, but I had to know if that phone was in service. Being a straightforward type of thinker, I grabbed Joseph's landline, dialled the prefix 141 to hide the number and then rang the mobile number. After two rings, it was answered. Nobody spokes, but the breathing sounded laboured and male.

'Are you on the Island?' I couldn't think of what to say, so I was vague.

'Who is this?' the voice asked. He sounded very upper class beyond a public-school accent. This man was nobility.

'Is Fabienne there yet?' I thought asking directly might make him think that I knew who he was. It didn't. He hung up. I looked at the telephone and then looked at the screen. I dialled it again and it clicked to a deadline. No voicemail, no engaged tone just static. Whoever replied to Joseph had lied, but why did he tell me that there was no reply? Maybe his contact did not want to break the law and so pretended there was no result, or was there a more sinister reason? I mulled it over and wondered what Joseph would say when he returned. I wanted to trust him, but this deceit threw me.

I was anxious to get going and frustrated by the delay, but I knew that going to sea without enough supplies was suicide. I wouldn't have thought about the return voyage, but Joseph obviously had more confidence than I did. He was right of course, because if we did survive the encounter which wouldn't go unnoticed by the inhabitants and the authorities, then there truly was no escaping the island. The sea was the only option. I flicked over the news and looked for another channel. The BBC was focusing on a drone attack which had wiped out the Syrian leader and his entire family. The Americans were denying any knowledge of the attack and British radar posts on Cyprus tracked the drone from somewhere north of Turkey. It looked like all hell was about to break loose somewhere else in the world. Funny, but it didn't seem as important as my predicament at the time. There was a dull thudding sound in the distance. The double glazing muffled the sound, but I'd heard it often enough to know it was a helicopter.

I jumped off the settee and walked over to the patio windows. Sliding them open, I stepped out to listen. I heard the noise much clearer this time. Then there was another more frightening noise. It was the crackling rattle of automatic machine gunfire in the distance. I guessed it was coming from the town somewhere. My mind ran through a hundred reasons why there would be a gunfight in the resort but none of them sat right with me. A trigger-happy policeman? A bank robbery? Terrorists in Barmouth? Someone thought they'd found the armed fugitive and opened fire?

A plume of white smoke spiralled into the air close to the fairground and all appeared to return to normal. At least from where I was standing. The dull thudding began again, this time it was coming from the north; from the farm below Nant-y-Col. A police helicopter came into view, a buzzing dot on the landscape. It was above the shoreline about five miles away from the town. I stepped back inside, an involuntary response to the sight of the aircraft which had hounded me so much. Even the most powerful binoculars couldn't see me, even if they did know where I was, and they didn't. It still made me nervous. I watched it flying towards Barmouth beach. Then there was another helicopter coming from a different direction. It flew from the river heading for the area where the smoke had been. It was a much smaller craft and I assumed it was a television crew looking for some aerial shots of any unfolding developments. They must have filmed the scene at the farm and the shots of the campsite.

I stepped back into the house and flicked back to *Sky News*. The banner headline described the pictures as breaking news. At first, I couldn't make out what had happened but as the helicopter circled the scene, my stomach tightened into a sickening knot. White smoke drifted from a crippled vehicle which I recognised almost immediately. Three armed police units blocked the exits and entrances to the funfair. Crowds of onlookers were being held back by uniformed police and the surrounding roads were cordoned off. A helmeted figure lay sprawled on the ground bleeding profusely from the chest. A dark puddle was spreading beneath his twisted body. A weapon was abandoned on the tarmac a few yards away from the prone figure. There was a second helmeted person crouched behind a large quad bike, cowering against the machine trying desperately not to get shot. Smoke billowed from the engine block.

I knew immediately it was the quad that I'd left on the playing fields. The police must have known that I'd escaped on Bryn's quad and then spotted it travelling along the road somewhere in the resort. I couldn't explain the rifle until the camera zoomed in on the scene. It was a paintball gun. They were kids causing a nuisance on a dumped quad, probably shooting cars on the estate with luminous paint balls. It would have been fun until the police spotted them. They must have recognised the quad, caught a glimpse of a weapon and hey presto, they thought it was me. After a long chase off the estate, through the town into the funfair a teenager was dead. I felt the air leaving my lungs as I slumped onto the settee. Another example that everything I ever touched turned to shit. Midas turned things to gold, and he moaned about it. He would have had good reason to complain if he lived in my shoes for a day and everything he touched turned to shite.

I sat there and watched the police move in and arrest the cowering figure. They cuffed the fugitive on the ground and then roughly removed the helmet. A dark black ponytail fell out and a teary teenage girl was unveiled. Nobody looked very pleased at all. I guess they were hoping that the body on the ground was me. I wondered how long it would take them to take off the helmet or look for ID. I thought that would be the ideal time to leave but there was still no sign of Joseph. His mobile was switching directly to the answering machine. The incident in town would have caused major traffic jams, so although I was anxious to leave, I wasn't overly concerned that he hadn't returned. The *Sky News* clock told me it was 2 p.m. I watched the incident every hour for the next four hours by which time, I was very concerned. Joseph still hadn't returned, and I had to make a choice as to the reason why.

Either he had decided that he couldn't risk his life on a doomed crusade or something very bad had happened to him. I dialled his mobile number once more and the answering machine kicked in again. Had he just been stuck in traffic; he would have called. I decided to go without him. I had no choice. Once again, I was alone but this time I felt no sadness at the concept. This time I was ice cold inside, numbed to the very core of my soul.

CHAPTER 34

I took a few moments to gather my thoughts. Joseph had planned the mission meticulously. All I needed to do was follow the plan. My instinct began to prickle me that whatever had happened to him was connected to the email he'd denied receiving. I was also aware that whoever he had contacted would probably be aware of where he lived. If I was going to implement his plan, then I needed to move quickly. He told me that his contact was ex-military. I'd made it this far by the skin of my teeth but tackling commandos wasn't top of my bucket list. It was going dark outside, so I switched on the lights and left the television on to make it appear as if someone was home.

I took the mobiles, the laptop, the map and the compass and headed for the stairs. Although I knew the island like the back of my hand, I thought I might need them. When I reached the landing, I glanced down the hallway to the bedrooms. Despite knowing that the house was empty, I tiptoed down the hall to Joseph's room. The door was ajar, but the curtains were closed, blocking out the light. I could see the shadowy shapes of a double bed and a dressing table on my right. The room was empty. I knew it was empty, but I felt the need to check, anyway. The light switch was to the left. Nudging the door open slowly, I checked behind it. There were no commandos, no vampires, nothing but a black towelling robe. My nerves were on red alert.

I switched on the light and made a cursory glance of his room. It all seemed in keeping with the rest of the house. I walked around to the far side of the bed and opened the bedside cabinet. There were two sets of keys, three paperbacks and a packet of tissues. The keys were marked, Jeep and Rib. It was a good start to my search. Underneath the bed yielded nothing but some fluff. I opened one of the curtains and checked outside. The garden was as immaculate as the house. A neatly trimmed lawn swept around the rear of the house to where the rock face met the garden. The borders had been dug with clinical precision and the shrubs were all pruned to the same height.

Happy that there were no assassins creeping through the grass, I searched the wardrobe. Nothing but freshly dry-cleaned clothes and polished shoes. The en suite bathroom looked like it belonged at an ideal home exhibition and I'd almost given up on finding anything when I looked at his pillows. One side was slightly higher than the other. For a man who lived inside a geometrically ruled house, that was out of character. I lifted the offending pillow and smiled. The Glock-17 had a reassuring feel to it. I hoped that I wouldn't need to get close enough to need it, but it was a welcome addition to the team.

I ran things through in my mind as I made my way to the garage. The lights were burning brightly, and everything was as I'd left it. I picked up one of the nail bombs and placed it gently into the storage box as if it was made of eggshell. Joseph had reassured me that the explosive gel was safe until it was sensitised, but I found it impossible not to be afraid of it. The remaining two devices fit snugly next to the first and once I'd clicked the lids onto all three boxes, I loaded them into the rigid beneath the boards which formed the middle bench seat of the boat. I had shotgun shells, 9mm bullets and three bombs. Not quite the traditional tackle recommended by the coast guard to be taken on to an outboard dinghy off the coast of Barmouth, but essential to my task all the same.

    I opened the back door of the Jeep and took out the two jerrycans, placing them into the rigid on opposite sides, to balance the load. I strapped them down and then set about looking for waterproofs. Joseph had said he had plenty of sets, but I couldn't see them anywhere. I looked behind the Jeep and there was a grey metal locker screwed to the far wall. Inside there were five sets of florescent orange waterproofs. I should have known that they would be stowed away neatly somewhere. Putting them on over my clothes was harder than it looks but I struggled into them, eventually. I thought back to the photograph of Joseph next to his boat. He'd been wearing a hat. On the shelf above the waterproofs was a vinyl baseball cap. I pulled it on to complete my seafaring disguise and with that, I felt ready to go. I unlocked the driver's door and took a deep breath. There wasn't much room between the Jeep and the wall, and I turned sideways to climb into the Jeep. I was about to step up when the automatic door whirred into life. Either Joseph was back, or someone else had his remote.

CHAPTER 35

I ducked down beneath the window and peered underneath the Jeep. Joseph's dark blue Jaguar pulled into the empty bay and the garage door rattled closed behind it. Instinct told me to wait where I was. I heard the car door open and then a second, followed by a third. Two sets of legs climbed out of the passenger side, neither belonged to Joseph. I couldn't tell if he'd exited the driver's side.

'Nice place, Joey,' a voice said sarcastically.

'Thanks,' Joseph replied flatly. He had brought people back in his car. I couldn't work out what was going on.

'Very nice indeed,' the accent wasn't local. 'How's the boat running?'

'She's fine.'

'Looks in good shape for the winter coming.'

'Let's cut the shit, shall we,' Joseph replied. His tone was flat but there was aggression in his voice. 'You don't give a fuck about my boat so don't pretend that you do.'

'Okay, Joey calm down. Where's the nutcase?' The first voice asked.

'The television was on when we drove up.' Joseph sighed. 'He'll be upstairs.'

'Lead the way,' another voice said gruffly. 'I can't wait to meet this psycho.'

I thought about what they'd said and the tone of Joseph's voice. He sounded as if he was under duress, but I couldn't help but think he'd turned me in. I had no idea who the other men were, but I knew they weren't here to wish us well on our mission. I had to assume at that stage that they were police. Whoever they were, I couldn't leave as planned and I really needed to go, so I had no choice but to confront things head on. I reached inside the Jeep and grabbed the Mossberg.

'What's going on, Joseph?' I aimed the shotgun over the bonnet. The three men turned quickly to face me. The strangers aimed automatic pistols towards me with two handed grips and a wide stance. They were either police or military. 'Have you turned me in?'

'Hands up, Joey,' growled a wiry built man. Joseph made towards the door but one of them trained their weapon on him. He had a dark flattop, greying at the sides. 'Over here, on your knees.'

'Who are your friends?' I kept my eyes on the two men not sure which one to shoot first if it kicked off. Joseph walked between the men with his hands up and his eyes on the floor. He looked embarrassed and annoyed as he followed their orders and knelt. 'I don't think they're Niners so I have to guess that they're with the police. You've grassed me up, haven't you?'

'Put the shotgun down and come from behind the vehicle,' the second man growled. He had a smooth-shaven head and blond eyebrows. He was the size of a small bungalow. 'I won't tell you again.'

'How does get fucked sound?' I grinned like a lunatic. They thought I was mad and maybe I was. 'Does that idiot think I'm going to put my gun down, Joey?'

'The nutcase is a comedian too, eh, Joey?' Flattop sneered. 'You never said that he was a funny guy.'

'Why turn me in?'

'I haven't turned you in.' Joseph shook his head.

'Who the fuck are Johnny Concrete and Charlie Bigspuds?' I asked.

'They're mercenaries.' Joseph looked up. 'They're a couple of greedy mercs.'

'Fucking brilliant,' I whispered to myself. I recognised them from the photograph of the boat. They'd been in the background. 'Friends of yours though, obviously?'

'We did a few tours together in the green and we've done a few private missions since we left,' flattop smiled thinly. 'They're pretty lucrative, you know. Anyway, Joey here asked me to ping a mobile didn't you, Joey?'

'And?' I decided flattop was in charge, so I pointed the Mossberg at his chest. I had more chance of hitting him if I aimed at his core.

'I always like to know whose phone I'm tracing,' he said matter of factly. 'You know, just in case they're someone who might have enough money not to be found. Turns out Lord Penrith is willing to pay shitloads not to have his number traced, and even more if we deliver you to him.'

'Sorry, Conrad,' Joseph said genuinely. 'I knew something was wrong when they replied to my email. I didn't want to walk straight into a trap, so I went to find out what was going on. This is all about money.'

'Very touching, but I've heard enough of this shit,' the bungalow said angrily, 'now put the fucking shotgun down and come from behind the Jeep.'

'Are they a bit thick?' I asked Joseph. He smiled and nodded. 'They're really are empty heads, aren't they?'

'You'd better watch your mouth, sunshine.' Bungalow blushed red as he spoke. 'Your smart mouth will get you killed.'

'You did say I was a cheeky bastard, Joseph.'

'You are,' Joseph agreed.

'Shut the fuck up, right now.' Bungalow was incensed. 'Put that fucking gun down now.'

'He is verging on retarded, isn't he?' I laughed and readied myself. My legs were shaking, and I tried to melt into the metal. 'Watch my lips, you ginger twat. I'm not putting the gun down.'

'Five seconds and then I'm going to shoot you.'

'You can't count to five, fucking retard,' I goaded him further. His face was almost purple. 'Anyway, I'm behind three tons of Jeep with a Mossberg pointing at your bum-chum here. What're the chances of you shooting me in the head?'

'Much better than you think, you psycho.' Flattop narrowed one eye taking aim. 'We've been following your little episode and to be honest, we've been impressed but don't overestimate your abilities. I can shoot you between the eyes any time I want to.'

'That would put an end to my troubles.' I nodded. I felt sweat running down my forehead. 'No point in me shooting you in the head though, eh? There's fuck all between your ears except fresh air, stupid twat.'

'Listen to me very carefully,' he said angrily. I was winding them up to boiling point. 'Our client wanted you alive, but he said that if we had no choice, then we take your body to him, anyway. So, for the last time, put the gun down and walk around the vehicle with your hands up.'

'No.'

'Do it now.'

'Get fucked.'

'Last chance.'

'That's why I think you're thick as pig shit, you see,' I said. They both looked set to explode. 'If you were going to shoot me, then you would have done it already. Lord Paedophile or whatever his name is wants me alive, doesn't he?'

Joseph nodded his head silently. His smile widened. Flattop stepped behind Joseph and pushed his pistol against his temple. 'Put the shotgun down now or I'll blow his fucking brains all over this garage.'

'Thick, you're going to shoot him anyway otherwise he'll come after you and you can't risk that.'

'Don't call me that.'

'Or what?'

'One more time and I don't care how much money is involved. Put the gun down and we'll let Joseph live. We could cut you in on the deal, Joey?'

'I don't work with snakes.'

'Snakes are far more intelligent. At least they know which end is their head, and which end is their arse, oh and they have a backbone, which is something you could use.' Something flickered in flattop's eyes. He was at his limit. I looked at Joseph's eyes and they told me what to do.

'Last chance. You come with us and Joey lives.'

'Do you think we're as stupid as you?' I shook my head and squeezed the trigger. All hell erupted.

I aimed high with the first shot. Joseph grabbed flattop's gun arm and I saw a chunk of flesh blown from the face of the mercenary. Shots exploded and in the confined space, they were deafening. The urge to curl up behind the Jeep was almost irresistible, but I knew that if I did, they would pin me down and I'd either be shot or have to give up. The only choice was to return fire. I felt the Mossberg kick three times. Nine-millimetre bullets whistled past my head and I could hear them ricochet off the walls behind me. A bullet pierced the bonnet eighteen inches to my left and at the same time Bungalow's knee erupted in a shower of blood and bone. A second blast hit him in the shoulder and knocked him sideways. He continued firing the nine blindly, as he spun. The Mossberg clicked empty, but I had no time to reload. I dropped her on the bonnet and grabbed the Glock from my belt. I aimed and fired. The windows of the Jaguar shattered into a million pieces. Power tools which hung on the wall exploded into shards of metal and plastic and the unrecognisable screams of the injured and dying were almost lost in the deafening gunfire.

CHAPTER 36

When the Glock clicked empty, I let the air out of my lungs. Sweat was stinging my eyes and I wiped them with the back of my hand. The smell of gunpowder and spent munitions filled the air. There was an eerie silence although the ringing in my ears was deafening. I grabbed the Mossberg and reloaded, leaving the Glock on the bonnet of the Jeep. Edging around the vehicle I surveyed the aftermath. Bungalow was sitting up against the Jaguar. His chest moved almost imperceptibly, and it was saturated with blood. His eyes had rolled back into his head. His hands were empty, but I couldn't see his gun.

Flattop was face down; his body sprawled on top of Joseph. A flap of skin hung from his cheek and the top of his ear was missing. There was blood pooling beneath them, but I couldn't distinguish who it belonged to. I kicked his leg but didn't get any response.

'Joseph,' I shouted. I grabbed flattop's ankle and dragged his body to one side. There was a bullet wound in the centre of his forehead. His eyes had the glaze of a dead fish. They stared at me accusingly. Joseph groaned and opened his eyes. His hands were covering a wound to his abdomen. Blood was running between his fingers. 'You're shot.'

'Thanks for that, Einstein,' he moaned.

'Is it bad?'

Joseph pulled up his sweatshirt to reveal a Kevlar vest beneath. There was a flattened slug embedded in the chest and a deep L shaped cut below the navel. 'A bullet hit my belt buckle. There's a field kit in the first cupboard along from the fridge. Can you get it?' he sounded short of breath.

'Good job you had that vest on,' I pointed to the slug. 'You must have realised there would be trouble.'

'I had a hunch, but I thought that once I'd explained who these people are that they would come around.'

'You should have taken the Glock.'

'I didn't intend on shooting them. I'm bleeding here.'

'Sorry.'

'I need that kit. I'll get patched up and then we need to leave.'

'Two minutes,' I said running for the stairs. The door was locked. 'What's the code?'

'Three, five, seven, nine,' he called breathlessly.

I had a feeling that he'd broken a few ribs. If he had, then he would be virtually useless for a week. I punched in the digits and the door clicked open. Taking the stairs two at a time, I bolted up to the living area. Inside the first cupboard was an olive-green rucksack. Behind it, the shelves were symmetrically stacked with crepe bandages, rolls of Elastoplasts and large gauze pads. I looked inside the rucksack and there appeared to be a selection of each already packed. I was about to pick up the bag when the gunshots started over again. There were two shots followed by four more. I had no idea who was shooting at who, but I had to assume that Bungalow wasn't dead. The gunfire died down replaced with the same deafening silence as before.

I ran to the stairs and cleared the top flight. I reached the landing and crouched against the wall. The door to the garage had closed behind me. If I hesitated, Joseph could bleed to death but what if he'd been shot again? What if Bungalow was alive and had his gun? If I stepped blindly into the garage, then Bungalow would get a free shot at me. I heard a thump on the other side of the door; then a dragging, sliding sound.

'Joseph.' I called.

Nothing.

'Joseph.'

Nothing. Then a shuffling sound. I was torn. Joseph could be bleeding to death on the other side of the door unable to answer me. The alternative was that Bungalow was alive. 'Joseph, knock on the door if you're there.'

Knock, knock.

'Are you shot again?'

Knock, knock.

'Is Johnny Concrete dead?'

Knock, knock.

'How many packs of cigars did you buy me?'

Silence. I thought it could be him.

'Three or four, Joseph?'

Knock, knock, knock. Then I heard someone punching numbers into the lock. Joseph had shouted the code to me. Bungalow would have heard it.

'Nice try but I don't smoke cigars.' I shouted and ran back up the stairs. I assessed my predicament. The Mossberg was loaded with three shells. I had no ammunition on this side of the door. Everything that I needed was in the garage, so I couldn't jump from the balcony and run away. The police would pick me up in hours. Bungalow was badly wounded but determined to get to me.

'We'll see who the retard is when I get hold of you, you little prick.' The door was open, and he was in the stairwell. I knew that his knee was shattered so climbing the stairs would be a long and painfully slow process.

I grabbed the settee and dragged it towards the top of the stairs. I used it to block the staircase and then knelt and peeped over the banister. He was slumped against the wall, crawling on all fours one stair at a time. He looked up and raised the gun. I pulled away as a nine-millimetre bullet hit the wooden rail, splintering it into a dozen pieces. A three-inch shard pierced the soft skin behind my ear. I swore under my breath and pulled it out. Blood trickled from the puncture wound forming a red stream down my neck. When it reached my shoulder, the stream split into two, running down my chest and my back. I decided not to look over the banister again.

I couldn't get a clear shot at him on the bottom flight and I didn't want to use my shells until necessary. If he reached the living room, then I would retreat to the kitchen area and use the granite breakfast island as cover. I could hear his breathing on the lower staircase. It was laboured and his progress was slow. I looked around for inspiration. Glass. I ran and lifted the top from the glass coffee table. Heaving it onto my shoulder, I turned and walked to the stairwell. I took a deep breath and tossed it over the banister.

There was a second of silence then it clattered off the wall. There was a dong sound like a bell. It resounded off the slate walls and for a moment; I thought the toughened glass was going to remain intact. Then it hit the stairs and shattered into a thousand tiny pieces. It sounded like marbles hitting a tiled floor.

'You little bastard.'

'Crawl over that, retard,' I shouted in response. Three shots rang out from the stairwell. The bullets ripped into the ceiling blasting huge chunks of wood away from the beams. I ran to the kitchen and opened the cupboard doors one at a time. The mug cupboard was full. I grabbed a tray and stacked as many as I could on it and then ran back to the banister. One by one I pelted the stairwell wall with them. I could hear Bungalow gasping for air. Encouraged by his protestations, I repeatedly ran back to the kitchen and emptied the cupboards. The glass cupboard was crammed. I tossed three trays full of wine glasses, pint glasses, tumblers, and flutes before starting on the plates. By the time I'd run out of breakables, the landing had three inches of sharp fragments covering it. Sweat ran from every pore of my body. The waterproofs were not conducive to keeping dry on the inside when the body was put under extreme exertion.

'You, scrawny little shit.' Bungalow screamed. 'I'm going to gut you, you bastard.'

'We'll see.' I said coldly. 'Unless you can stand up and walk, you'll be cut to ribbons before you cross the landing.'

I thought about setting fire to the stairwell, but I had to keep them intact. I had to get to the garage. There were crunching noises and muffled curses coming from the stairs. He sounded closer now. I guessed he was on the landing. The television was still running the news and when I glanced at it, a commercial break gave me another idea. I ran to the kitchen and pulled four large saucepans from the cupboards. Filling them with scorching hot water from the tap, I emptied a kilo of granulated sugar into each and lifted them onto the stove. I lit the four rings beneath them and then poured the contents of three bottles of sunflower cooking oil into the mixture. I filled the kettle and switched that on too. The crunching noises were slowly making progress across the landing. He would be at the bottom of the top flight in a few minutes. I poured every sticky substance that I could find into the pans. Ketchup, milk, butter, mayonnaise, chilli sauce, brown sauce, honey, and then I emptied the bleach from the cleaning cupboard into the mix.

Within minutes, I had four pans of scalding goo. I grabbed some oven gloves and picked up the heaviest vessel with two hands. The burning liquid threatened to slop all over me, and I slowed my steps as I approached the stairwell. Bungalow was still moving. From the sound of his breathing, I guessed where he was in relevance to the banister; I took a deep breath and tipped the concoction over the top. I missed his head, but the bulk of the liquid soaked his shoulder and right arm. The liquid struck and there was a momentary delay before his nerve endings registered the napalm-like substance. The oil and sugar made it cling to the skin and burned deeply. He wailed like a banshee and flailed about trying to escape the pain. 'You fucking bastard.' he screamed. The rest of his words were undecipherable; nothing but an incoherent stream of abuse.

As much as I could have watched him bouncing off the walls all day, I ran back and picked up the second largest pan. He must have anticipated my movements. As I neared the banister, three shots blasted the rail to smithereens. I tossed the pan and the liquid into the stairwell blindly.

'Bastard.' The abuse was high-pitched, more like a squeal than a shout. I glanced over quickly and a bullet whistled past me and ricocheted off the ceiling. The left-hand side of his face was red raw. He tried to wipe the burning liquid from his face with his hands, but the sticky substance stuck to the flesh of his fingers instead. He staggered backwards and flopped onto his back. Sharp fragments of pot and glass pierced his skin and he wriggled and flipped like a dying fish on the deck of a boat. The gun lay discarded in the glass. 'I'll fucking kill you.'

I turned and ran for a third time, retrieving the third pan. This time I had time to take aim, the gun wasn't a threat any longer. I poured the contents onto his upturned face, stifling his screams to a low gurgling sound. He clawed at his eyes and face, desperately trying to escape the pain. Shards of glass were now stuck to his hands and instead of relieving his agony by wiping his skin he ripped the scalded flesh away from the muscle below. He dug his heels into the floor and pushed himself backwards, trying to reach the end of the landing and the safety of the lower flight of stairs. It spurred me to get the job finished and I sprinted to the stove and picked up the last pan.

When I returned to the banister, Bungalow had made it a few yards, but his legs were just visible, and they were still. There was a trail of blood stretching along the landing where he had slid over the broken glass. The gun was in the same place. I'd made the mistake of thinking that he was dead once today, I didn't want to make it again. I tipped the last batch over him. His body from the waist down was saturated in the burning liquid. He didn't flinch. I sat with my back against the settee and fumbled with shaking fingers for my cigarettes. The menthol smoke calmed my nerves and I smoked it without pausing for a proper breath. Looking through the windows, I could see that the light was fading. It was time to go before it was too late, but I had to see if Joseph was alive or dead first.

CHAPTER 37

There had been no sound from the stairwell for a while. I picked up the kit bag and slung it over my shoulder. I didn't have the energy to move the settee, so I climbed over it. I kept the Mossberg aimed at the dead man and nervously retrieved his gun. Another Glock to add to the collection and after the events of the previous week, I couldn't have enough. I trudged through the sticky liquid which was congealing on the floor. Glass fragments had adhered to my boots as I crunched along the landing. The body literally blocked the gap at the top of the first flight. His face was deformed by huge yellow blisters that had bubbled up on every piece of exposed flesh. His eyes were no longer distinguishable, giving his face a hideous appearance. I stepped over him and sighed with relief that I could get on with the daunting task I had before me.

A hand grabbed my ankle and yanked me backwards. I tried to stay upright but when my other leg was tugged hard, I fell forwards onto my face. I felt fragments of cup piercing the palms of my hands. The web of skin between my thumb and forefinger was sliced in two. A dozen sharp fragments punctured my skin in the fall. My knees were lacerated by glass shards and lightning bolts of pain shot through my brain. The Mossberg clattered across the landing just inches from my clawing fingertips. The grip on my ankles was bone-cracking in strength. I kicked out, but he was too powerful for it to have any impact. I looked behind me and aimed a boot at his nose, but his grip took any momentum out of the kick and all I managed to do was burst a few blisters. Thick yellow puss dribbled down his face. Taking a breath, I sprawled forward for the shotgun. My fingertips brushed the metal and I almost had it until Bungalow let go of one leg. The release of pressure catapulted me forward and I knocked the Mossberg over the edge. I heard the gun clattering down the stairs one at a time. I cried out in pain and frustration.

I was dragged backwards a metre; every millimetre caused more lacerations to my body. I felt like a pincushion. Bungalow was inching further up my body and now had a grip on my belt and no matter how hard I struggled, I couldn't break free. He was very heavy and too strong for me. I reached for the Glock and grabbed the handle of the pistol. Bungalow dragged me by the belt with one hand and with the other he punched me hard between the legs. His huge fist felt like a sledgehammer and the pain in my testicles blinded me. White hot pain stunned my nervous system. The wind was sucked from my lungs and despite my mouth being wide open, I couldn't even scream.

'I'm going to fucking kill you,' he growled. His voice sounded thick with mucus. He aimed another punch but this time I twisted enough for it to strike my thigh. I kicked out again and my boot connected with the wound in his chest. I heard a hissing from his throat, and it gave me strength. He relaxed his grip enough for me to turn onto my back. I felt shards piercing the waterproofs, slicing into the flesh on my back. Pure adrenalin and fear drove me on. I aimed the Glock at his face and squeezed the trigger.

Click. There was no recoil, no bang and no blood. I squeezed it again.

Click.

Click.

Click.

'It's empty, who's the fucking retard now?' He chuckled manically and bit my left leg just above the knee.

I felt the pressure like a pinch at first but then it quickly built to an indescribable sensation that the skin was going to burst. Then his teeth penetrated the flesh and the pain intensified to unbearable in a millisecond. Teeth hit bone and my body went into a painful spasm. I felt my muscles jack-knife and my teeth clamped together so hard that I thought that they would crack. When you're feeling intense pain with the prospect of worse to come, then your instincts take over. Instinctively I brought the gun down on the top of his skull but all it did was infuriate him further. He bit down harder. My blood was dribbling from the corners of his mouth. Tears blurred my vision, but I couldn't give up. I changed my grip on the Glock, holding it by the barrel. Using the handle to strike his skull like a hammer; I smashed the gun into the top of his head.

Crack. The scalp split an inch, but he just bit harder. He shook his head like a Pit Bull killing a rabbit. I felt flesh and sinew tearing. My brain was beginning to give in to the pain but if I gave into it, I wouldn't wake up.

Crack. A deeper gash appeared.

Crack. The skull fractured audibly, and a chunk of scalp and hair stuck to the handle exposing the bone beneath, but the pressure of the bite didn't relinquish any.

Crack.

Crack. The skull sank visibly into the cranial cavity. The pressure of the bite was released a little.

Crack. The brains were exposed as the bones disintegrated beneath the brutal blows.

Crack. Grey matter and globules of pink sludge splattered onto my face.

Crack. The handle penetrated the mush all the way to the trigger guard like a hammer hitting mashed potatoes. A lump of grey sludge dribbled down my cheek.

Splat.

Splat.

Splat.

Splat.

Splat.

Splat.

Splat.

***

It was exhaustion that forced me to stop. I lay on my back staring at the ceiling and wondered if this whole thing was just a nightmare. My breathing was shallow, and I could hear my heart pounding in my chest. The pain from the bite was intense. It burned and throbbed and I could feel the swelling tightening the skin around it. I was aware of cuts and lacerations on my hands, elbows, knees and chest but the pain of the bite dominated them all. I made a conscious effort to calm my breathing down and then pushed Bungalow's corpse off me with my foot. He weighed a ton. Cautiously, I tried to stand with the minimum of movement and the maximum of concentration to make sure that I didn't incur further cuts from the glass. I looked down at the waterproofs and decided that I looked like an extra from a slash movie.

'Fucking great idea, smashing glass,' I remember mumbling to myself as I pulled a shard from the palm of my right hand. I retrieved the kitbag and walked gingerly down the stairs towards the garage. The Mossberg lay glinting on the bottom step and I made a mental note to make a strap for it before I left. I needed the gun attached to me from now on, just in case I went down again in a future confrontation. Something told me that I would.

CHAPTER 38

I felt a pang of guilt as I stood over Joseph's body. He'd taken a bullet in the chest near the armpit. The vest had stopped it penetrating but his right arm hung limply at an angle. Blood trickled from a glancing wound to his temple. I couldn't see any bullet holes anywhere. This was yet another example of what happened to those who tried to help me. I knelt by him and pressed a pad to the head wound. His skin was still warm to the touch and his pulse was strong. I strapped a thick pad to the bleeding on his abdomen and taped it to the skin. He'd given me a chance to end the nightmare and I wasn't going to let him down.

'You look worse than me,' he whispered. His eyes opened and the pupils looked dilated.

'Are you okay?'

'Stupid question.'

'Stupid answer.'

'I'm okay.' He shifted his weight and looked me up and down. 'You're a mess. Go and sort yourself out. Get a shower and then we need to get out of here.'

'I don't think you're going anywhere except hospital,' I shook my head. He was immobilised by his injuries and he would be a liability to me.

'You can't go alone.'

'I got this far remember.'

'Yes, but fuck knows how.' Joseph tried to get up, but his broken ribs would barely allow him to breathe. 'I'm fucked.' He sighed and lay back down. 'Sort out those cuts. I'm not going anywhere.'

'Are you sure you can hang on?' I took a few moments to think things through.

'First, you need to treat those injuries. You'll need every ounce of energy that you can muster, so bleeding to death will defeat the object. I'm broken up but I'll live.'

Walking back up the stairs to the bedroom was surreal. Like a journey through a haunted house. In stark contrast to the gore on the stairs, the bedroom was like a haven of normality. I peeled off the waterproofs and dumped them on the floor of the bathroom. Emptying the kitbag onto the sink, I found tweezers and antiseptic cream. The hot water from the shower soothed my body and my soul. At first, the water ran red, but it soon ran clear. Most of the wounds were superficial and didn't need dressing but the bite was nasty. In the real world, it should have been stitched and treated with antibiotics to fend off infection, but I didn't have that luxury. I plastered cream on it and applied a gauze pad. It wasn't ideal but the best that I could do. The wound behind my ear had started to scab already, so I covered it with antiseptic and a plaster.

I dressed in Joseph's room and the black combats kept the dressing packed against the bite wound. It was painful but would help to stem the bleeding. I glanced in the mirror and prayed silently that I wouldn't encounter a policeman or an observant member of the public. I looked like I'd been in a battle and without the beard and hair around the sides of my head, I looked like me. The original plan of getting to the launching ramp hidden in the rigid was out of the window. I'd have to drive and pray I didn't pass anyone. I'd need some luck.

'You have to make your own luck'. I heard my own voice talking in my head. I'd told Joseph those exact words. I would have to make my own luck and I had an idea how to do that. Everything that I needed was in the boat. I selected a clean set of waterproofs and took the remote from the Jag. I opened the garage door and walked back to Joseph. 'Are you okay?'

'I've felt better.'

'I need you to phone an ambulance and then the police,' I handed him the telephone as I spoke.

'The police?'

'Yes.'

'What am I going to say to them?' He nodded towards flattop's body. 'My house is trashed and there's two dead bodies belonging to Marines I served with.'

'Normally I would use my vivid imagination to come up with a blindingly believable lie but on this occasion, tell them the truth.'

'Have you had a bang on the head?'

'No,' I was adamant. 'Tell them everything including the fact that these two wankers contacted someone called Lord Penrith and that he's with a large number of Niners on Anglesey.'

'That doesn't make sense. It'll tip them off. They'll scarper.'

'If the police think that there is a peer involved in this and they can check out your story from his mobile phone records, then they'll descend on the island like a plague of locusts. The Niners will be spread all over the place in bed and breakfasts, campsites, caravan parks and hotels. They won't be together. If this hits the news, then the hangers on will run for hills long before I get there,' I explained my plan. 'Only Fabienne and her hardcore will risk staying. With most of them gone, I'll have more chance of getting to her. I need you to do this.'

'What about the Jeep and the rib?'

'Tell them that I stole the Jeep,' I winked. 'Don't mention the boat, eh?'

'They'll concentrate on the roads out of town?'

'That's the plan,' I thought out loud. 'You can put your selective memory down to the head wound. I'm taking your Glock and ammunition and all the Tovex is gone so there's nothing here that you can be done for. Tell the police that I killed both of them.'

'No. I'll tell them that I don't know what happened.'

'Whatever works for you,' I agreed.

'You see the black toolbox over there?' he pointed to a shelf beneath the workbenches. 'Take it with you in the boat. They're night vision glasses. Put them on as you approach the jetty and give it at least ten minutes to adjust to them. There's a camo-stick in there too, so black up before you land.' He looked very concerned as he spoke. 'Take this vest too. I don't need it anymore. Remember that you have the element of surprise. Make sure you take your time to reccy the place. Don't rush straight into a trap.'

'I need to go.' I nodded that I understood. I could tell that he thought that I was going to my death. It was in his eyes and written all over his face. 'Give me ten minutes before you call them. You take care.'

'Good luck.' He smiled, but it turned to a grimace as his broken ribs reminded him that they were there. 'Kill the bitch.'

'Joseph,' I said as an afterthought. 'Upstairs is a bit of a mess. I think it might mess with your karma.'

'Just fuck off, will you, or I'll tell them there's a nutcase in my boat.' He grinned.

'And thanks,' I shouted over the top of the Jeep as I climbed in.

***

Ten minutes later, when the sirens started wailing, I was navigating the one-way system through Barmouth. Three police cars and an ambulance screamed past me heading in the other direction. I knew it would be a matter of minutes before they were joined by every uniformed unit near the coast. The roads around the funfair had been reopened and I made it to the promenade without incident. Five minutes further on, I parked the Jeep at the top of the launch ramp. I saw why Joseph had said we needed to leave when it went dark. The tide was high, and the water was lapping at the sea wall just metres from the road. The wall ran for a mile in both directions and was designed as both seating and a barrier against the winter storms. A scruffy toilet block was the only building for half a mile and even from a distance it exuded the aroma of stale urine. A couple of winos occupied the bench in front of it, oblivious to the stink, cans of special brew in hand. The road was dead when I reversed onto the ramp and the Jeep purred as I lowered the trailer into the water. When the boat floated off it, I jumped out and tied it up. The two men eyed me intensely.

'Are you going fishing mate?' A pair of bleary red eyes tried hard to focus on me. His friend looked a little more sober.

'Mackerel are biting this time of year.'

'No this is a one-way trip. I'm emigrating,' I said. They looked at me as if I was mad.

'Where to?'

'I'm not sure, I'm just sailing that way and see wherever I end up.'

'He's taking the piss.'

'Are you taking the piss?'

'Nope,' I held up the keys. 'Here do you want to borrow my Jeep for a while?'

They looked at each other in confusion. Neither of them moved.

'What do you mean for a while?'

'The police will stop you sooner or later, but you could go for a spin in the meantime.'

'He is taking the piss.'

'Are you taking the piss?'

'Look,' I tossed the keys and the soberish guy caught them. 'I'm off so why don't you take her for a spin along the coast road. There's plenty of diesel in it.'

'He's taking the piss.'

'Are you taking the piss?'

They stared from the keys to the Jeep and then at each other. I untied the rigid and jumped into it. The outboard fired up on the second ask. I steered it forward between the guide buoys for a few minutes. The further out I went, the better I felt. As I turned the boat around and headed out to sea, I saw the Jeep trundling along the promenade. They were heading out of town, which meant they wouldn't be picked up for a while. The further out of the bay I sailed, the deeper the swell was and the darker the night became. I hugged the coastline using the lights of the coast roads and the seaside towns as my guides. As long as I kept them parallel to my right, I was heading in the right direction. The wind was biting, and the spray felt like tiny pinpricks of ice where it hit the skin. I was cold and alone but I wasn't down; in fact, the opposite was true. The freedom that the boat gave me felt liberating and exhilarating. I felt invisible to the rest of the world and invisible was good. My eyes adjusted to the darkness, so the cliffs and headlands were dark silhouettes against a darker backdrop and the ever-present yellow globes of light gave me the comfort that I wasn't lost in a black void.

When the lights and the land veered away sharply to the right, I knew I was level with the Menai Straits. In the distance, I could see the bridges illuminated between the landmasses, their structures made even more fabulous by the lights. From my position, the passage between the mainland and the island looked like a wondrous grotto, lights like diamonds twinkled on both banks but they belied the truth. The Straits are treacherous. There are powerful riptides and undercurrents as the sea is funnelled into a narrow channel and then squeezed out at the other end. Many an experienced sailor has come unstuck on the reefs and rocks which lurk just below the surface. I was a novice chancing my luck in the dark. My voyage was to be in the alternative direction along the south coast of the island which is less inhabited and therefore was less illuminated.

The rigid seemed almost indestructible as it ploughed through the swell relentlessly. Although it was a daunting trip in the darkness, it was also a nostalgic one as I passed the time identifying the villages and tiny harbours. The waters around South Stack were kind to me, although looking up at the lighthouse from the sea was alien to me. I'd only ever seen it from hundreds of metres above. Its white tower glowed eerily against the massive cliffs behind it and the mountain loomed above like a giant black colossus blotting out the night sky. There were white horses on the tips of the swell and salty foam floated on the wind like bubbles. It was cold and wet, but the most dangerous leg of the journey was pretty straightforward. As I sailed around North Stack, the lights of Holyhead twinkled like yellow jewels and the lighthouse at the end of the Breakwater shone like a beacon of hope for me. I used its beam to guide me along the rocky coast until the turrets and fortifications on the roof of Soldier's Point were silhouetted by the lights of the marina. It was the building, which had haunted my sleeping hours for months. Although I'd made it against all the odds, there was no glee in my arrival. I thought about turning around and sailing into the night, but I couldn't. This was where the final scene would be acted out. There would be no applause and no encores. When the curtain came down, it would be the end.

CHAPTER 39

Fifty yards offshore I killed the engine. I opened the black toolbox and took out the camo paint. My skin was cold and wet from the sea spray, but the waxy paint went on easily enough. I coloured my face, neck and hands before slipping the night vision goggles on. They fastened around my head and then I clipped the sights over my eyes. The world was transformed into video game mode. I scanned the breakwater from the shore out to sea. About a thousand yards along a green blob glowed. It sat and stood and then walked back and to for a minute or so. A smaller blob shadowed every move. A fisherman and his dog. I could see them even from that distance. Although he may have heard the motor on the wind, he was staring into impenetrable blackness. I was invisible to them.

My eyes adjusted to the goggles and I patiently studied the cliffy shoreline of Rocky Coast. I couldn't see anything untoward. The headlands looked clear. I decided to land in a sheltered cove that we used to call 'boulder beach' when we were younger. The beach was made from white, almond shaped rocks the size of melons, hence the name. I could hide the rigid there by pulling it onto the beach. If I climbed up the headland, I would be able to look down onto Soldier's Point. I would be able to see the remains of the outhouses and rear gardens and the approach road without too much effort but to see the much larger Porth-y-Felin House beyond it, I would have to navigate the overgrown grounds to search for a breech in the building's walls. The last time I'd seen the place, every window had been bricked up, to discourage both the elements and curious intruders from entering. With the engine running quietly, I took the rigid into the shore. The toughened hull held strong against the wave smoothed boulders. I jumped into the sea when it was knee deep and dragged the rib onto the stones leaving only the outboard in the water.

I sorted out as much as I could carry. The storage box with the three bombs inside was the heaviest and also the most important. I tipped the medical supplies from the kitbag and filled it with shotgun shells and spare 9mm clips. I fastened my blade to the belt and pushed the Glock down the back of my trousers. I cut some of the mooring rope from the rib and tied it around the stock of the Mossberg then I fastened the other end to my wrist. I didn't want to part company with her again. The throbbing from the bite on my leg reinforced the importance of it. I couldn't carry anything else and still remain mobile enough the run or fight. Taking a final look around, I set off up the beach. The stones clunked and clacked as I trudged along. I found a path through the thick grass, which took me to the headland, and I placed the storage box down on the grass. The clouds parted for a second and I could see broken glass along the top of the walls glinting in the moonlight. It was a testament to the times when we were allowed to defend our properties without considering the harm we might do to burglars. The vicious shards were sparkling green and white like emeralds and diamonds.

Forked lightning split the sky and blinded me for a second. Its path to earth was etched in my mind as I waited for the image to fade. Thunder followed seconds later and then the heavens opened. The rain bounced off the floor and deep puddles formed quickly. My clothes were drenched as I looked two hundred yards away to my left, where the breakwater meets the land. The rear walls of the hotel grounds met the side walls at right angles. A mock turret, complete with arrow slits marked the right angle where they intersected. The outer walls were in reasonable condition although the original white paint was only visible in a handful of places. Moss and climbing ivy dominated the vertical sections and the leaves looked like they were made from black wax as the rain dripped from them. Behind the wall were three oblong shaped buildings, which had been added to the main structure at various points in its history. The roofs were completely collapsed into the interiors making them almost irrelevant to my search. Only the insects and rodents could manoeuvre through the debris and the intertwined mesh of vegetation; thistles and nettles protruded through the empty windows. Another flash of lightning illuminated the scene. I couldn't see any sign of life.

The side walls followed the access road for a hundred yards, where the main gate led to a sweeping horseshoe drive. It was barely recognisable now. The gravel had been overtaken by greenery. The spiked iron gates were fastened with a rusted chain and a newer security mesh had been fitted in front of them to discourage trespassers. From what I could see, the security fittings were intact. The lane was empty, as was the area around the gates. I hadn't expected there to be guards dressed in sackcloth cassocks, their faces hidden by cowls, but I was almost disappointed by the lack of activity. I decided to circumnavigate the walls by following the rear structure to its end where it met the harbour wall with a ten-metre drop to the rocks below. The walls encompassed three sides; the sea formed a natural barrier to the east.

I carried the bombs in the crook of my left arm which left my right arm free to hold the shotgun. Progress was slow as I picked my way over rocks and boulders until I reached the breakwater. I rested beneath the turret for a minute and then followed the wall towards the sea. Coastal erosion had taken its toll on this section of the hotel grounds. The harbour wall was still well maintained by the port authorities, but they didn't extend their maintenance to the privately-owned properties which formed part of the marina. The section which met the hotel grounds had fallen away into the marina, leaving a perilous overhang. Water gushed over the edge in deep rivulets, carrying more of the land with it every second. There was no way that I could get around the walls there. I retraced my steps and took another breather beneath the turret and wiped the rain from my eyes, before ducking low and jogging down the lane as quietly as I could. When I reached the gatepost, I pulled the security mesh and looked at the fastenings. The clasps and bolts were pitted with rust spots. I was happy that they'd not been opened recently and then resealed. I thought about climbing over, but the bombs were too cumbersome and Joseph's warning to reconnoitre the area properly was fresh in my mind.

I carried on down the lane until the walls were interrupted by another turret, signalling that the boundary had been reached. I climbed through a hedge to follow the wall to the east away from the lane. Trees of different sizes tried to breach the wall, their branches reaching over defiantly. The canopy of leaves gave me some relief from the downpour. I scanned the area in front of me. I was in the grounds of Porth-y-Felin House now; the wall separated one dilapidated property from the other. I was also somewhere that I had no former knowledge of. This part of the properties wasn't visible from the road or the sea. I knew that the jetty which belonged to the RAF was in front of me somewhere. I scanned the thick undergrowth between myself and the humungous mansion, searching for any signs of sentries but the goggles showed nothing of any interest. The bushes and thickets which encircled the mansion looked alive with movement, but I knew that it was just the rain hammering the foliage. I pressed on until the trees gave way to a low fence and a five-bar gate. The gate gave access to the marina.

I climbed the gate and slid down a steep slope, which brought me to a rock outcrop above the jetty. I realised that I could use the metal structure to get around the hotel wall into its grounds although I would have to be careful. As I looked for the easiest way to go, I heard a whisper on the breeze. At first, I thought it might be a voice from the marina across the bay carried on the wind, but it was much closer. I froze to the spot and tried to melt behind the nearest tree trunk. Water dripped from the tree, running down the back of my neck but I couldn't move. There was a rhythmical rippling of the water below almost lost beneath the relentless rain and constant rattling of the rigging on the yacht masts in the marina. Ting, ting, ting, ting. I heard a splash below me. I thought that it may be a seabird or a conga eel jumping for an insect, but it was too persistent, and it was coming nearer.

As I watched, four green shapes emerged from behind the yachts. They were sat in a line, obviously in a kayak of some kind. Two of the figures moved in time, paddling the vessel towards the jetty. I sat and waited, my heart pounding, my breathing sounded deafening inside my ears as the boat came closer.

I clicked the goggles up, so that I could see the individuals in detail. My eyes struggled to adjust at first but then I focused clearly. Lightning streaked across the sky arcing from one black cloud to another. Ear-splitting thunder followed immediately. The sudden flash revealed that there were three men and a smaller figure, a female or young male. They neared the jetty and I tried to see where they'd gone but they were out of sight. I stood and peered from behind the tree. From my elevated angle, I could see them tying up the boat and I could also see two other boats already tethered there. We had planned to land at the jetty and if Joseph had come along, we probably would have. It would have been a mistake. I had a feeling that some things happened for a reason. Whispers drifted to me, but I couldn't understand what they were saying. My breathing was shallow as I waited for them to appear on the jetty. I could hear them climbing up the iron ladders. It took them forever, the rungs made greasy by the rain. When they reached the platform, they exchanged words and then walked up the boards towards the landing and to my surprise, headed in different directions. Three walked towards the old RAF building but one of them climbed over the railings and walked towards the hotel. I flicked the goggles back down when they split up, not sure who to follow. I needed to know where they were entering the buildings, but I couldn't see in two directions at the same time. The group of three climbed up the steps which led to the front of the mansion and then they took a path which led them left around the building, out of my line of vision.

That made my decision simple. I had to follow the lone figure. He picked his way through the thick undergrowth with remarkable ease. It was a path which he'd taken many times before. I remembered that this area was once a shrub garden about half the size of a football pitch. It was dissected by paved footpaths allowing guests to wander and enjoy the flowers and manicured rose bushes. Somewhere up ahead, there were wide steps which led up to the front lawns and the horseshoe drive. A huge triple fountain once dominated the upper lawns, the setting for hundreds of wedding photos. The contrast to what it had become was hard to comprehend. Mother Nature had reclaimed the area as her own. There was no symmetry anymore just a never-ending free for all, as bushes, trees, shrubs and vines all wrestled for light and space.

Using my memories, I tried to pick my way through the vegetation without making any giveaway racket. I heard a swishing sound up ahead, like the noise of supple branches springing back into their space and when I looked up, the green figure had gone. I crouched down and tapped the goggles as if they might not be working properly. If in doubt, give it a knock. There was still no sign of him. He had been about twenty metres ahead of me when he disappeared, so I edged a few metres closer. When I focused, I could just make out lines in the foliage. The tree canopy seemed to be much higher beyond which told me that the lines that I could see were the curved stone steps which led up to the hotel lawns. The figure had disappeared before the steps. He couldn't have climbed them without me seeing him. I remembered that there was an ornate wall with a stone balustrade which separated the gardens from the lawns above. Wherever he had gone, I couldn't follow blindly without covering my escape. I turned and retraced my steps. It was hard going; my clothes were clinging to me and the rain was sapping the warmth from my being.

Tiptoeing back through the brambles, I climbed onto the jetty and set the storage box down. Keeping the spot where the lone green figure vanished in sight, I took one of the bombs out and placed it tightly beneath a tree root against a rock. I twisted the top from the bottle and added some of the liquid metal. My hands were trembling as I fixed the detonator to the device, slipping the fuse wires into the liquid. I stood back to gauge the arc where the shrapnel would rip everything to shreds; the killing zone. I decided then that the jetty would be the escape route for me or for the Niners. I primed a second bottle and set it close enough to the first for it to be detonated by the other, but far enough away for it to impact a different area, widening the killing zone. The rocks would deflect the blast forward, aiming the metal fragments towards both the path and the jetty. When the number was dialled, anyone in that area would be torn to pieces. I could only pray that no one else would call that number before I did, or my plan was dead in the water.

CHAPTER 40

I made my way back to the gardens and crouched down under a bush. I could see the steps beneath the undergrowth but the walls either side were swamped by ivy. The wind was picking up, driving the rain sideways; the salty air was filled with the ting, ting of the yachts. I took the remaining bomb out and then slid the storage box into the leaves and crouched low as I searched the area. I studied the grasses and brambles for breaks, aware that every footstep caused the sound of cracking twigs. Although the noise was minimal, each tiny snap sounded like a bullwhip cracking in my mind. I heard something, but I wasn't sure what it was. The noise of the storm and the marina was drowning everything. I listened hard and there it was again, a sobbing noise.

I froze and listened intently, nothing but the ting, ting of the rigging and the rustle of the wind and the rain dripping from the trees. I relaxed and took another step and there it was again but this time it was more of a cry. The rain was distorting where the sound was coming from. I held my breath and waited; another sob and then the muffled echo of a door being slammed. I wasn't the only one who heard the noise. A rat the size of a toy dog bolted from the ivy thicket. The sudden movement stopped my breath and tested the strength of how anally retentive I was, but it also gave me a clue as to where the door was. I looked down at where the rat had come from and sure enough, there was an area of trodden ground. It was barely visible in the thick undergrowth but there, nonetheless. Muddy prints were visible beneath the vegetation. I used the shotgun to lift the thinner branches of ivy. Behind it, there was a narrow doorway, arched at the top. The cracked wooden door was decorated with metal studs and a plaited metal knocker. The frame was warped, and the rats had chewed holes through the weather bar. I took a deep breath and ducked beneath the ivy, pushing the door open with my foot.

I looked around a gardener's storeroom; the gardener himself at one with earth, his body long since riddled with worms. The image of his rotten skull jumped into my mind. Hideous millipedes slithered out of his empty eye sockets, pincers snapping closed. I could smell the stench of rotting flesh; it was almost overpowering. I blinked and the image was gone replaced by the web strewn room in front of me. My mind tried to comprehend what I'd seen and what I thought I'd seen. I focused on reality. A heavy grass roller stood against the far wall next to a dilapidated clothes locker. The floor was littered with broken terracotta pots. The vision of the rotting corpse had startled me. I hadn't experienced anything like it since the last time I'd been in close proximity to Fabienne Wilder. I wondered if she was aware that I was here, and she was playing with my mind or if it was just my imagination picking things up. She said that I had the type of imagination which could see more than most. I clung to that rather than believing that she could get into my head. I had to believe that, or I was finished.

A stifled cry shook me back to reality. I looked around. The storeroom was no bigger than the average bedroom. There were no doors and no windows. The floor was compacted earth. I looked up. The ceiling was vaulted and made from limestone bricks. If the lone figure had come in here, then I couldn't see how he'd got out. Voices murmured, almost whispers and then I heard the sobbing again. I walked over to the locker. It was made from tin. I pulled it from the top, but it wouldn't budge. There were metal fastenings bolted to the wall, the metal was warped and blistered by time. I opened the doors, hoping for a Narnia type door but there was nothing but spiders and rust. I jammed the second device into the corner of the empty locker, primed it with liquid metal and then set the detonator. I didn't know where it was but there was an entrance to somewhere in here. I just had to find it.

I tugged the grass roller, but it wouldn't move an inch. I grabbed both handles and yanked hard. There was a creaking noise and then a snap as the handle ripped off. I was sent backwards by my momentum and landed heavily on the soil. The noise was enough to awaken the dead. I held the Mossberg tightly against my shoulder and waited for the onslaught. Nothing happened. After long seconds, I put my hand on the ground to push myself up and felt a draft on my wrist. I flicked a large piece of terracotta pot with the back of my hand, but it didn't move. The soil around it felt spongy. I put my face to the floor and felt the draft once more. I could also hear sobbing. Not just one voice but several. I stood up and brushed the shards of pot with my boot. Some of it was stuck, fixed with some kind of adhesive. Then I saw a dull metal ring beneath the rim of a large piece. I pulled it and a trapdoor lifted. There was a rush of foul air and my video screen vision was awash with an orange light.

Slimy stone steps led down to a corridor below and although I could only see a small square, I could tell that the rock floor had been worn smooth by time and use. Candlelight flickered giving the place an eerie glow. I'd come too far and seen too much to be frightened. Whatever was down there needed to be equally afraid of me. I took the steps slowly keeping the shotgun aimed high. As I went lower, I closed the trapdoor above me. There was a bolt which fastened it to the joists around the hatch and I slid it home. It could delay my escape if I was in a rush, but it was better than allowing more of them to come from behind me. The steps curved to the left and then met the corridor. The walls were carved from the rocks, the floor was uneven and pitted with lips and ledges. The ceiling was higher in some places than in others. I knelt down and looked along the length that I could see. It looked like there were doors fitted randomly on both sides. The stench was stomach churning a mixture of animals and death. I could smell decaying flesh, but I could also smell the living. The smell of body odour and human waste was choking.

At the end of the corridor another set of carved steps led upwards. The murmuring voices were coming from that direction, but the sobbing wasn't. It was coming from somewhere much closer. I stayed low and edged down the corridor slowly. The first doorway was shoulder high. There was a hatch near the top of the thick metal door and a keyhole fitted halfway down on the left. The size and shape of the keyhole told me that it was very old. I listened against the door but couldn't hear anything. I slid the hatch open and peered inside using the goggles. I recoiled at the smell that came from the hatch; stale urine and excrement and the putrid odour of unwashed humans. I held my breath and looked again. There was a green figure in the far corner of a tiny cell which was nothing more than a two-metre hole in the rock. It cowered against the cold rock. I couldn't make out any features, but it had long, wispy, grey hair.

'Hey,' I whispered. The shape twitched but only made itself smaller still. 'Hey.' The figure trembled visibly. 'I'll be back to get you out, okay?'

'Fuck off,' it hissed. I couldn't tell what sex it was. 'I like it here. So, will you.' The creature cackled like a witch from a cartoon although it wasn't funny at the time. 'You'll love it when they come for you.'

I figured that they'd lost their marbles, sympathy replaced disgust. 'I'll come back,' I whispered. 'Just hang on.' There was no response. I slid the hatch closed and moved on. The urge to hammer the door down was almost irresistible but my primary goal would be compromised. The murmuring voices seemed to be growing louder; an incantation or a chant in a language which I couldn't identify. I reached a doorway on the opposite side of the corridor identical to the first. The sobbing which I'd heard was coming from inside. I slid the hatch open and stepped back to allow the worst of any offensive smells to dissipate.

'Help me,' a voice sobbed from within.

'Who are you?' I looked in and caught my breath. A young boy stood naked in the cell. There was a pentagram painted on his chest and his arms were tied behind his back.

'My name is David,' he whispered. 'Please get me out of here.'

'I will, David,' I kept my voice low but firm. 'I will come back for you.'

'No please don't leave me.'

'I promise that I'll be back.'

'Oh, God, please help me, mister.'

'I will,' I tried to reassure him. 'How did you get here?'

'I was hitch-hiking to Ireland to find my grandmother,' he began to sob. Tears rolled down his face leaving tracks in the dirt on his face. 'My mum died, and they put us into care. We ran away. We got into a van and they took us here.' He broke down and cried hysterically. Snot dribbled from his nose and dangled from his chin. His knees buckled and his head was against the damp floor. 'Please help me.'

'Who were you with, David,' I tried to calm him. 'You said 'we'. Who were you with?'

'My sister, Sarah,' he blubbered. 'They took her up there.'

'Where?'

'Up the stairs to the big room,' he sobbed incoherently. 'That's where they hurt us.'

'When was this?' I asked. 'When did they take her?'

'Years ago.' he screamed. His voice echoed from the rocks down the narrow corridor. 'Fucking years ago.' He threw himself against the door violently. His nose cracked against the hatch and his top lip split like a burst grape. Blood splattered against my face and I staggered back against the wall. 'She's coming, she's coming. I can hear her.' He screamed. His voice echoed down the tunnel. I aimed the gun at the stairs waiting for an army of Niners to rush down them. My breathing was shallow and there was a cold sheen on my skin. 'She said you would come,' David whispered. His voice seemed to float on the air. 'She said that you would come and save her, but you didn't. You didn't. You didn't. You didn't. You didn't.'

I stepped back to the cell door and cautiously looked inside. The rank stench of decomposition hit me like a baseball bat. The boy was gone or at least his image had. There were skeletal remains curled up on the floor in the foetal position. My mind was reverberating with his voice, the tortured pleas to release him yet he didn't exist. Not anymore anyway. I knew the remains belonged to a boy called David, the boy that I'd seen walking and talking just a moment before. He had been dead for years. I knew all this and yet I couldn't explain how no more than I could explain the vision of him begging for help.

I knelt and tried to gather my thoughts. I could no more explain what had happened than I could explain any of my living nightmares. I was dicing with evil, pitting my frail human mind against the most ancient malevolence known to mankind and yet I was searching for reasonable explanations. That was madness itself. I gave myself a mental kick up the arse and stood up. I was here to kill Fabienne Wilder and as many of her followers as I could not to provide answers or solutions as to how to remove cosmic evil energy from the universe. Even Stevie Hawkins would struggle with that one. I smiled to myself inside at the thought of him trying to explain that one and headed for the stairs.

CHAPTER 41

I passed the other cells and opened the next two hatches. There was a young girl in one, her hair matted with vomit and blood. Her teeth were missing, and her head was tilted at an impossible angle, yet she smiled at me as if I was her favourite uncle. 'Is it my turn again?' she cooed. 'So soon?'

'What's your name?' I asked cautiously. I didn't know if she was an apparition of something past.

'Whatever you want it to be.' She screamed like a wounded dog and spat in my face. Her saliva burned like acid eating into my skin and the rank stench of rotten meat sickened me. I wiped at it with my fingers but when I looked at my hand, there was nothing there. When I looked back into the cell, she was gone. Movement on the cell floor caught my eye. Maggots wriggled from the empty eye socket of a half-buried skull. Long grey threads of wispy hair clung to it, reluctant to let go even in death. I staggered backwards, shocked by the vision and by the fact that I might be losing my mind. Either that or the insidious evil which oozed from every inch of that place was controlling my thoughts.

I wanted to run away but I couldn't show weakness. I didn't want to look inside the next cell, but I had to. It held a middle-aged man shackled to a rusty metal ring which was drilled into the rock. He was tied up with a leather dog collar around his neck and a gag ball strapped tightly around his face. His muffled laughter disturbed me until I saw that he was masturbating. His face reddened, then turned blue and dark blood began to trickle from his eyes and nose. His head rocked backwards, either in ecstasy or agony. I couldn't decide which. A guttural noise came from his throat and his body went into spasm. I felt bile rising in my throat. I blinked the vile scene from my mind and slammed the hatch shut. I had no idea what type of hell I was seeing. I ran without stopping. There was no point. I wouldn't be able to tell who was real and who wasn't. I reached the end of the tunnel and crouched down to look up the stairs. The stone steps climbed steeply upward and then twisted to the left.

The incantations were louder now, more urgent, more sinister. A strangled cry echoed down the stairs and I decided that caution was no longer the key. When I reached the turn I ran, taking the steps in twos. At the top was an arched opening and as the room beyond came into view, a sickening vista greeted me. An iron chandelier illuminated the horror. It hung from the roof holding ever decreasing circles of burning candles. It was the only source of light.

There were six naked people, their faces hidden by wrinkled animal masks. A goat, a cow, a dog, a horse, a stag, and a cat. It was like stepping into the dreams of a twisted mind, except I knew that I couldn't wake up. A woman lay spread-eagled on an altar, her body painted with symbols of the occult. Her severed head was placed on her stomach, her eyes gouged out and tongue removed. My stomach churned and my blood pressure soared to boiling point. The others were occupied with a man who was suspended from the rafters, a heavy chain on each limb. His limbs were twisted at awkward angles, the shoulder joints dislocated. He was hanging above a pentagram which had been carved deeply into the rock. His blood was pooling into the symbol, filling each crevice with his life force. His head lolled backwards, his eyes open and staring at me. There was life in them. There was pleading and agony in them too. His lips moved silently as if in prayer. The chanting grew louder. They were oblivious to my presence, lost in the hysteria of the ceremony.

I aimed the Mossberg from the hip and fired three shots in quick succession. The candles splattered all over the entourage and then the chandelier crashed down from the ceiling. The Niners beneath were floored by its weight, crushed and pinned down against the rock. The lights were extinguished plunging the hellhole into darkness. I lowered the night vision goggles and reloaded the shotgun. The men at the altar fumbled about in the darkness. I closed the distance between us and blasted the first one in the lower abdomen, ripping the tip of his manhood off, leaving just a bleeding stump. I could see his lower intestine glistening through a deep hole in his side. He writhed on the floor screaming. As he slid along, his intestines unravelled like a slimy string of rotten sausages. The more he panicked, the more his guts spilled out. I thought about shooting him dead to end his suffering, but the thought was only a passing one. Fuck him.

The second man ripped off the mask and ran blindly into the wall, smashing his nose and breaking his front teeth. He dropped to his knees where I blew his head off with three shots. His headless body remained kneeling before the altar which at that moment seemed ironic. Blood spurted from the ruined neck in time with his dying heartbeat, making him like a morbid water feature in a garden from hell. The Niners trapped beneath the chandelier cowered and twisted in agony, their bones crushed by the massive weight. They could move but they couldn't escape. I thought about quietening their screams with a bullet to the face but again, it was just a silly passing thought. I left them limbless and sobbing for death to take them, begging for the pain to end. Fuck them too.

I checked but none of them was Fabienne and there was no sign of a baby. There were no exits apart from the way that I'd entered. It was nothing more than a high cave carved from the bedrock. I sat down on the steps for a while to calm my nerves and thought about what to do next. I tuned out their desperate cries and switched off the visions of carnage which were emblazoned in my mind. It was a wicked thing that I'd done but it felt right. I'd shown them the same level of mercy that they'd shown others. What goes around comes around. I knew that the Niners in the mansion would have heard the gunshots, there was no doubt about that. I pulled myself together and ran down the stairs. I banged my head on the low ceiling several times as I ran down the rock tunnel. When I reached the trapdoor, I climbed a few steps and listened for a moment. There were the footsteps of several people above. I heard voices whispering from the trapdoor above me.

'She wants him alive.'

'He can't get past four of us.'

'I'm not going down there. We'll wait until he comes out.'

'Give me the gun.'

'Fuck that, I'm keeping it.'

'Here, take this.'

'What is it?'

'A taser, just stun him.'

'But I'm soaking wet. I'll get a shock.'

'Shut up.'

'I won't shut up and I don't want a fucking shock.'

I banged on the hatch and the voices stopped. 'You're in for a shock but not the one you're thinking of,' I shouted. I took the mobile from the rucksack, ran back down the corridor and dialled.

***

When the device in the locker exploded, there was a whooshing sound first and then the sensation that the air was being sucked out of the corridor. Then the blast hit, and I felt the ground vibrating beneath me. I thought that I heard screams, but I couldn't be certain. The metal locker would have been shredded by the blast. Hundreds of shards of red-hot metal travelling at a thousand feet a second would have decimated any living being instantly. Smoke and debris filled the corridor and the fumes were blinding. My eyes streamed as I waited for the air to clear. When the noise settled down, I made my way back to the trapdoor. There was a gaping hole where it had once been, and I could see the moon shining behind the clouds and the raindrops splashed refreshingly on my face. The explosion had taken the wall and the ceiling off the gardener's store exposing it to the sky. It had also blown a fissure in the rock tunnel wide open. I'd missed it when I first entered the tunnel assuming that it ran in one direction.

I peered into the opening. It was like looking into the darkest pit of hell. The blackness was impenetrable. The tunnel ran in the opposite direction, heading beneath the hotel grounds towards the mansion. The desire to head up the steps into the fresh air was overwhelming, but I had to ignore it. I'd come to kill Niners and they were in Porth-y-felin House. The tunnel would take me there unseen. I squeezed through the gap and felt the atmosphere change immediately. It was like stepping into a void of desolation. The air that I breathed seemed to suck the life force from me. I felt hopelessness, desperation and infinite sadness running through my veins. Whatever was generating such negative energy was incredibly powerful. My body was saturated with despair. My legs turned to jelly, and my hands were shaking uncontrollably. I felt red-hot tears of anguish burning my cheeks. My breathing was laboured, and my strength was dissipating as every second ticked, by but I was drawn forward involuntarily. I was taken back to my dream where I was walking through mud.

The tunnel sloped gently and narrowed with every tentative step that I took. The deeper I went, the harder it was to breathe. My legs felt like they'd been injected with quick drying cement. They cramped and burned as if I was nearing the end of a marathon. My head felt too heavy for my neck. The pressure inside my skull was building to critical. White spots flickered in front of my eyes. The tunnel appeared to be filled with white bees. There was a high-pitched whine in my ears. I clasped the palms of my hands to the side of my head, squeezing, trying to relieve the pressure. I felt a gentle pop behind my eyes. Blood poured from both nostrils and ran down the back of my throat. Thick globules hit the tunnel floor with a splat. The coppery taste made me want to gag. I squeezed my nose between finger and thumb and tipped my head backwards to stem the flow. The bleeding took the edge off the pain momentarily and I pressed on down the tunnel. It dipped sharply, twisted to the left and ended in a rectangular opening which was far too symmetrical to have been built by the tunnellers.

As I approached the doorway, I could see that it was filled with a riveted metal door. It was a modern fitting, not in keeping with the doors I'd seen on the cells. I pushed it but it didn't give. There were no hinges and no handle, no keyhole or clasp. I assumed that it must have been bolted shut on the other side. I couldn't blast it open and I couldn't force it, so I did the next best thing. I knocked on it.

I heard shuffling on the other side. Footsteps neared. Whoever was on the other side was hesitant. I knocked again but harder this time.

'Open the fucking door,' I said. 'Someone has set a bomb off, hurry I'm hurt.'

'She said not to,' a man's voice whispered. 'Go the other way.'

'It's blocked, you idiot,' I growled. 'The entire tunnel has collapsed. Now open the fucking door.'

I heard a bolt slide. Then another. Then a third. The door creaked open a little and frightened eye peered through the gap. I rammed the butt of the gun into the face and kicked the door wide open. The man landed on his back, stunned by the blow. I looked around for any more Niners, but the room was empty. I shut the door, sliding the bolts home. I was in a cellar beneath Porth-y-felin House. There was a huge boiler the size of a transit van in the far corner. Much of the metal and most of the pipes had been ground off and taken away for scrap. There were burn marks and rents of fresh metal exposed on the walls and floor. It looked like the salvage crews had set to work stripping any valuable metals from the structure, but the work had been left unfinished.

'Stay down there or I'll blow your head off. Understand?'

The man lay still and nodded. His nose was broken, blood streaked his cheeks. There was an old Luger on the floor next to him. He must have dropped it when he was struck. I picked it up and tucked it into my belt, before checking the door on the opposite wall. It was much more akin to the rest of the building, blistered, peeling and warped. The wood was so dry that it would crumble under the slightest force. I opened it and looked down the corridor. Candlelight flickered somewhere at the far end, casting shadows which seemed to reach for me. The thought of wandering around the cavernous building searching blindly didn't appeal. My journey down the tunnel had sapped me. I knew that she was close because I could feel the evil, taste the violence and smell the tension in the air. I'd experienced her energy before, but this was tenfold. I noticed handcuffs hanging from one of the pipes, a coil of discarded rope next to a tatty old blanket and a stained single mattress. Someone had been held there.

'What's your name?'

'Colin,' he replied meekly. 'I know who you are.'

'Good,' I grabbed him as I spoke. 'Then you'll know not to lie to me then.' I dragged him across the dusty concrete to the shell of the boiler. His heels dug into the dirt trying to slow down my progress. 'Take off your belt.'

'Why? What are you going to do?' his eyes were wide and frightened.

'Just do it.' I hissed aggressively pressing the Mossberg hard into his cheek.

'Okay, okay,' he mumbled as he fumbled with his buckle. He held up the belt with a shaking hand. 'I didn't want to be here. I wanted to go home.'

'Why are you here then?'

'I had no choice,' he whispered looking around as if the walls could hear us. 'Most of them left this afternoon. The police were looking everywhere for her. I was going to leave the hotel too but one of them forced me to stay and we had to come here.'

'Put your hands on that pipe,' I ordered. 'Grab hold of it.'

'Okay, okay,' he said shakily as he held the thick pipe.

I fastened his wrists tightly to the pipe. His hands and fingers were curled over the top of it. He was sitting down, his legs and feet stretched out beneath the old kettle of the boiler. 'Why were you guarding that door?'

'They told me to.'

'Don't play stupid. Why?'

'Some of them went up the tunnel.'

'Why?'

'I'm not sure.'

I took out my combat knife and let the blade glint in the candlelight. Pressing it hard over his little finger, I asked again, 'Why did they go up the tunnel?'

'I'm not sure, honestly.' His eyes flickered up to the left. He was lying.

'That's your first lie,' I explained the rules as I pressed the blade through the knuckle until I felt it strike the metal beneath his finger. I gagged him with my left hand, closing his nose and mouth as he screamed. 'And that's your little finger gone. Nine more lies to go before I start on your toes. Get it?' He nodded furiously, his eyes wide open, set to pop out. Tears ran down his face, making lines in the congealing blood. 'Now, we don't want you to bleed to death, do we?' He shook his head in agreement. I took out my Zippo and clicked the flame alive. Placing the flame over the bleeding stump, I held his face tightly as his body jerked violently. The stump bubbled and sizzled as the wound cauterised. 'That will stop you bleeding out, but it hurts, doesn't it?' He sobbed and nodded. 'Now I'm going to take my hand off your mouth and we'll start again. If you scream, I'll cut your eyes out and leave you here. Get it?' His muffled groans led me to believe that he did.

'What do you want to know?' he gasped. Painful sobs racked his body. 'Please don't hurt me anymore.'

'That's up to you,' I smiled. My smile disturbed him. I could tell by his eyes. 'Now then, why did they go up the tunnel?'

'They were performing a preliminary ceremony,' he whispered. His voice was hardly audible. 'I was supposed to wait for them to come back but then she told me not to open the door for them.'

'Why?'

'The explosion.'

'So, she was here a few minutes ago?'

'No,' he said confused. 'It was over half an hour ago.'

'Half an hour?'

'At least.'

That meant that my walk down the tunnel had taken me much longer than I thought it had. It wasn't beyond the realms of belief the way things had gone. 'Who were the people they took with them and murdered?'

'I don't know, honestly,' he shook his head. 'They had them here already. I didn't know they were going to kill them, honestly.'

'Bullshit,' I mumbled. 'That's what you sick bastards do isn't it?'

'I haven't been to anything like this before,' he pleaded innocence. 'Normally it's just…'

'An orgy,' I finished the sentence for him. 'How many of them are here?'

'Ten or twelve, no more than that.'

'Where is Fabienne now?'

'They said that they had to get her away because of the explosion,' he blinked as he spoke. 'I think she's already gone.'

'I think you're lying again.' I grabbed his face again and sliced off his index finger at the knuckle. A garbled scream came from deep in his throat, but it was too muffled to attract attention from above. His legs kicked out in the air. 'Now that was your own fault,' I whispered into his ear as I took out the lighter and burned the bloody stump until the blood boiled and the flesh blackened. His vigorous twitching slowed and then stopped. He had passed out. 'Fucking hell,' I said to the empty room.

I let his limp body hang from the pipe while I looked around. The remaining pipe work ran behind the boiler and through the walls. It obviously provided the heating for the entire building once upon a time, pumping hot water around a mile of pipes and radiators. When the building was constructed, coal fires would have been the only means of heat. The central heating boiler, now antiquated, was a new edition when it was fitted. I knew nothing about plumbing, but I knew it had to be powered by gas or oil. I followed the pipes to the left and decided that they were heating pipes. The ones to the left looked the same. There was one pipe which was thinner than the others. It came through the back wall and ran beneath the kettle, but it had been sawn off and the rest taken for scrap. There was a handle fitted to a valve where it came through the wall. A severed gas main was just what I needed.

I ran back to Colin who was moving and moaning as he came to. 'Do you smoke?' I asked him patting his pockets. 'Wake up.' I slapped his face hard.

'No more, please.'

'Shut up whining,' I said impatiently. 'Do you smoke?'

'No.'

'No last cigarette for you then.'

'Don't kill me.'

'How many candles have you got down here?'

'Two,' he looked at them. They were nearly burnt down.

'Bollocks,' I wondered how long the gas would have to run before it was dense enough to cause an explosion. I ran to the gas main and twisted the valve handle. It stuck for a moment then snapped open. I waited for the sound of gas hissing, but none came. There was a gurgling sound and then oil trickled from the severed pipe. 'I'd never make a plumber, eh Colin?'

'What are you doing?'

'Well I was going to blow the place up, but I can't even cook a sausage with that.' Colin watched the trickle of oil slow to a drip and then it stopped completely. 'What's plan B, Colin?'

'I don't know. Take me with you.'

'What?'

'Take me with you, or she'll kill me,' he began sobbing again. 'She doesn't allow for mistakes. She'll torture me and kill me, or worse.'

'Worse?' I had to think about that one. 'Like the poor fuckers who were taken up the tunnel?'

No answer.

I grabbed the discarded rope and went back to the whinging Niner. 'Open your mouth.' He closed his weeping eyes and complied. I wrapped the rope around his head several times, gagging him painfully. 'I wouldn't worry about dying if I was you. I would worry about what comes after. If you lot are right and there's a sinister side to the universe, then you're about to experience it. I hope that it's all you thought it would be.' He struggled against the bindings and the pipes began to bang sending echoes along them through the walls and up into the house itself. Colin took comfort from his noisy achievement and rattled the pipe harder still. 'Now, what did you do that for?'

Suddenly I felt Fabienne's focus shift onto me. She wasn't in the room, but she was watching me. My muscles turned to lead weights and my nose started pumping blood again. Stabbing pains shot through my ears, piercing my brain. I dropped to my knees as the pressure grew. It felt like there was an invisible force squeezing the life from me. I heard footsteps above me, chairs sliding and raised voices. I thought about the young boy in the cell. 'She said you would come and save us, but you didn't.'

He wasn't real. He was an echo of the past replayed in my mind. He wasn't real. This was real. The pain in my head was real. The blood running into my mouth, dripping from my chin into the filth was real, but the force holding me wasn't. I knew it wasn't real. She was controlling my mind, but it wasn't hers to control. I blinked and shook my head. The feeling lifted slightly. Her focus had moved. Something had distracted her. I ran to the corner and picked up the dirty blanket and dragged the mattress with the other hand. It was coarse, horsehair maybe. Grabbing it, I dropped it onto the floor where the oil had leaked. I wiped it around the concrete soaking up every drop. I flung the oily blanket over Colin's head and placed the mattress over him. He started shouting at the top of his voice.

'He's down here,' he screamed. 'Help me. He's down here.'

'I think they know,' I said, sourly. 'Shall we see if they come to help you?'

I ran to the wooden door and booted the middle, panelled section. The ancient wood splintered down the side. I ripped the bottom half of the door away, the cracking sound boomed off the crumbling walls. 'No sign of the cavalry yet, Colin,' I shouted over his screams. I dropped the dry wood on top of the mattress. Voices echoed through the corridor. I ran and blew out the candles, clipping the night vision goggles down. Peering through the missing door panels, I saw shadowy figures at the end of the corridor. I waited for a clear sight of one of them and aimed the Mossberg.

Movement on the left.

I raised the gun and fired. Plaster and wood exploded off the wall and a cry rang out. I fired again.

'Fuck this, I'm not going down there.' The figure withdrew quickly, and I heard footsteps rattling up wooden steps. 'We'll wait at the top. He can't get up the stairs past us.'

'She said to wait here.'

'Why isn't she here then? Fuck it. I'm not getting shot for anyone.'

Their courage inspired me. I fired another three shots to encourage them to retreat and then reloaded quickly. A shadow ran across the corridor. I fired another three-shot volley, just to make sure and then I melted to the wall and moved up the corridor slowly. The floorboards felt brittle and fragile beneath my feet. They'd taken up a defensive position at the top of the cellar stairs and they were right that I couldn't get up them without being shot. The pressure in my head increased again and my vision blurred. My arms felt weak, barely able to hold up the gun. I crept back into the boiler room and ripped off the remaining pieces of the door.

'See,' I said to Colin as I placed the splintered panels against him. 'They're not coming to help you. But you can help me, Colin.'

'Yes, yes,' he gasped. 'I'll help. What can I do?'

'Burn, you bastard,' I whispered through the blanket. I put the Zippo to the corner of the material and lit it. The oil caught quickly throwing up plumes of thick black smoke. 'See you in hell, Colin, save me a seat.'

'No.' Colin started to scream, but the flames cut his wailing short. As he inhaled, the burning fumes frazzled the delicate tissues in his trachea. The flames spread quickly to his clothes and the tinderbox-dry floorboards. They crackled into flames in seconds. I watched his terrified struggles for a moment and then ran for the tunnel door.

Unbolting it, I felt her focus on me again. My knees buckled. I fell to the floor and scraped the scabs from my wounds. I spat phlegm mixed with blood onto the wall and watched in fascination as it dribbled down. Maggots appeared and devoured the globule before becoming blue-bottles and buzzing straight onto my face. I swiped at them and tried to tell myself they weren't real. It was her creating the images in my mind. I felt that I needed to go back the way I'd come. Back into the house. Back into the flames. I was magnetised to the source of her energy. It was commanding me, controlling me. It was violently dominant, brutally forceful, yet undeniably desirable. The image of Fabienne naked, writhing in blood flooded my mind. The images were sadistically passionate, cruelly beautiful, intensely addictive, yet terrifying. I had to follow the lure. I knew that I was a fish heading for the hook, a moth to a flame, a lemming to the cliff edge, but there was no denying the desperate need to follow. I felt myself taking a step. Then another. Each step sucked my will and sapped my resistance. Smoke was filling the tunnel and breathing was painful. I heard the questions in my mind. How could I not want to go to her? How could I not want to be part of her forever? The evil, the violence the torture and the sweet agony of others were all there for the taking. My heart was blacker than theirs, so why didn't I just give it up and add my evil soul to the greater power, the ultimate malevolence and enjoy eternity suffering?

'Give in and come to me.' Her voice whispered inside my head.

'Fuck you.' I said to myself.

'You want me.'

'You're scum.'

'You love me.'

'I despise you.'

'Stop fighting me. Come to me and we can be one for all time. You've proved that you're evil enough, sick enough, black enough inside to be mine. Come to me.'

'I'm coming to you,' I said in the darkness of the tunnel. Her voice hadn't had the effect which she desired. In fact, it had the opposite effect. 'I'm coming to blow your fucking brains out.'

I heard screaming. Loud, high-pitched screaming. Deafening, tortured screaming which pierced my very soul. I covered my ears and closed my eyes. The pain in my head was excruciating. I dropped to my knees and gritted my teeth. The screaming dropped an octave and became muffled. As the sound became more bearable, I realised the screams were my own, but I couldn't stop them. The images in my head were too explicit, too visceral, too hideous to ignore. We were entwined in a passionate embrace. She scratched my body with yellowed nails, tore at my throat with lycanthropic fangs, ripped out my innards with skeletal hands and it was such sweet pain. I wanted it. I wanted her again. I wanted her once more before she tore me to pieces. The putrid visions reverberated around my head. I couldn't take anymore.

I opened my eyes and slammed my forehead against the tunnel wall. White light flashed behind my eyes. I smashed it again. Damp lichen stuck to my skin. I was blinded by the impact. Again. The images exploded with the pain. Again. Blood ran from a cut above my right eye. Again. The pain replaced everything, numbing the disgusting desires, the filth, the vileness which was seeping into my soul. Again. I fell onto my back breathless and bleeding, but free of her. She was gone for a moment, but I knew the spell was only broken for now. The evil in that place was overwhelming, omnipotent, suffocating and smothering. I wasn't strong enough to get physically any closer to her. She'd try to bend my mind again and this time I wouldn't be able to resist. I couldn't split my skull open repeatedly to expel her projections. She was too strong, and she was becoming stronger by the minute. I could feel her presence fingering my skin, tainting the air I breathed, reaching and prodding for a way into my soul. It was like a weight pressing down on me. I had to go back and get out of the tunnel before she swamped my mind for good. I wiped the blood from my eye with the back of my hand and walked quickly back to the steps. The closer I got, the more the weight lifted. I sucked in a lungful of fresh air and felt the oxygen invigorating my body. The blackness began to leave me and as I climbed the steps, I felt tinges of hope. I lifted my face to the rain and laughed like a lunatic. I clambered over dirt and debris to reach the edge of the trapdoor. I sidestepped a severed arm and noticed with some amusement that the dead hand was still gripping the taser. I reached the top and peeped up over the mound of remains.

A bullet blasted into the rock behind me, sparks flew into the air. I crawled away from the entrance, using the bricks and rubble as cover until I reached a point far enough away to risk looking again. Through the night vision goggles, I could see a group walking from the mansion. There was smoke rising from the vents above the cellars. An orange glow came from the cracks in the brickwork. The dry joists and floorboards had caught fire; the blaze had spread to the floors above quickly. I watched as they fled, five people huddled together. They were heading for the gate to the jetty. A green blob appeared from behind the wall and another shot rang out. I was pinned down with nowhere to go. I felt her focus upon me again but this time it was suffocating. She'd aimed every evil ounce of strength that she had on me. I couldn't fight her like this. The game was over. In close proximity to her, I was powerless. Enough was enough. I couldn't finish this on my own. She was too strong. That's when I knew how this would end.

CHAPTER 42

I took out the mobile and dialled 999. The operator diverted the call to the police, and I explained who I was and what I was about to do. They thought that I was either completely mad or telling the truth, which pretty much amounted to the same thing. When they were convinced, I hung up and I peeked up again. The five people were next to the gate at the edge of the jetty. Three of them were armed, one was making a call and the other was carrying a bundle. The bundle glowed green, but it was a different hue. It was the size of a baby, but the shivers down my spine told me that it might not be. I lifted the goggles and saw the woman holding it. Her skin was black, and she turned to look at me. Her eyes glinted in the moonlight like black diamonds. As her eyes met mine, I was transfixed. It was Fabienne Wilder, although she looked very different. Her skin once flawless, was creased and wrinkled, deep lines started at the corners of her eyes and then criss-crossed her face. Her jet-black hair was streaked with grey and her back was stooped. She looked a hundred years older than when we had last met.

'Fabienne,' I shouted from behind my mound. 'You look a bit rough.'

'Oh, I just need some 'nutrition' and I'll be as right as rain,' she sounded angry but fragile. 'The souls you released tonight are making me stronger already. I must thank you for that. You kill without thought and each one makes me stronger, you fool.'

'Is this what it's all about?' I shouted. 'All this cosmic energy and sacrifice bullshit, is it all to keep your body from turning to dust?'

'All you have achieved is to delay the inevitable.'

'Good.'

'The child will still be taken by the beast on Lammas Day and when she is, I'll be rewarded with her youth. You, nor any other mortal can stop that from happening.'

'I can't let that happen, Fabienne,' I shouted. A bullet ripped into the wall behind me just to remind me not to stand up. 'The police are on their way, Fabienne.'

I heard startled voices arguing. Most of her followers couldn't afford to be outed. I peered over the top again. They were heading onto the jetty and angry words were exchanged.

'You're a liar,' I heard her scream. Two of them were guiding her towards the jetty. 'He's a fucking liar. He wouldn't risk it. He'll be locked up for the rest of his miserable life.'

The familiar sounds of sirens came from the distance. I used the noise to sneak another look. A bullet whistled past my ear. I took out the Glock. I was too far away to use the Mossberg with any significant effect. The rifleman was a good shot, but he was getting on my tits. 'Can you hear the sirens, Fabienne?'

'There are twelve days until Lammas Day, you idiot.' she screamed. Her voice was cracking. She was scared of dying. 'There's plenty of time. I will find you and you will die. The child is already dead.' She shook the bundle violently. I heard a whimper, but it didn't sound human.

Something told me that she was right. The baby would die regardless and so would I. I put the gun over the mound and fired off four shots. I looked over the rubble and saw Fabienne and her cronies at the edge of the jetty. I fired five more shots which ricocheted off the metal rails. They ran back towards the gate. The shooter fired again missing me by inches. I emptied the clip in his direction with little to no chance of hitting anything of use. I saw a muzzle flash, and then a train hit me. My left arm felt like it had molten lava in its veins. I felt blood pumping from the entrance wound at the front of my shoulder and more pouring from the exit wound in my back. I fell backwards and stared at the moon. The cold numbed my broken body and I could feel every single raindrop hitting my face. As they rolled down my cheeks, they mixed with my tears and made icy rivulets across my skin. My nerve endings were on fire, every inch felt scorching white pain. I felt unconsciousness claw at my mind dragging me down.

'She said you would come, but you didn't, you didn't, you didn't, you didn't…' a voice whispered accusingly. I felt my eyelids becoming heavy. Numbness seeped through my veins. I felt cold fingers on my right hand, lifting it. Flashes of pain shot through my tortured brain. My hand felt like it had pins and needles deep in the sinews and tendons as it moved to the mobile phone. Something or someone was guiding it. The number that I needed to dial flashed into my mind, but I couldn't move. The moon faded as my eyes flickered weakly and then closed. Only my hearing was functioning. 'You didn't come…' As I drifted into oblivion, two massive explosions shook the ground.

EPILOGUE

It was two weeks later when I came around. I thought that I was dead. Although I was drugged up to the eyeballs, I recall a succession of familiar faces standing over me, brother, sisters, mother, and friends, smiling and happy faces, their voices reassuring. There were also unfamiliar ones too. Serious faces, asking questions, frowning, and accusing faces. My left arm was strapped across my chest; the right was handcuffed to the hospital bed. There were uniforms, lots of uniforms, police, nurses, doctors. And there were the needles. More fucking needles than you can imagine.

As the mists of pain and medicine cleared, there was only one question on my mind, but no one could tell me what had happened. I asked it a hundred times, but no one would answer me until, one day, a senior detective cleared the room. It was deemed that I was well enough to give a statement. They offered me a lawyer, but I didn't see the point. The detective refused to give me any details about what had happened at Soldiers Point until I'd given a full statement. It took the best part of two days to recount my side of the story; they tape recorded the entire sorry tale. At the end of it, he was good to his word.

No one was found alive at the scene except me. The police examined the underground cells and the skeletal remains of fourteen people had been recovered, although they were struggling to identify some the victims. I didn't think that they would. The Niners picked their victims carefully. The explosions brought the ceiling down on the ceremony cavern. Thousands of tons of rock had collapsed, liquidising the remains in there. They didn't think that the investigation into what happened there would ever reveal any evidence. They simply couldn't justify spending millions of pounds to recover mush. All they had was my word for it. My version of events was taken very sceptically.

Porth-y-felin House was gutted. When the inferno died down only the walls were left standing and the remains had been searched thoroughly. Signs of occult activity had been recovered but the police wouldn't release all the details. Although the mansion was a landmark, it was demolished a few days later.

Fabienne Wilder and her followers were blown to bits. The jetty was nothing more than a pile of twisted metal. The investigation was limited to testing the DNA of a few bin bags of rotting flesh recovered from the metal stanchions of the jetty, or remnants floating on the sea. The rain washed most of the evidence away, leaving the forensic teams with mush. Any larger pieces of human remains, which had landed in the sea, had been gnawed at by the dogfish in the marina. Four of the six Niners who were killed on the jetty were identified. Fabienne Wilder was one of them. The police were left with more questions than answers, especially when a shredded blanket was recovered from the marina. It was stained with blood and there were chunks of skin covered in thick black hair. When the DNA was tested, they couldn't identify it, but they said it was derived from the lupine family tree; it was the remains of a young wolf or something related to one.

They told me that Joseph survived his injuries and escaped any criminal charges. I have it on my list of priorities to call him and offer to replace his crockery. In the grand scheme of things, it's important to me that I at least offer to pay for it. He was lucky to walk away a free man, whereas I don't think that I'll be afforded the same leniency. I will do some time once they decide exactly what I'm guilty of and I'll embrace the experience with both arms. It will give me the time to write again. Being locked behind concrete and steel doesn't seem so bad anymore; I'll be fed, showered and given a bed to sleep in safety. They know that I'll be a target, so I took a deal. They will guarantee to put me in segregation if I plead guilty, 'on the grounds of diminished responsibility'. That would mean admitting or pretending that I lost my mind and went mad.

I can't do that. I was never mad at any point. I knew what I was doing at every stage of the horrific journey. I thought that it was all over, apart from serving a few years, but once again, I was wrong. I received hundreds of cards from well-wishers, many promising to sign an online petition which was designed to put pressure on the courts to apply leniency. I can't remember all of them but one stuck in my mind. It said,

'Colin has saved you a seat in hell.'

When I asked him to do that, there was nobody in that cellar but us. My mind tells me that it's a coincidence, but I don't do coincidences. My gut instinct tells me that despite Fabienne being fish food, it still isn't over.

Am I mad?

No.

Am I evil?

That's a different question all together.

These articles are taken from Internet sources and the links are live. Please be careful if you access their websites as they're dangerous and Internet 'savvy' as to who is watching their communications.

Order of Nine Angels

The Order of Nine Angles (ONA; O9A) 'represent a dangerous and extreme form of Satanism and first attracted public attention during the 1980s and 1990s after being mentioned in books detailing fascist Satanism. Presently, the ONA is organised around clandestine cells (which it calls 'traditional nexions') and around what it calls 'sinister tribes'. They are human vampires in that they sacrifice non-believers and drink their blood. The hearts are used in ceremonial 'eating' and the donors: men, women, and children, are chosen dependent on the Satanic calendar.

As recounted by Goodrick-Clarke in his book Black Sun, the Order of Nine Angles assert that they were formed in England in the 1960s with the merger of three neopagan temples called Camlad, The Noctulians, and Temple of the Sun.

Printed in Great Britain
by Amazon